THE
PARTY
WALL

By the same author

Rule Three: Pretend to be Nice
Dawn Sugar, or Someone to Sleep With

THE
PARTY
WALL

ANNABEL DILKE

ANDRE DEUTSCH

First published in Great Britain
1989 by André Deutsch Limited
105–106 Great Russell Street, London WC1

Copyright © 1989 by Annabel Dilke

British Library Cataloguing in Publication Data

Dilke, Annabel
The party wall.
I. Title
823'.914 [F]

ISBN 0 233 98389 9

Printed in Great Britain by
Ebenezer Baylis and Son Limited, Worcester

For Sasha

PROLOGUE

'Shipka Avenue is definitely on the move now,' estate agents always told prospective buyers.

It was as if, from the moment the council planted sycamore striplings at exact intervals down it a year ago without asking any of the residents, the broad street could be taken seriously. In spring 'For Sale' notices sprouted like the buds on the sycamores: disappearing almost as quickly as the purple-streaked cones unfurled first into apple-green frilly balls and then into large dull leaves. Pigeons and aphids settled into the trees, spattering and dribbling the cars parked beneath with frosted smears and stickinesses.

There was usually at least one skip to be seen and, after builders had filled it with bits of old brick and plaster and rotten timber by day, shadowy figures would emerge at night to stuff in bulky items that the dustmen refused to take away for nothing.

A scaffolding palisade enclosed the house on the corner which was being entirely repointed and the father of the only black family left on the street was painting the windows of his house brilliant white each fine weekend.

The street lay south of the river and it was generally accepted that it was not safe to walk around the neighbourhood at night. But it took only ten minutes by car to find oneself in Chelsea (something strangers to the area never believed); there was a common at the end of the road, a tube station only two blocks away. The estate agents were right: sooner or later, houses in Shipka Avenue would be worth a bomb.

1

Set along the road in blocks of two joined at one side like Siamese twins, the Victorian double-fronted houses had changed their look over the past few years. They could be middle-aged widows now, setting off on summer cruises in a last brave search for love. Old red bricks were no longer left to fade and gather grime. Now they were painted the colour of Italian ice-creams: strawberry pink, banana yellow, pistachio green. And the net veiling which had swathed the windows in the past was gone, all gone, even in the bedrooms.

It was as if the residents were shouting in one great happy chorus: 'Look at us! We've nothing to hide!'

If you walked down Shipka Avenue in the early evening – as dozens did each weekday, briefcases tucked stiffly under their arms – then you could see people drinking, chatting, reading, playing the piano, cooking. In the mornings you could even see people dressing. There was no spying from behind net curtains as there had been in the past: there was no need. Besides, if you looked through those gleaming double-glazed bay windows set behind orderly strips of garden then you could see that, inside, each semi-detached house was much the same.

They had stripped wooden doors with brass knobs; Indian rugs in primary colours scattered on polyurethaned stripped floorboards; heavy old furniture in the sitting-room, stripped pine in the kitchens; spotlights studded into high ceilings painted the same shade as the walls; Berber wool stair carpeting chosen because it did not show the dirt, but which was never allowed to get dirty. It was as if everyone, all at once, had decided to be similar. This, if you thought about it, was a much more subtle strategy for concealing the truth than the net curtains of the past had ever been.

Only one house – Number 11 – was different; and because of the extreme neatness of the house to which it was joined, Number 9, its dilapidation was all the more painful. Two lime trees loomed in bushy freedom either side of the cracked and sinking concrete path which bisected the front garden, weeds straggling from every crevice. Because of the trees, you couldn't even see the house's upper windows which were, anyway, masked by ancient and dirty net curtains; a ragged privet hedge boxed off the lower half of the house from view.

There was a sign on the peeling black-painted front door which said 'Thompson'. This was because a man who had once owned the house, many years ago, had been called Thompson and the sign had never been unscrewed. It should have been substituted with one reading 'No Circulars' (which many of the other front doors in the street displayed), for an unremitting unsolicited stream of paper poured through the letterbox of Number 11. There were letters from firms which specialised in replacing old roof slates with concrete interlocking tiles, or the wooden frames of windows put in a century ago with aluminium ones guaranteed not to rust. Anyone trying to sell such modernising equipment was inexorably drawn through the rotting sagging wooden gate of Number 11 and towards the letterbox which, for many years now, had not sprung shut as it should have done. This meant that after a heap of leaflets had been forced through – often concerning insulation or central heating – a cold draught would stir the already chill air of the house until eventually the letterbox was snapped shut manually from inside. Recently a new firm of estate agents in the area had also taken to stuffing heaps of paper through. 'Dear Owner/ Occupier,' their Roneoed sheets made to look like individually hand-written letters read, 'we have a client who is particularly interested in your property . . .'

Who lived here? A stranger to the street would probably have replied that it could only be someone very old. Only an elderly and frail owner would make no effort to wash the net curtains which fell in grey folds inside each window; would let rain and wind crumble and flatten the faces, naked of paint, of the ornamental plaster caryatids which supported the windowsills and were such a feature of the houses, and allow the greenery in front and back gardens such licence.

You could imagine this solitary occupant of the house

3

retreating finally to just one room, crowded with the junk of the past, dark, with maybe an old cat or two creeping about in the stillness. You could picture a bent figure shuffling to the kitchen that was not labour-saving to open small tins of old-fashioned soft food like steamed puddings and creamed chicken, heating the tins themselves on the pitted rings of a greasy cooker to avoid washing up. You could imagine their decay paralleled by that of the house, hidden away behind windows that were never cleaned or opened, even in summer. You could see in your mind cobwebs sodden with grease clinging to the old strip lighting in the kitchen; rain trickling down outside walls whose guttering had collapsed, to seep through brick and plaster and peel off layer after layer of faded but still garish old wallpaper in rooms where silverfish flashed in and out of coconut matting that had not been disturbed since it was put down years and years ago.

While deploring the state of the property, which let down all the others in that up and coming street, you could feel sorry for such a person. You could picture their discomfort and loneliness and, at the same time, offer up a prayer that you would never find yourself in the same circumstances.

But, as a matter of fact, though much of this imagined picture of the inside of Number 11 was accurate, no one in Shipka Avenue ever felt sorry for its owner, who was neither elderly, nor infirm, nor ever lonely in the conventional sense of the word.

CHAPTER ONE

'But of courrse not, darrlink,' Stefan replied to the English girl who sat, quiet and fearful, on the edge of a chair in his saloon. 'Neverr I rregrret it defaecatink to West – neverr' and he added after a pause finely timed to allow for the laughter which did not, in this case, follow: 'Many epologies forr my etrrocious Enklish. I em illiturrate.'

There were five guests tonight in his saloon. Stefan would have preferred to call the room 'the lounge' except that, issuing from his chapped and nicotine-stained lips, the word always became 'lunch' and by now he was bored of the resulting misunderstandings. 'Peas' and 'sheets' were tricky words too, so Stefan had learnt ways of avoiding them also, much as a man with a stammer finds synonyms for the words he cannot utter. If Stefan went shopping for peas or sheets, they became 'small round green vegetables' (often he was offered Brussels sprouts instead) and 'cotton blankets'.

Four of the six people present came from the same obscure and tiny East European country and, besides the English girl, there was an Irishman who had been one of Stefan's lodgers for more than six months now.

On such evenings, Stefan was happy though it was against his nature ever to admit such a thing. The saloon was his stage, his guests the audience. Most of the guests had seen the play often but for the English girl it was a first night. She watched and listened as if at one of those experimental dramas where the audience is hideously vulnerable, waiting only for the moment when she might leave – never halfway through, because that would be rude, but the moment the curtain began its trembling descent.

Stark, lit by a hanging shadeless lightbulb, the saloon was a stage on which any play might be enacted. The walls enclosing a seventeen-foot-square space had once been painted a shade called 'fondant green' but were now marked with splashes of red wine which had turned purple, scratched with dark horizontal lines where chair backs had been dragged against them. Bottles and glasses were grouped in confusion on the mantelpiece whose chipped surface showed that the fine pink marble had been painted different colours on at least three separate occasions. There was a greying goatskin rug – an old gift from Greece – on the dull wooden boards of the floor, and only a divan bed to sit on beside several hard wooden chairs without cushions which were sprinkled with fondant green.

All this the English girl absorbed, sitting in her dark loose clothes the colour of earth which looked as if they had been bought second-hand, while contrasting it with the neat house in which she lodged next door. As with a real stage, she did not see the worse seediness behind the scenes such as ancient wiring. Sometimes this caused terrifying flashes and the smell of melting caramel when too many people boiled kettles for strong black coffee to be steeped with white sugar, ironed shirts and cooked on the encrusted stove in the kitchen at the same time. There was dry rot too. Even at this moment, multi-headed tendrils were snaking greyly round the base of the saloon behind the skirting board, forcing portions to buckle outwards. The divan bed had recently been shifted to conceal the worst of the dry rot's ravages. Each time Stefan thought he should do something about it, he went to see a friend or had a drink, depending on whether there was any in the house.

'My house is a disaster,' he would say, usually between noon and early evening. But the house had been a piece of luck: an omen, he had believed at the time, for the future. Fifteen years ago, just arrived in Britain and destitute, Stefan had filled in a row of crosses at random on a free football coupon. It was the first time he had played this strange new game, something to while away the time there was suddenly so much of. But the coupon had won Stefan £50,000 and, because he was living in a hostel for immigrants, he had invested a quarter of the money in a Victorian double-fronted semi-detached house in what was then an undesirable street the wrong side of the river inhabited mostly by the poor and elderly. Life in the West was to be like Christmas every day, Stefan had believed. But he had never won again, though much of the rest of the £50,000 had gone on trying.

After some alcohol, Stefan would often say: 'Besides, I am sitting on gold.' He would discuss selling his house for a large profit and moving to a small flat nearby which would give no trouble. But he lived on the rents from lodgers in three of the four bedrooms which were habitable (he himself slept in the front reception) as well as on the social security he claimed while keeping quiet about the lodgers.

Not all the lodgers paid. No one would have guessed, from the affectionate way in which Stefan addressed the Irishman, that he was owed three months' rent by him. Nor that the Irishman had threatened to shop Stefan to the Department of Health and Social Security if he persisted in nagging him about the money. From his tone, it did not appear he regarded himself in Stefan's debt at all.

'Hey Stefan, where's the nosh then, mate? You're always telling us about your bloody bean soup. It better be good.'

'A few moments morre is all,' said Stefan with a smile, quitting his stuffy saloon for the kitchen which was always cold and damp: even now, at the end of June. But when he was alone in that tiny room which, unlike every other in the street, had not been merged with the third reception, his smile vanished as if a stage mask had been removed.

This sudden change suited his style. Stefan had a face with no shadings of expression. Either it was deeply taciturn, dark, bitter – the sort of face which looked as if it had never smiled, and which also knew of an unpleasant secret. Or it almost

7

cracked apart with radiant bonhomie. He seemed, even to himself, to be two entirely separate men.

'This Irish peasant is poisoning my life,' he muttered into the oily orange depths of his soup. There was an electricity meter connected to an electric fire in the Irishman's room but Stefan was convinced that he plugged the fire into the electric light socket, thus obtaining free heating for himself even during the hot summer months. 'Cheap stuff,' he said as he scattered bright green curling fragments of parsley into the pot.

Standing at his stove with a terrifying glare on his face, he presented a strange mixture of elegance and shabbiness. A short thickset man of fifty, he wore a raspberry-coloured polo-necked sweater and grey flannels, both of which needed mending as well as cleaning. But his black kid lace-up shoes were shining new. Stefan believed that a man is judged by his shoes. He held his feet well back from possible splashes as he tasted his food, sucking noisily on the spoon. His bean soup was famous. If English people invited him for supper, which was hardly ever, he would make a pot of it and take it round so as not to embarrass them if he could not eat their food, which was always.

The sharp spicy smell of tomatoes, garlic and parsley, the sound of the soup swishing heavily back and forth in its pot, drew every guest to the unsteady trestle table covered with a green plastic cloth melted and blackened in places by forgotten cigarettes. It was already set with light metal knives and spoons and an assortment of bowls. Stefan sliced up a long French loaf and began to ladle out the soup.

'Could we open a window please, Stefan?' Almost the first words the English girl had uttered, but she thought she would faint from the stuffiness.

'Of courrse, darrlink.' He gave her a blue and white container like a miniature old-fashioned washbowl. There was too few oxygen, he told her understandingly: she was probably feeling sophisticated.

The back garden on to which the saloon's French windows

gave was dominated by a vine, a *Polygonum baldschuanicum* planted by the previous owner of the house in an unthinking moment. Like the dry rot in the saloon, the vine was allowed to sprawl freely and, unclipped, it had enfolded the small square in a close green embrace. It rampaged over flowerbeds crowded with pale weeds, weighed down tottering wooden fences, shot up in bushy sprays against the pitted bricks of the house.

'That's nice,' sighed the English girl. Just now feathery bunches of ivory flowers hung from the vine. The fresh smell of vegetation flavoured with a trace of cat drifted into the saloon to blend with the garlic and tomato of the soup and the stale dusty whiff of too many cigarettes smoked in too small a room.

'Tis trree is disasterr,' said Stefan, as a vine tendril swiped at his wettened quiff of black hair. If he had been on his own, he would have shut the French windows again straight away.

The other guests were all regulars and British citizens.

On Stefan's immediate right was Luli. Luli occupied a secret position somewhere in her early forties – 'She is forty few,' said Stefan. Luli was scented and full-blown and, like the vine, she moved unpredictably. Now, her wide flat face still as she brooded on some private thought, Luli looked sulky, fat, finished. Then she laughed and slanting bones appeared in her cheeks and her shining red upper lip flattened and lifted above her very white front teeth until there was only a narrow strip of deeply tucked flesh separating it from her small nose which curved downwards like the beak of a budgerigar.

Luli had black eyes the shape of soles when she was not laughing and tumbling black hair with a strangely matt dead quality to it. Stefan was the only man in the room Luli had not slept with, but there was a special intimacy between them nonetheless. Only Stefan and Luli knew that the blue stains on his thumbs had been caused by massaging dye into her hair, three nights ago, over her bathroom basin. Stefan was a party to Luli's dark moods, too: the times when she cried

'Oh God, I am in God's black books!' Even so – 'He is a drunkard', she would say contemptuously of him and he in turn would describe her cosy bedsitter two streets away which was stuffed with painted wooden plates and dolls in national dress as 'a spies' nest'. But two or three times a week the drunkard dropped in at the nest of spies and was warmly welcomed unless he had behaved exceptionally badly on the last occasion.

On Luli's other side sat Christo: sallow-skinned, stiff-backed, elegant in Pringle jersey over Jaeger slacks, and with a head on which everything appeared to be moving backwards. Christo's frizzy brown hair was gradually edging off his skull, leaving an increasingly intellectual forehead in its wake; his nose was wide and flat as if someone had pressed it in with a casual thumb, and when he showed his many gold teeth in a smile the corners of his mouth appeared to be trying to touch his ears.

'He is more English than the English,' Stefan would say, not intending it as a compliment. Christo had a large English vocabulary precisely delivered, a well-paid job as the manager of a local carpet shop, and a mortgage on a thoroughly carpeted flat. Christo worked out his finances on neat squares of paper cut for the purpose; he made sporadic attempts to keep away from the other exiles though, like Luli, he had settled nearby; and, in the evening, he sometimes watched several hours of television. On an occasion like this, with an English person present, he strove to give the impression that he was one apart, dropped there by chance and viewing the others with amused curiosity. But every so often, when Christo forgot about himself, his carefully constructed cara-pace would shatter and he would laugh at something in the same way all the exiles laughed: as if caught up in a desperate hurricane of mirth.

Next to Christo sat Dimiter – younger, thinner – who had been a lodger in Stefan's house for almost two years. Dimiter was so quiet that he seemed but a shadow of a person. On an evening like this, with a stranger present, he would say nothing unless coaxed. He was like an old-fashioned maiden, darting occasional disturbed glances from under a heavy fringe, but most of the time staring expressionlessly down at his checked trousers bought in a Selfridges sale. However, behind the mask of sweet diffidence there existed a terrible determination. Dimiter had made the decision to leave his homeland after being badly beaten up by its police and imprisoned on a false charge. He had escaped clinging on to the underside of a goods train engine. He had known that he risked death or, perhaps worse, mutilation; but he had also known that, because of its danger, it was a place the border police were unlikely to search. Dimiter had qualified as a doctor, but now made his living doing all kinds of odd jobs, often for the other residents of Shipka Avenue. He was cheap and reliable and he wasted no time in chatting, it was said.

The English girl, who was called Helen, knew nothing, as yet, of the differences between the exiles. To her they were still as one person – strange, dangerously spiced like the bean soup – and in this warm and noisy environment she felt both threatened and a trespasser.

Helen was mostly frightened. She was afraid of not being liked and of giving offence – but also secretly, still, of nothing ever happening to her. It was a combination of all these fears which had caused her to accept Stefan's invitation to dinner tonight when many others had refused. As a lodger in the house next door, she had heard a great deal of Stefan, and she had passed him often in the street. Yesterday she had stopped when he had stopped because otherwise it would have been rude. They had talked – or he had talked while she had tried to untangle his strange speech – and, caught by surprise, she had said 'Yes, all right, I'd love to.' There was no way of getting out of the invitation without giving offence. So, reluctantly and with trepidation, Helen had come.

Now she found to her surprise that the evening was not so bad. She could not forget the squalor of the surroundings but she liked the way her bowl of strangely delicious bean soup

11

had been filled to its brim; the way Stefan asked her constantly and anxiously, 'Is okay? You like it the soup?' as if it really mattered to him; the way no glass at this table could become less than half-empty without being immediately replenished. She liked the warmth that beamed from all the exiles, though felt less comfortable when it was directed at herself; the constant hum of talk occasionally flipping between languages; the explosions of laughter. Everything seemed double strength here: tastes, reactions, emotions. It didn't even matter not being able to understand much. But when Stefan said in English, after several glasses of wine, 'I em gettink ocularr pleasurres from you, darrlink' or warned, with a sly wink, 'My lips arre tekkink kissink dirrections', she cast her eyes primly downwards, pretending she had not heard and wondering when she could go.

Helen could have talked in English to the Irishman, who sat next to her but he was already quite drunk and, anyway, as an only child she was more used to observing than sharing. She rather liked sitting here passively while incomprehensible and monotonous language swirled about her like flood water.

Certain words recurred again and again: one sounding like 'slooshi', uttered in a cajoling bark as if to say 'listen!'; another which might have been 'loju', said in a nodding, tut-tutting sort of way. But, in this language, everyone sounded as if they were reciting tables.

Now Luli was droning on in a husky smoker's whisper. Her black-pencilled black eyes blinked, stared, narrowed to glistening slits as her cheekbones rose to meet them. Her plump white hands clapped together, twined themselves in densely black ringlets of hair, patted and tweaked the thighs and arms of Stefan and Christo on either side of her, now clasped her own elbows under her bosom that was like a pillow.

What was she talking about? What did they all talk about at such length with never a silence falling? Stefan and, particularly, Christo translated for Helen every so often, but it was a wearisome process for both sides. It was usually an

12

anecdote concerning a person they had known years ago before they ever came to this country. It never seemed to have anything to do with the life they all lived now in the environs of Shipka Avenue.

Without warning, Stefan sprang up and began to sing an old Slav hymn. The mournful passionate bellowing drifted through the open French windows and out into the fresh night, rising and falling.

Helen cringed with embarrassment, trying to pretend it was not happening though, as a lodger next door, she ought to have known what to expect. Then she shut her eyes, as if to block it all out, for now, like a parody of a character in a musical, Stefan was kneeling at her feet, holding her hand and kissing it moistly in between breaths, singing directly to her and enfolding her in a cloud of garlic and spicy after-shave.

When the front doorbell rang, everyone present including Helen assumed that it could only be the neighbours complaining. This was normal. When he had guests, Stefan usually burst into song soon after eleven o'clock. Roughly a quarter of an hour later one or other of the neighbours on each side came around enraged, rumpled, and dressing-gowned to protest.

'Leave it,' muttered the Irishman, slumped in a curve over his drink. 'They'll go away.'

The bell rang again: first a short trill as if the person pushing it was not certain it was operating properly; then a long buzz which vibrated throughout the carpetless house.

'Someone should answer it,' said Christo, who was pleased by the idea of Stefan offending his neighbours yet again.

But Stefan carried on warbling, his bulging eyes straining into Helen's, his arms flung out in dramatic entreaty. Like the dry rot and the vine, the neighbours might go away if ignored.

'I'll get it,' said Helen, seizing on the excuse to escape and slipping from her seat. Outside the front door was an angry neighbour, no doubt – but a fellow countryman all the same.

Bewildered by the evening, Helen craved normality. Though if it was her landlord Stephen Johnston at the door, as was very likely, then he would probably regard her presence in this house as a gross betrayal.

Through the dirty whorls in the square of patterned glass set into the front door she could see a thin black shape silhouetted against yellow light from the lamp-post which stood directly outside. The shadow moved closer to the glass, put the edge of a hand against it, using it as a shield to concentrate all its sight on penetrating the smeared and distorting glass. Frustrated, it moved back, became less defined, and Helen saw the thin wavering shape of an arm raised to the side, ready to press the bell once more.

She opened the door.

An unknown man was standing outside. Helen clicked the old-fashioned light switch that was like a varnished, ridged black cupcake and, in the light which now flooded the bare dirty hall, saw a blinking white face of sharp angles, a slenderness and grace like an animal's. He was at least thirty-five, perhaps more. The grey eyes, which slanted upwards, were tired and his black hair lay flat against his skull. He looked as if this was his last stop.

Then, all of a sudden, the man's face altered as he registered the singing pouring through the half-open door of the saloon. He smiled to himself as he listened. This was no neighbour.

Then he uttered Stefan's full name, making it into a question, and she realised that he spoke no English whatso-ever. She beckoned him into the hall, put up one hand to indicate 'wait' and went into the saloon.

Still singing and now sweating profusely, Stefan danced over to Helen and, she was sure, was about to clasp her to him. Immediately she told him about the stranger, raising her voice.

'Na?' asked Stefan. 'You open it the doorr?' And straight away he went out into the hall.

Hovering in the background, Helen listened to their flat

14

interminable speech. There was a long passionless explanation from the stranger; a staccato gabble from Stefan; another toneless monologue from the stranger. Finally Stefan uttered a word, the form of which sounded like 'trook', but the meaning of which was clearly 'so be it'.

'Heerre is Mikhail,' he said to Helen in English. 'He defected' (it seemed he could pronounce the word perfectly when he wanted) 'since shorrt time frrom my countrry. I hev it frresh lodgerr.'

CHAPTER TWO

The two builders came into the kitchen of Number 9 Shipka Avenue like unfamiliar guests, tentatively and with a faint air of surprise. Yet it was they who had brushed the wrong shade of yellow on to its walls before allowing the plaster to dry out properly, thus ensuring that the job had to be done all over again a few months later.

It was they, too, who had laid the cork floor, put in the pine units and fashioned the large pin-board which Caroline Johnston used to remind herself of her life. 'B.F. – Tues.' read one scrawled message on the diary of the month speared there; 'Order more N.S.' another. Caroline Johnston had stopped working part time when the second of her two children had been born eleven months ago, but she had volunteered to become an unpaid breast-feeding counsellor for the natural childbirth group which had guided her through both pregnancies. 'B.F.' stood for bra-fitting, 'N.S.' for nipple shields.

There was also what might have been a crude portrait of Caroline pinned to the board, the work of James aged two. The artist had caught the vague stare with which she often confronted life and the rosy roundness of her face framed by a dark scribble of curls. There was a card advertising an exercise studio which, each week, Caroline intended to contact but never did; and a Xeroxed sheet headed 'Baby-sitting Circle'. This supplied the names, addresses and telephone numbers of local parents who regularly babysat for each other in exchange for squares of cardboard cut from Cornflakes packets. Most of those on the list were from exactly the same socio-economic group as Caroline and her husband Stephen and they looked much like them but, even so, the list was an interesting guide to small changes of behaviour within that group. There was one single parent, a divorcee and two couples who had different surnames, not because they were unmarried but because the women had chosen to retain their maiden names as a symbol of independence. There were strange androgynous Christian names like Bolly, Vivian and Louie; odd surnames like Bazalgette and St John Brookes.

On this particular morning, Caroline Johnston had had to call in the builders for the second time in a month because the drainage pipe from the washing machine had become blocked and, in consequence, had overflowed, flooding the beautifully polished cork floor. Caroline could see dark freckles forming on the tiles where water had seeped underneath them and, as always when something went wrong with the house, she felt aggrieved, picked upon.

In spite of unremitting attention, Number 9 gave constant trouble. It was like a petulant invalid cherished with nourishing snacks who inexplicably suffers a fresh relapse as soon as pronounced fit by the doctor. Or was it that, like a cancer, the decay of next door was permeating the common wall?

'Oh you are *sweet!*' said Caroline suddenly to the family pet, an elderly Scottie, which had crept out from under a clothes-drier draped with damp nappies. 'Who's a beautiful boy, then? Who is? *You* are! Who's my Fred?'

The two builders sat down at the pine table, not even making a pretence of being interested in the ruined section of floor and, obediently, Caroline served them both with tea. They liked Bourbon biscuits too, and a proper chunk of conversation before getting down to work. Like royalty, they selected the topic but, as a matter of fact, it was always the same and needed very little to activate it.

'Shocking, that,' said the elder one, who was called Jack, catching sight of the newspaper on the table which led with a story on soccer violence.

'Dreadful.' Caroline wished she had thought to remove the newspaper. She tried to offer her son a pile of bricks but he struggled away and walked stiffly over to the damp cork which made interesting sucking noises when trodden on. *Why* were even tolerable builders so impossible to find? Caroline mused in a panic-stricken way. Several of her neighbours had used Dimiter next door and said he was good, but Caroline's husband Stephen had forbidden her to in view of the state of Number 11 (which detracted from the value of their own house) and the number of times they had had to complain about the singing.

Pieces of Jack's familiar diatribe seeped through a porridge of preoccupations, much as the water was now filtering upwards through the cork. 'If I was Prime Minister. . . Makes me laugh when people say flogging's no deterrent . . . Look what happened when they got rid of hanging . . . I'd have messages flashing on to the TV every five minutes. "Muggers will be flogged, muggers will be flogged" they'd say . . . We'd see, dear, we'd see . . .'

The telephone mounted on the wall near the cooker started to ring and the conversation came to a stop because Jack's partner Bill, who was also his brother, had been deaf and dumb since birth. Stirring their well-sugared tea, the brothers sat silently waiting for Caroline to give them her full attention once more.

'Yup,' she was saying into the telephone, 'you simply must persevere. It's essential for the baby . . . Oh yup, *everyone* can do it, that's simply not true . . . No, there's absolutely no such thing as scheduled feeding. Give it him whenever he wants it . . . Well, it *is* painful to begin with . . . Abso-lutely!' (a glance at the builders) 'Like rocks? Poor old you, well so were mine . . . Yup, even if they're bleeding, you *must* . . . Look, I'm having a bit of a crisis right now. Can I call you back in' (another glance) 'ten minutes? Right. And don't worry – we'll sort you out. That's what I'm here for.'

'Do you think you can finish the floor today?' Caroline asked Jack when she had hung up.

'Oh no, dear! Can't do it before the beginning of next week.'

'Oh God! This is perfectly dreadful! I thought the whole point of coming this morning—'

'Can't do it today, dear.' Jack had high blood pressure. His cheeks were veined with crimson, his hands like overstuffed pork sausages. 'We've got to get over Croydon way to do a tank burst. Next week, dear – I give you my word.'

The toddler had disappeared and it was unusually, threateningly quiet. Caroline sprang from her chair and, flinging open the kitchen door which gave on to the hall, saw that he had dismantled the lamp on her husband's bicycle propped there.

Normally Caroline would patiently have explained to her son why this was unacceptable behaviour, defusing his rage with a wholemeal digestive biscuit. Now she snatched the pieces of lamp away and, tucking him under her arm, ignored the screaming and kicking. Like an echo, there came a thin wail from upstairs. The baby had awoken.

'Another thing,' Jack went on, 'I'd cut down on immigration. *I* don't want any more of them here and I'm not alone' – and his brother Bill, who had been studying his lips, nodded solemnly. 'Don't get me wrong, dear, I'm not a racist. But I'm a patriot. Keep Britain British, that's what I say.'

'Oh that reminds me,' said Caroline, her voice rising, 'could you take a look at the fence in the garden? The people next door have let their own garden get into a perfectly frightful state and their creeper's pulling down our fence. I've asked them to cut it but the one who owns the house simply pretends he doesn't understand. It seems jolly unfair that *we* should have to pay for the repair of a fence that *they've* broken. I mean, we've worked like stink to get this house right. Right?'

'It does, dear. It does.'

'If he says "It's not a fair world, dear, let's face it",' thought Caroline, 'I shall jolly well explode.' But even as Jack parted his lips, the door opened and her lodger Helen, who had been working upstairs, came into the kitchen.

'I'll be in tonight, Caroline,' said Helen, meaning could Caroline provide her with supper at an extra cost of three pounds on top of the forty pounds a week she paid for bed and breakfast?

'Oh – right,' said Caroline, thinking, 'Can I do cheese soufflé again – so soon? And would it go with those mushrooms which have got to be eaten? And perhaps apple crumble for pudding . . . I've got some apples.'

'And I must give you a cheque for this month.'

'Super. Can you hang on a minute while I sort this out?' She turned to Jack and said firmly: 'Could you possibly come and look at the fence now if you've finished your tea?'

Good-humouredly, the builders gathered up their cigarettes and lighters from the table and they all went out into the garden, the toddler still struggling in his mother's arms, Helen following on behind because, in this hot clear weather, it was nicer to be out than in.

'You see?' said Caroline. 'You see?'

Trellis woven with compliant, neatly trimmed honeysuckle and clematis topped the three wooden fences bordering the Johnstons' orderly forty-foot-square garden with its brightly coloured flowerbeds, its sandpit and miniature pond with water lilies. But on the longest side, which was adjacent to Number 11's garden, the trellis leaned backwards, the creepers entwining it throttled and dragged down by bulky masses of vine. The fence which supported the trellis looked frail too. Jack gave it a push and, when it swayed, said 'Dear!' in a shocked way under his breath.

Helen could almost touch the anxiety emanating from Caroline. When things went wrong with Number 9, Caroline felt singled out by fate and of course it all meant having to have Jack and Bill around for even longer.

'Whole of it could come down any minute,' said Jack. 'It only needs a bit of wind' – and the fence cracked and billowed as he dealt it another sharp shove.

20

'Oh *do* be careful!'

'If I was you, dear, I'd cut their plant now. Do it with a pair of clippers. Cut the main stem from this side. I'll do it for you. They'll not notice.'

'Oh no! It's against the law to cut on their side of the fence.'

Something stirred through the untidy shawl of vine flowers and leaves flung across the trellis. They all moved closer. Through the dusty tangled branches overlaid with bright green leaves and hung with shedding ivory blossoms they could see a man on his knees scraping at the earth with a piece of broken slate. He had obviously been working on it for some time for he had cleared a large space and there was a big heap of uprooted dandelions, chickweed and nettles by his side.

'Oh, it's Mikhail!' exclaimed Helen without thinking.

The man looked up at the sound of his name, rose, brushed the soil from his knees and came right up to the other side of the trellis. He smiled as he recognised the girl who had admitted him to Stefan's a week ago. No one uttered a word. Then Mikhail said 'café?' to Helen. He pointed to the ruined battered shape of Number 11, then made a circle of forefinger and thumb and tilted the hand towards himself.

'Okay,' said Helen, nodding.

'You're not going next door?' exclaimed Caroline, fears about the fence and the cork floor blown away, for the moment, like dust.

'It's all right. I know him.'

'Guttering's shocking,' said Jack, casting a professional eye on as much as could be seen of Number 11 through the matted greenery. 'Pipe's coming away badly. Roof's going. Chimney stack's going to be a problem. Half of that's yours, dear. Look at it! – it's leaning right over. Needs repointing, that, else it'll topple and then you *will* have problems. Dear!!!'

'Oh God!' Jack was right. Why had she not noticed before? Why had her husband not noticed before? Had they never looked up? 'This is too appalling for words!' Panic began to build up in Caroline and she rushed for James, now content-edly uprooting pansies, and folded him into her arms like a mother bird, as if the stack might come crashing down at any moment. A memory nibbled at the outer edges of her mind – and then she forgot it as she tried to pin Jack down to a time when he and Bill could mend the stack. 'I mean, it might come down at any minute – right? Can't you possibly fix it tomorrow?'

'It's all *right*, dear! Don't *worry*!' said Jack in exactly the same calming tones as Caroline's husband sometimes said 'Don't get your knickers in a *twist*, Caro!' 'Put it like this, dear – it's been that way for quite a while. Because we've only just seen it doesn't mean it's coming down tomorrow, now does it, dear?'

'Well, maybe not . . .'

'It's common property, dear, so that means you pay half and the people next door pay half. Well, it's only fair, isn't it? – even though you and I know it's not a fair world, dear, let's face it. It's in the middle of both houses – see? Best get your husband to have a chat with them. Let him sort it all out and *then* we can get going.'

'Well, I don't know how . . . It's jolly difficult . . . Oh why do the most appallingly frightful things always happen to *us*? . . .'

Quite unfazed, Jack picked up the threads of his favourite conversation and started telling Caroline that there was no real unemployment problem. So Helen slipped out of Number 9's thickly varnished front door with its square of original stained glass, swung back the well-oiled and painted wrought-iron gate, and dived through the almost impassable barrier which was the privet hedge that shielded the front of Number 11 like a hedge in a fairy story.

CHAPTER THREE

The inside of Number 11 looked worse by day, the dust and grease and the piles of circulars behind the front door spotlit by thin rays of sun which struggled through the unwashed fanlight. The door immediately to the left was closed and a faint odour of stale tobacco and old gin seemed to seep through its cracks. Mikhail, fresh and handsome in jeans and a scarlet cotton open-necked shirt pointed to the door, said 'Stefan', and clasped both hands in prayer, leaning one cheek against them.

There was an unhealthy hush over this house, broken only by the sound of boiling water rushing in a frenzied stream up the tube of a coffee percolator on the kitchen stove. The night she had come for supper, Helen had caught sight of the dirty pots and dishes in the kitchen overflowing the stone sink and covering every surface. Now all was cleared away. Even the sink looked less grey (though more scratched) and the blue and white flowered pattern of the linoleum on the floor could be clearly discerned, perhaps for the first time in years.

It was obvious who had effected the change. His sleeves pushed up to his elbows, Mikhail still held a damp cloth in one hand. He put it aside, filled two unmatched cups without saucers with coffee and hot milk. Then he pointed through the sagging open back door at the garden and looked at Helen with his head on one side, like a bird.

Seated on two wooden chairs collected from the saloon and balanced on the bumpy surface of what might, once, have been planned as a minuscule lawn, they sipped their coffee. This lush little space where vegetation pressed in on all sides was an oddly pleasant contrast to the pruned square next door, from whence she could hear the low burble of Jack's voice. Here, it was like being caught in a fresh green net. Now Helen could clearly see how much work Mikhail had done. Where creeper had threatened to close over the garden like flesh over a wound, he had cut it back so that sun could reach the freshly dug soil. It was dark, the richer for having been uncultivated for so long.

'What will you plant?'

'Uh?'

Helen repeated the question slowly and distinctly, as if Mikhail had only to concentrate and then he might grasp the meaning.

A jumble of chatter burst from him, delivered with the sort of intensity which indicated that he, too, believed it only required sufficient effort and goodwill to communicate.

Impasse. Regretful shakes of the head on both sides. Every so often, as if approaching the problem from a fresh angle, Mikhail would begin again, only to fade away like a car that will not start, then shrug his shoulders in good-humoured resignation.

So they sat in silence, part of a shifting dappled pattern as sun filtered through bundled swatches of creeper, smiling tentatively at each other. 'Yes, he is like a cat,' thought Helen; and he: 'I think I know what sort of studious obedient child she must have been . . . Her strange drab clothes must be some kind of new Western fashion.' 'He has good eyes,' she thought; and he: 'I wish I was able to make her laugh. When she laughs she breaks through herself.'

Mikhail's face – all angles and slants – could have belonged to an Eskimo or a Japanese except that it was narrow. His thick black hair curled around the back of his ears; his grey eyes flecked with gold aimed themselves at his temples when he smiled, which was often, showing beautiful even teeth.

He rose suddenly, motioned Helen to hang on a moment

24

and went into the house: disappearing into its crumbling darkness from the fresh green garden as if for ever.

'A dictionary,' thought Helen. 'That's what he's gone to find.' And she sat passively waiting for him to return, watching as a breeze scattered white down from the dandelions which huddled together for protection on a patch of ground Mikhail had not yet attacked. This garden left to itself reminded her of the country garden of her childhood which had been a jungle of surprises.

There was a crash and a rattle from above as a blind shot up. The heavy white face of the Irishman, set in a cross rumpled expression, framed by woolly dusty hair, looked out. There was not a glimmer of recognition as he stared down at Helen. He scratched his head thoroughly, then was gone.

Now Mikhail was back, not carrying a dictionary but trailing Stefan, hastily dressed and unshaven. On his feet Stefan wore burgundy slippers with gold chains slung across them. Here was the interpreter.

'Oh Stefan. I'm sorry. I didn't know he was going to wake you up.'

'Is okay. Is let?'

'Twelve o'clock.'

'Uh.' He accepted a chair and a cup of coffee from Mikhail without thanks, blew his nose thoroughly on a dirty handkerchief, fumbled for a cigarette. There was no trace of the lechery of the other night; none either of the energy which had propelled him through anecdote after anecdote, each more vulgar than the last, until light began to creep across the sky. This person seemed submerged under an enormous mass of apathy and despair.

Helen looked from his face – dark, pitiable, folded in on itself, encrusted with sleep – to Mikhail's, alert and shining with purpose. Mikhail gave Stefan no chance to recover himself. He aimed a long monotonous question at him. Stefan raised a hand as if to ward off a blow. A verbal prod from Mikhail, then:

25

'He tellink you he is poet.' A deep sigh. 'He want know what worrk you arre mekkink.'

'I'm a freelance cookery writer. I compose cookery tips for *Her* – that's a well-known women's magazine.'

'Wrriterr?'

'Yes.'

A minimal sentence squeezed itself from Stefan's lips, as if each word was a stupendous effort and all he wanted to do was close his mouth for good, allowing just enough space to clamp around a cigarette.

Mikhail looked interested, impressed. He nodded several times, his eyebrows raised.

'What will Mikhail do here?' asked Helen.

'Uhhh!!' As if to say: 'Well, yes, that's quite a question: some question indeed!'

But Mikhail was not going to let Stefan get away with failing to translate. He delivered a short lecture. Stefan drank most of his coffee noisily, seemed to gather a little more energy and then spoke at greater length.

An argument appeared to develop – not serious, but certainly a difference of opinion. There was more fluctuation in the sound of the language now: irony in Stefan's tone, protestation in Mikhail's.

'What were you saying?'

'He want to be poet.' Stefan sniffed hugely, gathering up phlegm from the depths of his throat. 'I em tellink him is not possible.'

'Is that all?'

Another throaty sniff. 'Uh.'

What Stefan had actually said to Mikhail in their own poetic language was: 'Look at us. We are like vines. Torn from our native earth and transplanted we wither and die.'

'Nonsense!' Mikhail had replied vigorously. 'We are like seeds borne by the wind. We spring up and flourish wherever we land.'

'Look at me! I invite you to look at me!'

'I am not you.'

26

'You are a madman. You cannot speak one word of this crazy language. How will you ever be able to write poetry in it?'

'We shall see . . . She has a beautiful mouth, this girl. But so unsure of herself. She believes she is not attractive. Are all Englishwomen like this?'

'Ah, Englishmen! They don't know what they have. But you leave this one alone. She is my discovery.' A sly smile. 'As a matter of fact, I have had her.'

'Really? I believe you!'

'Well . . . At least I believe she enjoyed my kisses the other night.'

'Why did Mikhail leave? How did he leave? I hope he won't mind me asking him this.'

'No. He don't mind. But I em tellink you: Mikhail was firrst-class poet in my countrry. A favourrite of rregime. Tey trrustink him . . .'

There was an interruption. Wrapped in an old pink towelling bathrobe belonging to Stefan, the Irishman spread bare dirty feet on the strip of paving-stones outside the back door which might once have been a tiny patio. 'Is there no coffee left or have I to make it myself?' As he spoke, he unpeeled a clementine, one from a large bag Stefan had bought yesterday.

'Mikhail mek it coffee. Mebbe we drrink all. I hev parrcel wit morre,' said Stefan politely with a smile. To Mikhail he said: 'This Irish peasant is poisoning my life. I cannot rid myself of him. He is a blackmailer. My nerves are destroyed. He is a vulture.'

'Gabble, gabble, gabble,' said the Irishman, winking at Helen. 'Doesn't it get you down? They're in England now.' And since he was not prepared to make his own coffee, he helped himself to more clementines and went back to bed, unable to go out and enjoy himself until his next social security giro cheque arrived, the day after tomorrow.

'Ah,' said Stefan to Mikhail, 'now he has poisoned my mood for the day. This pathological meanness. Always I buy the finest, always he helps himself. But when I ask him to replace what he has taken, he buys the very cheapest if he buys at all. And I am a pauper because of him. He owes me thirteen weeks' rent now . . .'

'You were saying, Stefan? About Mikhail leaving?'

Gently bullied by Mikhail, encouraged by flattering interest from Helen, Stefan unfolded the story.

In a land where most make do with little, Mikhail had had unheard-of privileges, including a second house in the country, a Mercedes car and, greatest of all, permission occasionally to travel abroad. Even so, Mikhail had decided to defect at least one year ago. He had told no one: not even his parents, whom he loved dearly, nor his wife. Being a favourite of the regime, trusted, he had been given permission to attend an international poetry festival in York and had secretly packed his entire works, published and unpublished, in two old-fashioned cardboard cases bound with leather straps which had not been searched by the police at the border.

Once in York, he had immediately sought sanctuary at the local police station. It had taken some time for them to find a suitable interpreter, but then a retired civil servant living in the area who had learnt Russian in the Army had been asked to assist. Mikhail understood Russian: his country and the Soviet Union shared the same alphabet.

The Home Office had arranged for him to stay at a hostel in London but it was apparently deeply depressing – worse even than Number 11 Shipka Avenue, said Stefan with a smile like sunlight gleaming through a barrage of hailstones – so Mikhail had sought out Stefan, learning on the grapevine that he sometimes had rooms of a sort to let.

'So – can he never go back?' asked Helen.

'Ohhh!' Stefan looked shocked by her ignorance, but not altogether surprised. 'He will be kilt, I em surre. I em not jokkink. If don't be executed, in prrison forr tis life – end I em not tokkink about it prrison like heerre wit all the convenients. *Terre* is *rrill* prrison: no fourr mills a day, no TV wit colourrs end so end so. Rrill serrious business.'

Now one could see vestiges of pride appearing on Stefan's dark veined features, amidst the gloom. 'Many pipple don't hev it nottink to do wit perrson like Mikhail. Tey arre coowarrds. I em tekkink it bick rrisk hevvink him in my house. But the tinks what I done to help I done forr yuman rrisons, you know? I know I em lost cause but I em not chip stuff. Many pipple frrom my countrry what cem out – tey arre chip stuff, rrill chip stuff. Tey don't cerr of nottink but matterrial tinks, livink in fency pless end so end so.' And Stefan added the extra piece of information that while the Home Office considered Mikhail's application for sanctuary it was paying his rent and a bit extra for expenses, commenting: 'We arre socially securre house.'

What turn does a conversation take when a man has just revealed that he has abandoned his entire life: torn it up into bits like an improperly phrased letter? Because she was very English, Helen smiled almost pleadingly at Mikhail, shifted her position on her wooden cushionless chair in the small untidy garden, smiled again.

Mikhail was waiting, as optimistic and alert as if he were even now taking up his pen to write the first words of his new life on a fresh and empty sheet of paper.

'Did he have children?' she asked after a moment, only to fill the silence.

Stefan relayed the question and a curious blankness passed over Mikhail's face. He answered briefly, and Stefan translated.

'No. In such case, he sayink, he don't neverr liv it his countrry.'

Now Mikhail was speaking again: urgently, rapidly, enthusiasm sparking off him. He must find a proper translator for his work among his countrymen scattered in this strange new land; he must talk with publishers soon, explain the rarity and interest of what he had brought with him, in his head as well as his suitcase. His eyes glittered. There were to be no problems. Certainly there would be no lack of interest in what he had to say.

29

'Mebbe you cen help even, Helen,' Stefan suggested with a sigh. 'You arre wrriterr. You know it tis worrld. Mikhail nid much help. He don't know it tis. Tis is trregical tinks. He is virrgin.'

'Well, I'll try,' said Helen, making an effort not to let her doubts show. 'I'll certainly try and think what I can possibly do to help.'

CHAPTER FOUR

Mikhail had yet to learn that few in his adopted country knew anything of importance about the one where he had been born and shaped.

'How fascinating!' would be a common response when he told them from where he had come. 'Now where *exactly* is it? . . .'

And after he had patiently explained its exact location – set like a dark green butterfly with ragged irregular wings in the centre of the Balkans – they would say: 'They do very cheap package tours there these days, don't they? Advertise them on the tube. Seen them often. Drunk their wine too. Very acceptable for the price. As a matter of fact, we've often thought of going there though we haven't got round to it yet, I'm afraid' (a laugh here to put Mikhail at his ease). Then: 'I suppose *you* go back a lot, take advantage of those cheap prices. You must have family there? – parents, brothers and sisters, that sort of thing?'

Or sometimes, perhaps, from those who did know where it was: 'Of course it's really quite separate from the Soviet Union, isn't it? – Pretty liberal now, I was reading only the other day. Yes. Funny coincidence meeting you like this.'

Once even – from an ambitious young diplomat with more brains than common sense or heart – 'Of course, in its own way the system is democratic. What I mean is, they don't know any other and I believe the ordinary working man is proud of it.'

The exiles were rude about all these reactions. They would call their adopted countrymen 'children' and make comments like 'They have a sort of poetic naïveté.' But in truth they could not really blame them for their ignorance. So little information, accurate or otherwise, had appeared about their country in the Western press. So few of themselves, in any case, had ended up in Britain. And those who had, like Stefan, were not enlightening. When asked by English people to place his old country, economically and socially, Stefan said it was a peasant dragging a dead sheep by its back leg through the snow. The sweetest tomatoes in the world were grown there, he would add; and it was extraordinarily beautiful with a much more ancient and illustrious culture than was generally understood. They had invented their alphabet and not, as was often believed, the Russians, who adopted it. And, by the way, it was a country where homosexuality was unknown.

They were not as the Polish exiles, who numbered one hundred thousand in London alone — who had their own government (with some ten successive elected Prime Ministers since the war), their own daily newspaper, their own club where, over stuffed cabbage leaves and dumplings, they reinforced their already strong sense of true nationality. They were not like the Rumanians either, whose exiles' association held well-attended annual dinner-dances in a conference hall somewhere in the City. And neither did they have anything in common with the Hungarians, many of whom occupied key positions in the media and almost got away with being mistaken for English because of a peculiarly detached quality which was not really coldness but more a precise sense of their own worth.

Many of those in exile from Eastern Europe met once a year at the Easter service in the Russian Orthodox church at Emperor's Gate (and not the other church, so near by, in Ennismore Gardens which was rumoured to be run by the Russian Embassy). In this crowded little church that was less like a church than a vaulted galleried room, they would stand at the back and gaze at the rich carpets on the floor, the icons, the yards of brocade, the rings of lighted candles and the mounds of Easter cakes and painted eggs presented by the faithful. They would savour the overpowering scent of incense, bow their heads as they listened to the choir's singing and chant 'In truth he is risen' over and over again after midnight when the priests announced 'Christ is risen.'

The burning candles they held (and sometimes inadvertently set fire to those in front with) symbolised the faith that had survived a formal ban on religion in the countries of their birth. 'It's barbaric!' English visitors to the Easter service sometimes said of the bowing thrice to the altar, the kisses bestowed on the brocade under the Bible and the Bible itself, the candle-lit procession round the square led by the priests while neighbours' heads popped out of windows and doors to watch this annual routine. 'What does it all mean?' But you had only to look at the faces of the exiles in that church – intent and awed – to know what it meant to them, and Mikhail's countrymen were no exception.

Those who came out of that country had courage and determination, certainly. But the most determined went to Canada and the United States. The exiled community in London, which numbered perhaps only one hundred, lacked cohesion. At any rate to begin with, they concentrated on the practical business of making a living; or they made a successful attempt to forget their beginnings altogether. This applied particularly to the women, some of whom married influential or wealthy Englishmen and whose attitudes and aspirations, within a few years' time, became English. There seemed to be no one who looked further, who perceived that strength might come from organisation. True, some of the exiles – like those around Shipka Avenue – clung together in blobs, the glue their common language and past. But it was a random business. There was no community spirit.

It was the boast of the President of their old country that it had no dissident movement, and certainly little hint of it (or, for that matter, the various attempts on the President's life) had ever surfaced in the Western press. In that country, artists of all sorts were accorded extraordinary rewards. The President was cunning and far-sighted. Early on in his unusually long reign, he had understood that all revolution begins among the intelligentsia and therefore fostered a relationship with his artists, particularly writers, like the relationship between an indulgent married man and his pampered mistress. He aimed to prevent the possibility from the beginning.

For Mikhail it was different. He had always chafed at the lack of freedom and, like a mistress who spots all the signs that her lover's interest is declining, had done the rejecting before being rejected himself.

In Mikhail, the bitterness of being unable to write or speak freely had grown and grown until it had poisoned every pleasure and forced him ever closer to the line which separated what he had learnt was allowed and what he knew was not. So finally he really had no choice but to leave his exceptionally comfortable life style, his status and his literary reputation – in favour of the unknown.

In his wake, Mikhail had left a joke which, like a bomb, had been timed to activate the day after his defection. He had submitted a poem to the leading literary magazine which seemed entirely ideologically correct. Only after it was published, hours afterwards when Mikhail was well across the border, was it noticed that the poem contained an acrostic which was a damnation, in the coarsest terms possible, of the President. Now, as Mikhail imagined the shock waves, he felt alarmed as well as amused. Why had he done it? He knew it was to ensure that the break was for ever.

Mikhail, at the moment, was in a state of extreme elation. It seemed to him that he had realised a common dream in giving himself the chance to begin his life again. No one could return to the true start. But here, in this utterly foreign environment, he felt he could be and do what he wanted. He was a lucky man.

Two weeks later, when Luli went back, he would begin to understand that, even among his compatriots in exile, he was set apart. Now, at the beginning of it all, even the house in Shipka Avenue shrouded in the cobwebs of the past, the strange pocket of immigrants he had found himself in, seemed part of the realisation of his shining dream.

34

CHAPTER FIVE

Luli was packing. It was a seemingly endless process since all the other exiles kept adding to it.

The first to arrive at Luli's stuffy cluttered bedsitting-room with its crocheted mats draping every patterned armchair was Dimiter, who woke her up.

'My God, what is the time!' exclaimed Luli, surprised out of her warm double bed bound with a heavy tartan wool blanket. She was sallow and slit-eyed without her make-up, like an older Chinese version of herself. Her black hair was tucked away under an elasticated net to protect it from the cream she smeared on her face at night when she was alone. Her body overflowed a pink satin nightdress.

'Half-past eight only,' said Dimiter, who usually began work at eight. 'Don't fuss.' He kissed her on both cheeks and unobtrusively wiped the cream from his face with a handkerchief afterwards. Small and slender in pressed jeans and white shirt he seemed like a boy to Luli, who did not see the lines of sadness under the thatchlike fringe and always used the diminutive of his name.

'My God!' said Luli again. She had caught sight of a plastic bag Dimiter swung behind his legs. 'This is impossible, Mitko. Impossible. Always it's the same.'

'Please Luli, it's not so much, you'll see. Only some coffee beans and a warm sweater for my mother. It weighs nothing.'

'Well, okay, okay. But you know, this is a big problem for me. Nobody realises' and, still grumbling softly, Luli indicated the three large suitcases outspread on the floor: clothes and parcels tied with string flung all over them; more clothes

35

draping every piece of furniture in the room. Luli pushed two long cardboard containers of cooking foil off one chair, swept a heart-shaped box of chocolates off another. Then she screamed suddenly as if she had been shot.

'Arrghh! Mitko, do something! This disgusting creature! Get it out! Ah, for God's sake get it out!'

A large ginger cat belonging to the owner of the house had crept into Luli's room, attracted as much by its cosiness as by the knowledge that it was not wanted.

Dimiter picked the cat up, holding its long struggling body as far away from himself as possible, and dropped it outside the door, which he shut with a bang.

'It poisons my life, this animal,' said Luli, as she set the table in one corner of the room after sweeping several pairs of black woollen tights off it. She clicked on the radio and light dance music filled the room. 'So unhygienic.'

She hummed and swayed and licked her fingers as she took from a small refrigerator slices of peppery dark red salami, fat black olives glistening with oil, sheep's—milk cheese imported from home (Luli got her supply from a secret source, the embassy in London) and soft crusty white bread kept fresh overnight wrapped in a cloth in a drawer. As the coffee percolated, she wiped her face with a sheet of kitchen roll, pulled off the hairnet so that her hair sprang over her shoulders, dropped it on a corner of the table. Then she and Dimiter sat down to breakfast.

Luli was going home. Luli was the only one of the exiles who ever did return home and this was her second trip this year. How could Luli afford it on her meagre earnings as a receptionist at a West London hotel? Luli's situation was — peculiar.

Admittedly none of the other exiles had ever applied to return home on a visit, being pretty sure what sort of a reception they would get if they did. But every one had tried, some harder than others, to bring out elderly parents or other relatives on visits and none had succeeded.

It was Stefan who voiced widely held suspicions when he

called Luli's bedsitter a 'spies' nest'. For to receive such favours, to be allowed to go back and forth, Luli must surely be involved in some sort of a deal. But it was only Stefan who dared to say what the others merely thought, and they put this down to his famous self-destructiveness. They were too afraid Luli might refuse to take messages and gifts for them. Luli's help was essential. A nice sweater or a pure cashmere scarf – so prized in the country of their birth – often vanished if sent in the ordinary way. Once a tube of anti-wrinkle cream Christo sent his sister arrived emptied and entirely flat. 'Squashed in the post,' insisted the authorities when his sister complained.

Luli brought presents back too. Her suitcases would set off so stuffed that they could hardly close with Marks and Spencer's sweaters and tights, bags of coffee beans, economy rolls of cling film, boxes of Brillo pads, packets of Technicolor condoms for brothers and nephews, and other valued Western goods. They would return packed with bottles of home-distilled plum brandy, heavy glass jars of clear syrup studded with whole cherries or strawberries which sometimes burst with sticky consequences on the way, and tiny painted wooden flasks containing plastic phials of sickly sweet attar of roses, which was another local speciality.

'Give my mother this too will you, Luli,' said Dimiter, handing Luli an envelope which, she guessed, contained money. 'Tell her I'm okay, please. Say she mustn't worry about me.' He offered his sweet smile, the expression in his eyes hidden under downcast lids. 'Say I haven't found the right girl yet.'

'I'll get this to her,' said Luli, tapping the envelope, 'and those, Mitko. But I may not have any time to talk to her.' Her voice took on a plaintive note. 'After all, I haven't seen my family for six months, darling. Think! My little niece must be walking now. See what I have for her, the pumpkin' – and she stirred the contents of one of the suitcases until she turned up a minute smocked dress and a pair of matching pink kid shoes with ankle straps.

There was another tap at the door. This time it was Christo, who had brought chocolates for a wife abandoned long ago, a coffee grinder for his sister, a pipe and Virginia tobacco for his old father, a widower now. Luli put up no objections. Christo always drove her to the airport in his scarlet Ford Fiesta and could be counted on to sort out problems of excess baggage (afterwards reclaiming exactly calculated contributions from the other exiles). He sat down at the breakfast table and Luli added a bottle of plum brandy to it.

'Stefan is coming,' he said.

'This drunkard!' said Luli. 'How did he ever manage to get himself up after the night he had yesterday?' Then: 'I should dress myself soon . . .'

The clothes she would wear on the trip were laid on her sofa which, itself, was covered in unbleached linen squares embroidered in red and yellow and orange silk thread by her mother and sister. There was a smart emerald wool suit bought in the last Harrods sale; size four scarlet very high-heeled shoes, also new; and, Luli's pride and joy, a silver fox fur jacket, a present from a rich Arab she had met through her work whom Stefan had nicknamed 'the cash dispenser'. Luli would arrive in splendour but return from the visit wearing old clothes. Her best outfit would remain behind, adorning her unmarried sister, Ivanka, whose dearest, only wish was to join Luli in the West. It was the special ambition of Luli too, who saw in the much younger Ivanka the daughter she might have wanted, had things been different. She was working on the problem, but it needed the co-operation of the authorities in Britain too.

Another knock on the door, a feeble one. As they guessed, it was Stefan, but Mikhail had come along too with a bag of gifts.

Muttering to herself, Luli dealt with Stefan first. She accepted the photographs Mikhail had taken of him in his newly tidied garden a few days ago, the lamb's-wool waistcoat, the thermal underwear, the chocolates.

Then, with a shy smile, Mikhail proffered his parcel.

'Oh Mikhail!' wailed Luli, sounding as if it was agony to utter the words. 'You should have come earlier! You really should!' She gazed into his eyes: such attractive eyes in such a vital, handsome face, and so much harder therefore to say what she had to say. 'The fact is, my darling, that I cannot take any more. See? – I'm over the limit as it is. Well over. I dare not take any more. Now if you had only come earlier, like Mitko here. Next time, my darling. Next time I shall be delighted.' Then she suddenly touched her untidy hair and her unmade-up cheeks, looked down at her semi-nakedness as if surprised.

Dimiter did not look pleased to have succeeded where Mikhail had failed. Rather, he appeared embarrassed and unhappy.

'I must start work,' he said, getting up from the table; and, as he passed Mikhail on his way to construct a window seat for the owners of Number 26 Shipka Avenue, he gave his arm a secret squeeze.

'You are disgusting, Luli,' said Stefan. It was an enormous effort to form such a sentence at this time of day. To lubricate his tongue he poured himself a glass of the plum brandy and emptied it at one gulp. 'You are contaminating my air this morning.'

It was time to go, too, for Christo, who usually enjoyed this sort of scene but now wanted to fill his car with petrol and so thought he would put up a show of detesting trouble, like most Englishmen. He edged out, promising to return in a couple of hours to take Luli to the airport.

'Why you don't tek it tis forr Mikhail?' demanded Stefan, lapsing into English for some reason and then instantly rephrasing the question fluently in his own language.

'I can't, Stefan.' Luli looked truly heartbroken. 'I wish I could, Mikhail. I am so sorry. I know what it would mean to your family to receive these gifts. I have family too, Mikhail. I understand these things. My family is my life. You know this. I feel bad, Mikhail – as bad as you. But see how they have all loaded me down. See!'

Stefan snorted into his third glass of plum brandy, misting Luli's white embroidered tablecloth with tiny drops of deep sticky crimson.

'They can't know it's from me,' said Mikhail, cutting right through Luli's protestations that she could not fit his parcel in. 'Not at the customs. Not anywhere. I'll give you a telephone number separately. Here—' and he passed across a slip of paper. 'Someone will come and collect it from you.'

Luli dropped the pretence too. 'Someone will tell them,' she wailed. 'Don't ask me to get my own family into trouble, Mikhail. Don't ask me to make my own situation difficult . . .'

'You are cheap stuff, Luli,' said Stefan sternly. 'Who will tell them? No one knows but we three. I won't say a word. Mikhail won't for sure. Now – don't disappoint me.'

'I'm sorry, Stefan,' said Luli firmly, as if she had gathered new strength from somewhere and now the matter was closed. 'I really must go on with my preparations if you'll excuse me. My God, what is the time?'

Silence. Then: 'Luli, I am warning you!' Stefan's dark veined face was a terrifying sight, totally changed. 'You know what I mean! I am warning you!'

'I don't understand you,' said Luli, but her plump face looked anxious and sly as she patted astringent lotion on to it.

'If you don't do this thing for me – and for my friend Mikhail here – I am warning you, Luli.'

Luli glared at Stefan, who waited impassively. Mikhail looked down at his shoes.

'Well, maybe I can find the room after all,' she said sulkily.

Stefan would have liked to say triumphantly 'That's better' and Mikhail wanted to plead 'You will be sure to deliver my parcel safely?' But they both knew it was best to leave now and not risk making Luli either angrier or more anxious.

40

They did not notice, as they slipped out, that the ginger cat slid back in.

'Thank you,' said Mikhail to Stefan as they walked along hot bright pavements to Number 11 Shipka Avenue where a lunch of stuffed tómatoes (prepared by Mikhail) awaited them.

'It's nothing. This little dictator. She really enjoys playing with us all.'

'Is that so?' asked Mikhail, who had already learnt that Stefan found this sort of casual and seemingly disinterested comment irresistible.

Stefan stopped abruptly in the street, his face purple with fury and disgust. 'This cheap bitch goes back twice a year!' he bellowed. 'Do you think she gets those privileges for nothing? Come *on*! You know this world. You are not a child of the West. Oh, we all love Luli but you must be careful what you tell her, how you deal with her. You know this. Actually' (Stefan was fond of using this word in both languages) '*I* play games with Luli. This is the real way round. Often I tell Luli lies to amuse myself. She's not too bright, our Luli, though I have to admit she has a wonderful pair of tits. It makes me laugh when I imagine her repeating my lies about this and that to the embassy here or the police over there. After all, the poor girl has to tell them something, doesn't she? I'm doing her a favour.'

They passed the pet shop on the corner which, though they had not compared notes, both considered a shocking waste of valuable space.

'Do you have some sort of hold over Luli?' asked Mikhail casually. 'What did you mean when you said you were warning her?'

Stefan smiled to himself. It was obvious that he longed to tell Mikhail: particularly because scoring over Luli had put him into a good mood, which was unusual for so early in the morning. Finally, he tapped the side of his nose.

'Yes of course,' he said importantly. 'But the reason is a secret between Luli and me. Better it stays like that and she knows it.'

41

CHAPTER SIX

A great deal more than a shared wall and a common wooden fence separated the crumbling back of Number 11 Shipka Avenue from the immaculate rear of Number 9. But in both attic rooms overlooking the very different gardens, work was in progress.

In his bare but newly cleaned room, Mikhail was copying out words selected at random from an elderly *Sun*, the only newspaper to be found in the house, which he had discovered scrumpled up and stuffed behind the divan in Stefan's saloon. Each time he copied out a word he looked up its meaning in the battered bilingual dictionary Stefan had lent him. Several words could not be found, however; sometimes whole sentences remained a mystery. An example was the headline 'GUTSY STRIPPER FLOORS MUGGER'. Yesterday, searching for the meaning of 'defend', Mikhail had stumbled upon 'defector'. 'One who falls away,' he had read, 'a deserter'.

In her comfortable but somehow characterless room next door, yards away from Mikhail and at precisely the same level, Helen was trying to compose lively and original copy for her cookery column.

She had written: 'It's as important nowadays to give your guests a dish which looks pretty as it is to tantalise their tastebuds. Try creating heads, bodies and legs out of slices of kiwi fruit, chunks of papaya and strips of rhubarb, and then set your fruit men in a delicate cranberry jelly (frozen cranberries can be found in most supermarkets). Your dessert will certainly be a conversation stopper, and the blend of sharp and sweet flavours is yummy and different.' Now she studied the sheet afresh, crossed out 'men', replacing it with 'people', and substituted 'piece' for 'stopper'. There were strict conventions attached to this type of journalism. You never put a dish in the oven, but popped it in; herbs were always measured in generous pinches; black pepper was never anything but freshly ground. You also had to master a breezy and faintly bossy style. But the main requirement of the job was an ability to dream up ever more novel combinations (last week, Helen had suggested roasting turkey in orange juice and then decorating it with slices of strawberry glazed with apricot jam). It was more difficult than it appeared.

In his effort to learn English, Mikhail had pinned useful words selected from his dictionary all over his little room. 'Bread' and 'milk' were attached to the bare wall by the window which, in Helen's room, was mostly taken up by a large radiator; 'want' and 'please' were on the wall facing his bed. On the part of the ceiling which sloped downwards, Mikhail had pinned a long timetable on which every hour of the day from eight o'clock in the morning was accounted for. He would study English for two hours. Then he would work on his poetry. Then he would return to the English for a further two hours. Then he might tackle the problems in Stefan's house. 'Conversation' he had written against the hours which covered the afternoon and evening of that day.

All his adult life, Mikhail had operated on the premise that everything is possible provided you try hard enough to achieve it. His own experience had proved it to be true. Mikhail had come from a poor family, had done spectacularly well at school and, with one book of poems, had bounded straight into the ranks of the favoured and celebrated. Now he knew that if he struggled with this foreign language persistently enough – if he concentrated all his considerable intelligence on listening, copying, memorising – then there was no doubt he would master it, and quickly.

In his native language, Mikhail had written the outline of a new poem during yesterday's allotted time. It was about the room in which he now worked. Mikhail had contrasted it with his old study. There had been sun and space there and a cool green view of willow trees. There had been an Italian electric typewriter, shelves full of his own books and friends', stacks of the thick shiny paper he liked, a deep sofa on which he could rest and listen to Bach and Mozart played on his fine stereo system.

There was nothing here: no trace of that former life, except that Mikhail had pinned to the cupboard door the dust jackets of several of his published collections of poems, a photograph of himself receiving a top literary prize, and a four-leafed clover protected in a plastic wallet which had always been his good luck charm. 'I did this, I was this,' said the book jackets and the photograph.

In his poem there had been no nostalgia for that room of his past, no self-pity about finding himself in this cramped and stuffy attic with its narrow bed, its ancient springless armchair and the small metal table with uneven legs on which he now worked. There was no expensive equipment here in this room which was too hot in summer, too cold in winter. Mikhail had only a cheap lined exercise book and a Biro pen to work with. But for the first time in his life, he knew with a thrill of joy that he could write exactly what he wanted for publication. There was no longer any necessity to write in a code which, with frustration and despair, had become ever more dangerously explicit. Now he could set out his thoughts without fear of reprisal and this new freedom was what his new poem was all about. For what help were all those enormous privileges of his former life if a writer could not perform the one function he felt he had been created for — write from his heart?

An image of the girl next door came to Mikhail. Always a fatalist, now he was sure it was destiny which had entwined his new life with that of this girl who was a writer also and could therefore help him so much.

He knew that she was working too because she had told him in the pitifully restricted French they had eventually discovered as a basis for communication. Yes, she had said, she would enjoy coming out with him, but first she must work.

He saw her pale brown hair falling straight around her serious unmade-up face; her reddened hands with their bitten fingernails resting on the keys of her typewriter; the outlines of her body obscured by loose dull clothes. If her desk stood under the window like his then they were looking at the same orange, black and grey pattern of bricks, roofs and chimneys that was the back of the houses opposite. If she looked down into the gardens, then maybe she was watching the same tabby cat slink like a hunchbacked tightrope-walker along the wide top of matted sprouting trellis, its fierce yellow stare never leaving a sparrow which bounced bright-eyed and casual a few yards away.

Next door, Helen was no longer at her desk, which did look on to the gardens just as Mikhail had pictured it. She was standing at her open wardrobe, touching clothes and thinking with one part of her mind how lucky she was to have her job when she did not have the use of a kitchen. In her imagination she tested her recipes thoroughly; but of course her editor did not know that none were ever tried out in reality.

She extracted a straight olive-green dress which might be suitable for a sightseeing trip around London followed by a visit to the reasonably priced Turkish restaurant in Bayswater which Stefan had recommended. She held it against herself, looking at her reflection in the long mirror set into the wardrobe door.

'What difference does it make?' she thought, seeing only the face that was too round, the hair which fell too straight, the body that was too plump. 'There's no point.' And she scraped her hair back from her forehead and pinned it with a metal clip. 'I hate all my limitations. I'd like to change everything about me: become someone else in the mirror and someone else inside.' Then the idea followed: 'How would I be if I were set down somewhere completely different where not one person knew of my previous self? Could I escape from this me?'

'Dimiter is comink?' Stefan sounded anxious as he opened the door of Number 11 to Helen, who had arranged to pick Mikhail up for reasons to do with the Johnstons.

'Oh, is he?'

'No. He is comink? You see it him comink in strrit?'

'Oh no. No sign.'

'What's to do it if he comink? I hope he don't be comink forr lonk time.'

Stefan looked smart, she now noticed. Though she didn't know it, he had on his best shoes (dark grey with silver buckles), the moth-hole at navel level in his raspberry wool jersey was not too obvious and his grey flannel trousers were creased in the right places if shiny in the wrong ones.

He appeared altogether brighter since Mikhail's arrival. He seemed to appreciate the changes in his house: the way the tessellated floor in the hall now shone without a trace of dust, the absence of the enormous pile of circulars which had been dumped in the dustbins.

In this house of apathy Mikhail rose early every day, using each minute to achieve something either for himself or for others. Now even the garden was quite different – the vine clipped back and ranks of sweet-smelling furry tomato plants springing up in the flowerbeds he had created.

'Where's Mikhail?'

'Mikhail prreperrink it himself forr you.' Stefan managed to instil much innuendo into this. 'I stay in' – and in case she had missed the lubricious meaning here too, Stefan explained 'I em hevvink it visitorr, a 'oman.' He went on: 'I tink I hev to get merrried. My house is disasterr in winterr. The cold is terrrible, terrrible.' He watched her face for a reaction as he told her: 'She comink frrom Compooterrdet.'

'Computerdate?' In her astonishment, Helen forgot her usual awkwardness, her anxiety about whether Mikhail and she would be able to communicate adequately, and the unease Stefan always produced in her because of the violent variations in his moods. 'Do you belong to Computerdate, Stefan?'

'I? You hev to be jokkink! I pay it cesh forr mit wit a 'oman!' Stefan snorted with mirth. No, he explained, it was Dimiter who had paid the membership fee to Computerdate. Yesterday, he went on with a sly smile, a woman had telephoned when Dimiter was out and he, Stefan, had answered. When she had called him Dimiter, he had not put her right. They had had a pleasant conversation: she liked a joke, the same as he did. Today she was coming all the way from Birmingham to see him. He had cooked real good veal and green beans for her; and he chivvied Helen into the kitchen and displayed the dish proudly. It was real food. Good food. Not like English people had. Didn't she agree?

When the woman had asked for his prescription, Stefan went on with a self-conscious smile, he had subtracted ten years from his biography and added six inches to his length. He had said he was six foot, and an occupational therapist.

'Well, you look very—'

'Rreprresentatif,' supplied Stefan. He seemed pleased to be considered thus. 'Yes, I tink.'

There was a sound at the door and they both turned to see Mikhail: all spruced up like Stefan. He had put water on his newly washed hair to smooth it but it was not easy. This was because, from the day of his arrival in England – for no reason he could express even to himself – Mikhail had taken to parting his hair on the left rather than the right, and it had not yet grown accustomed to the change.

A lengthy gabble more full of expression than usual spilt from Stefan and Helen felt acutely uneasy at identifying the same note in it as had been there when he discussed his visitor from Computerdate.

There was a flat monologue in return from Mikhail containing no answering innuendo at all.

'I must learn it,' thought Helen. She had already tried

without success to find in the local bookshop a manual which might help. 'I can't go on hoping that one day it will translate itself for me; that I'll suddenly comprehend it as babies understand their parents' speech.'

They were ready.

Mikhail opened the front door for Helen and, searching for the right parting phrase, emboldened and protected by Mikhail's presence, Helen said, surprising herself: 'If you can't be good, be careful.'

A totally blank response from Stefan, then: 'Tis is good!' He chuckled with genuine delight as if he had heard the saying with fresh ears, for the very first time. 'I like it tis. I em not beink good, I em tellink you. But I rremberr it beink cerrful!' Still giggling to himself, he shut the door behind them.

Mikhail and Helen walked up Shipka Avenue, which appeared foreshortened and hazy in the heat. The common lay flat and tired at the end, shrivelled and brown like an elderly sunbather after so many hot weeks of supporting footballers and joggers and bicyclists. The pond was dull and finished too, full of scum and paper and fished to the limit by the hordes of optimistic anglers who turned up with tins of maggots, waders, large green heavy duty umbrellas and picnics the moment, in early May, when the council took away the board planted in the water which read 'Fishing Season Closed'. The aggressive grey and white Canadian geese which lived there in winter had gone also: fearful of the lead weights which had poisoned so many of their number.

'Where?' Mikhail uttered the word proudly, stressing its h and giving it many rs.

'Très bon,' said Helen. With difficulty she outlined the itinerary she had planned and they halted at the bus stop under the massy shade of a huge chestnut tree, its candelabra blossoms faded pink skeletons now. It was a long wait for a Number 88 but the day was blue and warm and the rest of it lay before them charged with a sense of the unknown.

If you had to try and translate every single thought you wished to impart into a language you were not at all fluent in, Helen quickly discovered, then what was inessential and indecisive got sieved out. In a way, it was like communicating in a pure new language, though deeply frustrating too.

Showing Mikhail the sights of London was like teaching a small child, because all information had to be rendered down to its simplest form. Like a teacher, Helen also tried to see it through his eyes, selecting what she believed would interest him most.

'Anything? One may say anything there?' he exclaimed in disbelief as their bus rolled past Speakers' Corner at Hyde Park; and outside Buckingham Palace he stared for a long time at the guard who was largely ornamental, the facade which shielded the real living quarters two courtyards away.

But it was Harrods which made the greatest impression on him. Mikhail was a sophisticate: one who had travelled far more widely than was usual for a native of his country and, indeed, his part of the world. Even so, something in him still found it hard to believe that this magnificent opulence, this wasteful show, was permanent: that it had not been laid on by deceitful authorities especially to fool him. There was a primitive suspicion, planted long ago, that people in the West did not really enjoy this standard of living: that, as with Buckingham Palace, the reality was masked.

It was so difficult to believe that this profligacy existed day after day whilst, back in the country he had fled, ordinary people must queue for hours to buy what were not even considered luxuries here. The shop was so brightly lit too: Mikhail thought of the dim lighting everywhere in that other world.

Was all this flesh sold? he wondered, passing through the huge cool food hall with its faint pleasant smells and clean white aprons where the corpses of half a dozen different animals and birds lay behind glass, elegantly putrefying. And the other, worldly, side of him added: 'I suppose they throw away that fine dark red venison, those pale pink slices of veal, if they are not sold at the end of the day.'

Mikhail did not view Harrods as a place for the rich to shop: he saw only that its many doors opened to the streets and that all who wished could push through them. How come they looked so unimpressed? he wondered; and, as he and Helen passed a rack of mink jackets chained each to the other, he brushed their silky fur with one hand as people are said to pinch themselves to check they are not dreaming.

Dinner at the end of the day was reassuring. Mikhail had obeyed Stefan's instructions about avoiding the Russian restaurant a few streets away. It was a haunt for staff from all the East European embassies, Stefan had warned, and Special Branch policemen – offered free drinks by the proprietor – sometimes went there too.

In the Turkish restaurant, Mikhail could speak basic Turkish to the waiter and, knowing the cuisine well because his native country's was derived from it, took pleasure in ordering a meal he hoped would please Helen.

In this foreign environment, having to come to terms with a completely downgraded life style, he consciously had to fight hard to retain his self-esteem. Now he found it soothing to his spirit to sit at a table and be served with a fine meal that had not been cooked by himself. He enjoyed the illusion that the waiter recognised his superiority, even though he fully appreciated it was mere illusion. He was so grateful that, at the end of the meal, he gave the waiter a tip he could not afford which was over and above what he and Helen (who had insisted on splitting the bill) had already paid.

'Are you content, Mikhail?' she asked him, using the formal '*vous*'.

'I am very content'; and he took her arm as they went down the draughty litter-strewn steps of Notting Hill Gate tube station.

Being able to communicate only at a very basic level, with no subtleties, meant that when they arrived back at Number 11 Shipka Avenue and Mikhail took her hand and said 'Come with me', Helen replied simply 'Yes.'

She did not want to say 'No', but she was afraid. 'I'm not

50

ready yet,' she would have liked to say; and 'Let me be sure you're serious about this.' But her French was not up to it and, even if it had been, she knew it was fatal to reveal either caution or intensity – even though her own experience had taught her to take care of her emotions, having instilled in her, a loving person, a fear of love. As it was, she did not even say that she dreaded encountering Stefan.

They met no one. The door of Stefan's bedroom, on the ground floor, was closed though light edged its outline. As they tiptoed past – Helen treading in time with Mikhail so they would, if detected at all, sound like one person – they heard a tinkling giggle from within and a voice imprisoned in flat vowel sounds: 'Oh Dimiter, you are awful! Really you are!'

In Mikhail's sloping-ceilinged little room – the shape of an old-fashioned cheese cover, just like her own – the sash window was pushed right down and a warm breeze fluttered the pieces of paper stuck all over the walls. Mikhail did not switch on the light, so she could not read 'want' and 'please' neatly printed in English; or see the timetable for that day scribbled in his native language.

'Beautiful,' he said proudly.

'Oh no!' She sounded almost horrified. There was no need for him to say it, she meant. But now he was sliding the clip from her hair which, released, fell in a straight curtain obscuring one anxious blue eye. His own, having completely dried during the evening, sprang up like a black wing.

'Helen,' he said. Just her name pronounced 'Heln' and, she imagined, uttered with a certain tenderness. She could not read the expression in his almond-shaped eyes which gleamed in his pale face in the dusk. Then, with none of the hesitancy he had shown previously, he began to kiss her, edging her towards his narrow bed; and she stopped thinking about anything else except this moment which seemed snipped from the rest of her life, embellished, then pinned back on to it, like a jewel.

CHAPTER SEVEN

In the street outside his immaculate house with its strip of garden planted with petunias, marigolds and pansies, Stephen Johnston was washing his three-year-old grey Volvo estate car. On Sunday mornings this activity filled the space between returning from church and having lunch.

Often his son James helped him. James's idea of washing the car was alternately to scrape at it with a stick and throw buckets of dirty water at the wheels. If Stephen did not allow him to do this, he would refuse to eat his lunch.

So – 'James darling, don't scratch the paint, darling, will you? . . . I've got a good idea. Why don't we take that nasty stick away?'

'No!' James's first and almost only word and an effective one, he had discovered.

'Well, nice stick then. *He* doesn't want to help wash the car. He wants to sit in the garden instead, with all the pretty flowers.'

His son looked at him curiously, pityingly. He jabbed at the car again. With a sudden uncontrolled movement, Stephen took the stick away. James started to scream: a peculiarly intense high-pitched sound. Stephen gave the stick back and James went on jabbing, still sobbing under his breath, every so often looking defiantly at his father. Then Stephen remembered the sponge at the bottom of the bucket and lifted it out, squeezing it sensuously so that dirty soapy water dribbled noisily back. James stopped jabbing and looked. Stephen went on squeezing the sponge casually. James dropped his stick, toddled over and snatched it away.

52

'Good morrnink.'

Stephen looked up and saw the case from next door, which was what he and Caroline called Stefan.

'I see you hev it choffyurr forr clin it yourr carr.'

Stephen nodded, smiling tightly. Stefan looked appalling: obviously only now returning from a night out and bundled up in an old raincoat. On his head he wore a peaked tweed cap; on his feet black lace-up shoes that gave off soft gleams of light.

'He's drunk,' thought Stephen contemptuously.

Stefan would phrase it rather differently when he got in.

'I em hevvink it lonk monoloc wit bottle of liquid frrom Scotland,' he would tell his Irish lodger. 'Goodbye, clearr conscious.'

'How you arre enjoyink it tis pleasent wetterr?'

'Very much.' How had the man the effrontery to discuss the weather – at least, that was what this jumble of rolling rrs and mispronounced aas and misplaced pronouns appeared to mean – when only the night before last Stephen had had to complain yet again about the singing? But unfortunately, just for the moment, Stefan had the upper hand.

He bent to talk to James, eyes sunk in puffy mounds of bluish flesh, the rims of his lips smeared brown by too many cigarettes. 'I see you arre good Enklishmen – washink it carr on Sunday. Well, I em endink it my day na you arre starrtink it yourrs.'

'Er,' Stephen began, smile still pinned to his lips, 'could we discuss the repair of our common chimney stack? I did put a note through your door to that effect, together with a copy of a very reasonable estimate from our builders. I don't know if you got it? It is a matter of some urgency.'

'Leterr. Leterr I will be plizzed. But na I em not slippink it one blink since tirrty-six hoorrs.'

'Damn!' said Stephen to himself as he watched Stefan's bundled-up tottering figure disappear through a screen of privet, the rotting wooden gate making a soft crunching sound as it closed behind him. Then: 'Something's got to be done about that singing too – maybe a petition? Yes. But not before we've sorted out the money for the repair of the chimney stack.'

But how could you sort out anything with someone who never replied to notes, who always said 'later' and anyway spoke quite unintelligibly, who didn't seem to care if his house crashed around him? It was like trying to negotiate with a being from another planet, so great was the gap between them. And, to relieve his feelings, Stephen roared 'No boy!' at his dog which had crept out of the front door and was quietly urinating on the marigolds.

Encountering Stefan was one more blot on the day, always Stephen's least favourite of the week. What he longed to do was behave like a bachelor; to slump in a soft armchair with a glass in his hand reading a thriller or watching an old film on the box. What he would do was play the role of good father and give Caroline a break. That was how Sundays were spent, just as Saturdays were for carrying out minor repairs to the house and tidying the garden and helping with the shopping. After lunch there would be a walk full of impatience and drama on the flat triangular common with James and the baby. It was Caroline who would have the reward of the house to herself for a precious hour.

Church had been bad enough. Stephen and Caroline had put their boys down for the only good free primary school in the area, which was run by the church. (Naturally, they would be removing them at the age of eight to send them to a proper prep school.) But in order to qualify for consideration, a child must have staunchly church-going parents. So the local church on the common – used by the school – was one of the few in central London full to bursting on a Sunday morning. The Johnstons were amongst scores of other middle-class young couples with pre-school-age children who sang hymns loudly and made sure they shook hands with the vicar after the service (the same young couples Stephen would see later on the common, calling 'Daisy' or 'Caspar' to their children and 'Fred' or 'Mac' to their dogs as they walked off

Sunday lunch). It was becoming harder and harder to be sure of gaining admittance to this excellent school with traditional teaching methods which had originally been set up to educate the poor children of the parish. So Caroline now undertook to dust the church each Wednesday evening and had agreed to man the cake stall at the church fête next month. Once they had got the children in, of course, they would relax. They might not go to church again.

Neither Stephen nor Caroline were true believers, and they did not much like the vicar. He gave poor sermons, they considered. Also he had not yet taken the trouble to organise a Sunday school for the children, who fought with their mothers for the right to run up and down the aisles where there was an exciting hot air vent which blew up their clothes; and hid under the pews when the vicar suggested 'Let us pray' and wailed if they were thwarted.

But Stephen and Caroline would never have shirked their duty towards their children, just as they would never have discussed the degree of their disbelief in God with each other. They lived a life whose pattern they did not question. Though neither was particularly well educated, they agreed that education was the key; that you lived in a house only to turn it into a means of being able to afford to move on to a better one; that divorce was out unless absolutely unavoidable. They knew the rules and, for all his anarchic behaviour now, they knew that James was cast in the same mould.

When Stephen looked at James asleep, he caught a glimpse of the man he hoped his son would be. That small plump face, so often distorted by rage in the day, seemed noble in its sweet purity then. Sometimes, as he stood transfixed by fearful love, Caroline would join him in the darkened nursery and put her arm through his and they would stare down at their sleeping children and not need to say a word. But those moments of true communication were rare these days.

'Lunch!' called Caroline from the front door. Returning to the kitchen, she picked up a collection of magnetic letters which lay in primary coloured confusion on the floor. Each day, Caroline constructed suitable words out of these letters which she stuck to her refrigerator so that James might gain a reading advantage over other children. Heaven knew, the competition began early enough and, hard to believe, he would be starting nursery school next year. But James was only intent on picking the letters off. To him, it was part of an amusing game his mother had devised, however often she told him: 'No James, look! D-O-G – like Fred, see?' Now she wearily rearranged what had been BIN to read NIB.

Meanwhile, Stephen persuaded James, who did not at all want to leave the sponge, to come inside and, by degrees, they all sat down at the round polyurethaned pine table tucked into the bay window in the kitchen-cum-dining-room.

Mealtimes in this house were ordeals. Even the food was not to be enjoyed, being primarily designed to appeal to very young children. Today Caroline had cooked overdone unsalted lamb which would be cut into tiny cubes; liquid mashed potato, also unsalted; and over-boiled Brussels sprouts. Apple purée with home-made custard would follow.

Stephen and Caroline would not eat their own food until they had coaxed James and the baby, who was called William, to eat at least half of theirs.

Both children suffered from different feeding problems. James did not appear to eat at all these days, though his chunky body never seemed to lose weight, whereas William only enjoyed feeding from Caroline, who maintained that breast was best even when a child was almost a year old. Caroline had read that breast milk loses its nourishing properties after six months but she believed in the soothing nature of breast-feeding, for herself as much as for the baby. She could feel the intense joy of new motherhood slipping away from her now: that feeling of having partaken in a miracle. Continuing to breast-feed – and voluntarily supporting others who were trying to – was a way of prolonging it; for, like so many friends of theirs, Stephen and Caroline had decided it was only sensible to stick at two. Often after giving hours of encouragement to one of her breast-feeding mothers,

Caroline felt quite irritable and emotional, just as she had straight after giving birth to James and William. Life had been rich and dramatic then.

The frilly edges of teeth were beginning to sprout from the baby's gums now, so feeding him was increasingly painful. But there were still few moments in Caroline's day she enjoyed more than her private sessions with her younger son: relishing the clasp of his small mouth on her body and the tingling sensation of the milk being drawn from her breasts, doting on the sweet powdery smell of his hair and his greedy dreamy eyes.

'You really should stop feeding him,' said Stephen, not for the first time. 'He won't start eating properly until you do. Remember James?'

James had gone on feeding from his mother until his brother had been born. That had been a mistake. One moment her breasts were more or less his exclusive property. The next, a tiny interloper had muscled in. Who knew what terrible feelings of rejection James had suffered as a result, which were bound to surface later if indeed they were not surfacing now?

Stephen was pretending that the spoon piled with bits of cooling lamb and sprouts cemented together with mashed potato was a train hoping to enter the tunnel which was James's mouth.

'Quick, James! Open the tunnel or the train's going to crash! Quick!'

James's lips clamped shut and hundreds of passengers perished in a bloody pile-up.

On the other side of the table, Caroline was engaged in the same sort of game with the baby, who was greedier and also less self-willed. His mouth opened apathetically like a reflex action whenever the spoon approached, though afterwards the food mostly spilt out in a lumpy avalanche over the plastic bib with a shelf he wore clipped round his neck.

Deprived of sleep for most of the night, having to wait for the unappetising food they nevertheless wanted, the two

57

parents looked at each other drearily like prisoners waiting for their professional torturers to take pity on them. 'I would give my soul for a decent night's sleep,' thought Stephen; and Caroline: 'It's not their fault.'

'Oh, knew I had something to tell you,' she said, looking across the smeared table at her sandy-haired freckled husband who was like a large, creased, well-behaved version of James. 'Guess who came in at four this morning? And you'll never in your entire life guess where she'd been!'

Stephen evinced mild interest by raising one pale orange eyebrow.

'Next door!'

'How do you know?'

'I heard their front door shut just before ours was opened. And then the light went on in their kitchen. I mean, where else could the girl have been?' Brewing tea to keep herself awake, holding the sated and temporarily satisfied William on her hip, Caroline had looked through the bay window of their kitchen and seen chinks of light in the scramble of creepers draping the trellis on the fence which divided the gardens of the two houses. Then she had heard Helen's key softly softly turn in the lock; the front door close with a click one could catch only if one was listening for it; and her feet, shoes off, creeping stealthily up the stairs. 'It's not the first time, either.'

'Where is she now?' mouthed Stephen, suddenly realising that Helen might be in the house.

'Out,' said Caroline in a normal voice. 'While we were at church, I think. Maybe even next door. There's a new one who's moved in, you see. I told you. *Did* I tell you?' Since having her children, all powers of memory seemed to have deserted Caroline. 'My mind's an absolute sieve,' she often said.

'Yes. I've seen him. Thin. The one who was doing the garden, if you can call it that.'

'A bit like that film actor . . . Oh, what's his name? *You* know! The dishy one in that film we went to the day that

58

perfectly frightful hospital doctor told me William might have to be induced . . .'

And Stephen said immediately: 'Oh yes. A bit. Mouth's different, though.'

Caroline released the children from the table: William out of his highchair and on to a woollen rug laid on the floor, James to hit a saucepan with a soup ladle. She took their own two plates of food from the oven where they had been keeping warm.

'Well, I'm staggered,' said Stephen. 'Staggered. I never thought of Helen like that—'

'We're all human, darling.'

'But *they're* not, are they?' Stephen laughed immoderately at his wit. 'Saw his friend the case just now. You should have seen him! I could smell the alcohol from six feet. Said he hadn't slept for thirty-six hours – leastways, I *think* that's what he said. Could hardly understand a word. Well, that's a lie! Do you know, he's been here fifteen years, so someone told me – fifteen years! – and he can't even speak English yet. Of course he wasn't going to discuss the chimney stack. Not a chance.'

'Well, Jack seems to think there's no immediate danger.'

'Come to think of it,' said Stephen, 'Helen might have done us a good turn.'

'Oh?' Caroline kept one eye on the children as she ate her food quickly, the way she had learnt to do everything since they were born. She could have a bath in two minutes flat these days.

'Yes. Maybe she can use her influence to stop the singing *and* get him to pay for his half of the stack.'

'As long as she doesn't bring whatshisname here.' No visitors had been a house rule ever since the Johnstons had decided to capitalise on their spare room and take in a suitable lodger. There was quite enough infringement of their privacy, as it was. 'Apart from anything, it might be bad for James,' Caroline went on. 'He notices things now.'

Why would it be bad for James? Stephen mused briefly, downing a bowl of apple and leaping from his chair to prevent James from hitting William with the soup ladle. It might be no bad thing for James — who allowed no door to be closed against him, no secret to be kept — to learn that people expect, as a right, to have private emotional lives.

Caroline decided to try and remember to talk to Helen in a tactful way about the general suitability of Mikhail. Then she began to stuff her children's passive limbs into small waterproof garments so that Stephen could take them for their walk and leave her a fragment of peace out of the day.

•

CHAPTER EIGHT

Whilst the children next door were striking a fine balance between being allowed to enjoy themselves uninhibitedly and flooding the bathroom floor, an evening of entertainment was being prepared at Number 11.

There was a different pattern to life here. At Number 9 the day started early, with a sudden jerk, when the children woke each other up. It came to full force just before lunch, and there was an echo of this intensity at six o'clock when the children were bathed. Then it petered out, slumped into exhausted torpor as soon as the children fell asleep. There was no vitality left in Number 9 by the evening whilst, next door, things only began to get going.

As empty milk bottles were set with a scrape and a clink on the swept stone doorstep of Number 9, the first wine of the evening would be uncorked at Number 11 and put to breathe on the warm top of the cooker which was almost, but could never be quite, clean. While Caroline washed the dishes and Stephen dried them in the kitchen of Number 9, aromatic heat would blast from Number 11's oven as its door was opened and re-opened to baste, stir and re-season. And as, one by one, the lights blinked off at Number 9, red candles stuck to saucers on rippled pools of wax would cast uncertain shadows over the feast laid out on the trestle table in the saloon at Number 11.

Every meal was a feast here and usually a reason could be found to justify it. Tonight it was Luli's return. Everyone wanted to hear news from her and so Stefan, Mikhail and Dimiter were combining to create a banquet and Helen, who

61

suddenly seemed to be part of this household, had volunteered to make a pudding. ('Poddink? What it is?' Stefan asked. 'Ahh! Desserrt!') Christo would bring more wine soon.

'Perrsley,' said Mikhail now, looking to Helen for approval.

'No Mikhail. Parsley.' Earlier in the day Helen had used the shopping trip to the twenty-four-hour supermarket nearby which was run by a family of exiled Ugandan Asians as an opportunity to give Mikhail another English lesson.

There were too many people in the small kitchen chopping, mixing, tasting, rolling: each sure that he was the only true cook. The different smells drifted towards the low peeling ceiling, blending like the separate conversations.

'Pippairrs.'

'No. Peppers, Mikhail. Peppers.'

'Pyeppairrs.' He had toasted green and red peppers under the grill until their skins became crisp and black. Now he lifted off the skins with care, cut away the pith and seeds, and sliced the warm cooked flesh into strips. He dribbled best olive oil over them, added the juice of half a lemon, salt and black pepper and the parsley, chopped.

'*Qui s'appelle?*'

'Chushki,' replied Mikhail, or so it sounded.

Dimiter was making the savoury pastries which, as a child, he had so often watched his mother make. He tucked a mixture of sheep's-milk cheese and beaten egg into thin dough wrappings, stroking each layer with oil and butter before rolling them into long fat sausages. He brushed the pale shapes with more butter and oil until they glistened, ready for the oven as soon as Stefan removed his lamb spiked with garlic and roasted in red wine and more oil.

Helen's pudding, trifle laced with sherry, seemed, even to her, an embarrassing relative in this company. But she had wanted to show the exiles something essentially, typically English. They had looked on knowingly as she mixed egg yolks and warm milk to make custard (which they made delicate cream caramels out of) and with growing astonishment as she swamped bought sponge fingers and tinned raspberries and peaches with it.

Stefan and Dimiter began gently bickering over the use of the oven, so Mikhail and Helen retreated to the saloon.

In its privacy he kissed her. She hugged the whole length of his thin body to hers, grateful for this tender and passionate relationship which bore no similarity to any previous one: in which there was no tussling for emotional power, no flinching away from commitment, no bondage to the past. If Mikhail had been English, Helen would probably have told him about her other disastrous affairs: that was what usually happened, like laying out cards on a table. But it was all curiously simple when you couldn't speak the same language. Besides, she believed that by some strange alchemy she and Mikhail understood each other very well.

It was just six weeks since he had arrived at this house and it was astonishing how much change he had wrought. The walls of the saloon had been washed as had the goatskin rug Mikhail had pegged on a washing line in the garden and left to whiten and fluff out in the sun. There was a jam jar of bronze chrysanthemums on the mantelpiece, swept clean of bottles and glasses. Evening sun, no longer blocked by the rampaging vine, cast a kindly old-gold beam over the room, remarking on its gleaming windows and polished wooden floor. Mikhail had found a length of Indian cotton somewhere in the house which now draped the divan bed, its scarlet and yellow colouring clear and fresh after a thorough wash.

But the greatest change was in the fireplace, previously blocked off by a square of hardboard. Mikhail had removed the hardboard (as, by the way, had every other resident of Shipka Avenue) and found a set of elegant cream and brown tiles. He had cleaned the chimney with a broom attached to the long pole Dimiter used to roll out his pastry, collected wood from the skips in the street and chopped it up with an axe he had found in the cellar. Now a fire burned energetically in the grate: the focus for a circle of chairs scraped clean of fondant-green paint. Mikhail planned to persuade Stefan to buy prints to pin on the walls and would ask Luli, who had an old sewing machine, to make cushions for the chairs.

Christo arrived with a case of wine.

'It is becoming cold,' he commented to Helen who, being English, would expect a remark of this kind. 'For August. Ah, a fire! How pleasant.' He unwrapped himself from his Burberry raincoat and slung it carefully over the bannisters in the hall. 'Something smells appetising.' He went into the kitchen to check the food.

Another difference of opinion developed over whether or not Dimiter should have mixed the sheep's-milk cheese in his pastries with cream cheese. Christo said they would be too salty without, upsetting Dimiter who flung out a small speech and then became completely quiet.

'I am only telling him how this should be done correctly,' explained Christo to Helen in self-defence.

Luli's entrance a few moments later was spectacular and emotional. She came into Number 11 like a scented breeze, darting kisses at the men's ears. They seemed to breathe deeply as if, thought Helen, watching, they wanted to inhale a tiny piece of where she had been. Or did they instead, perhaps, sigh?

'I am back,' she said – not 'I am home' – and there were tears in her black eyes.

Christo took her coat, Stefan ushered her into the saloon, Mikhail gave her a glass of wine and Dimiter carefully took from her the large plastic carrier bag she was holding.

'But Luli, what have you done to yourself?' asked Christo, for, instead of clustering stiffly in jet black curls, Luli's hair hung straight and lank. It suited the clothes she wore: a simple black jersey and skirt, not at all new. She looked as if she were in mourning and also younger.

'Well, I gave my Carmen rollers to my little sister Ivanka, didn't I?' she said with a smile and a shrug. 'She wanted them so. Why should I be so selfish as to keep them when I can buy more as soon as I can save the money? The poor girl. She has nothing there.'

Now Luli took in Helen, who stood in the background close to Mikhail, holding his hand. Luli gave her wide tucked red smile and, at the same time, accorded Helen the sort of look a restaurateur might cast at a piece of meat in a butcher's shop.

'But all the same you look good, Luli,' said Stefan; and he gave her two more kisses.

'Well and why not?' Indeed Luli's eyes were bright and clear and her skin fresh as if she had not sat up until dawn drinking and talking talking every night for the past two weeks. It was always like that. She never believed she would see those dear people once more even though she had been back over and over again at regular intervals.

'How was my mother?' asked Dimiter, as if it had been an effort to hold back the question even until now, and threw a longing glance at the carrier bag.

'Wait, darling, wait. I tell you everything. I give you everything. We have the evening.'

It was the first time Helen had been together with all the exiles since that disturbing first evening when Mikhail had arrived. As before, their incomprehensible chatter eddied about her and she could only guess at what intonations and gestures really conveyed. But the difference now was that she felt she had a claim to be there. She no longer seemed like a trespasser and nor did she feel afraid that they would encroach on her. She was comforted by the richness of their company: it was something to warm oneself by, like the fire.

Luli was pulling gifts from the plastic bag. There was a dark blue cap and matching gloves for Dimiter, who came first. Because it was forbidden to send home-made items (which, curiously, came under the category of works of art) out of the country, his mother had pinned labels from shop-bought goods on to her own beautifully knitted creations in case the parcels were opened by the customs, though Luli's

65

never were. Dimiter caressed his presents for a moment and then slid them back into the thin red and white patterned paper his mother had used to wrap them, as if that too was precious.

'How is she?'

'I saw your mother, darling,' said Luli. 'Let me tell you. I went to her house one evening to take your gifts. At first I thought she was out because there were no lights – not one. But she was there after all: sitting in her parlour with her sister and her cousin, watching the sun setting over her garden and eating figs from a big bowl. Well, I couldn't stay long, Mitko, the time was so precious – you understand? Your mother says she is living for the day when she can visit you and the two of you can be together once more. You have to go on sending her invitations, she says. She does not despair even though they have refused her permission for an exit visa so many times. I told her you are a good boy. She says she knows it already' – and Luli pinched Dimiter's cheek affectionately.

'Ah!' There would be more, to be coaxed out in driblets over the next days and weeks and months.

Dimiter half-closed his eyes, conjuring up that room he knew so well, all dusky now. He saw the blacker shapes of his mother and her relatives, knees apart and hidden under shapeless skirts as they sat well back in chairs facing the window with embroidered cushions at the base of their spines. He saw their rough hands with wedding rings thin from half a century's wear embedded in the wrinkled flesh reaching out to squeeze plump figs split pink by the sun before popping them into puckered unpainted mouths while the soft gossipings about this and that went on and on and the purple and orange painting outside the window was overlaid with a wash of darkening blue.

Christo's father had sent a jar of sticky morello cherry jam which had survived the trip and a large gherkin in oil in a small bottle. Luli told him his father's eyesight was failing fast.

'But this is an old person, Christo. What can one expect?' And she looked sad, thinking of her own mother.

There was home-made aniseed liqueur for Stefan, whose mother had remembered his tastes well; a piece of local pottery, a brown and white and blue striped coarse-grained sugar pot with a lid; and photographs in exchange for the ones he had sent. Stefan exclaimed over the beauty of a teenage niece born since his defection and the baldness of a brother who, the last time he had seen him, had had 'a head like a bull's'.

There was nothing for Mikhail.

'I am sorry, Mikhail,' Luli said. 'It was impossible.'

No matter. He had not dared to hope for anything.

'But I brought this to show you,' Luli went on, waving a rolled-up newspaper. 'You have to know what they are saying about you . . .'

'They' were seldom named, but Mikhail knew who they were all right. Was there pleasure or pity in her voice? Hard to tell with Luli who did wrong things for right reasons, like love of her family.

'I'll read it later,' said Mikhail. 'I don't want to spoil my appetite.'

Luli shrugged. 'I'll tell you more when we've eaten. I saw several of your friends when I was there . . . Well, Mikhail, you have to know what those people are saying too.'

'You didn't see any of my family? You gave them the gifts I sent?'

'Your brother came to fetch them. He brought some things for you but I couldn't take them, Mikhail. You have to understand this. You have to know the things they are saying about you . . .'

'Are my family all right? Did you discover that?'

'They have taken your car and your house in the country,' said Luli; then, as she saw the look of terror on Mikhail's face, the kindness which lay uncorrupted at her centre impelled her to add truthfully: 'But your parents are all right – they have not

67

touched them – and so is your wife and your brother. I believe you must be thankful for these things.'

Helen, who understood none of this, felt Mikhail's hand in hers tighten and then relax. She looked from Luli's soft black eyes to his fearful pale grey ones. Then he drew his hand gently away and sat down by the fire like someone who needs time alone to recover.

The trestle table was set up in position and covered with red crepe paper for the occasion. Stefan and Dimiter began loading it with dishes of food. There was a small plate of fresh scarlet chillies (without which no meal was complete) to accompany them, and a basket filled with more bread than the Johnstons next door ate in a week. This wasn't the wholemeal variety to be found at Number 9, but crusty white stuff. Eating was a serious business here. .

Luli returned to her major preoccupation: the misery of her younger sister Ivanka.

'The poor girl. The poor poor girl. She lives only for the moment when she can join me here. She said to me this time "Luli, what should I do? Tell me, Luli. There is a nice man who wants to marry me." Well! – she is twenty-eight now, my baby. It's hard to believe, I know it' – and, as so often before, Luli passed around a wallet of photographs. 'She wants to have children – well, it's only natural – but how can she have children there? It would be like giving them a life sentence. I said to her "Vanya, you must have faith. Somehow I will make it so you can come to me." So she told the man – a good man, nice, attractive, oh yes! – that she cannot marry him. Over there it is like a living death for her.' And Luli repeated: 'She is existing only for the time when she can be with me.'

Silence fell in that room of flickering shadows, lit only by candlelight and the fierce flames in the fireplace. Each person seemed in a dream, or another place.

Then, suddenly turning to Helen, Luli said earnestly: 'Listen, I em heppy beink heerre. Rrilly. I hev med sometink of tis life. I wek up end I em heppy only to brreate tis frree airr. I hev good jop: enoff forr my nids. But is too trregic to brrek wit tose you lof – end morre when you see tey arre soo unheppy. My poorr sisterr, she soo want to be wit me.'

'I am sure that she enjoyed your beautiful fur,' said Stefan in their own language, his lips pursed as if for a kiss, his little eyes gleaming.

'Oh yes, of course!' Luli's husky voice took on a doting, whining timbre. 'The poor girl, she needs to have these pretty things. But of course the other girls don't like it. My mother says to her "Vanya, *don't* go out like that!" She is like a fashion plate – always so smart because of me. And of course they are jealous. My poor baby. She suffers so. Her eyes! – the look in her eyes when I had to leave her behind this time. It haunts me.'

'Well, maybe soon . . .' said Christo.

'I hope so. I really hope so.' Luli ate a chunk of crisp lamb with care, mindful of the caps on her front teeth. 'When I am in bed at night I am in another life, you know? Well – it does no harm, does it, to dream? In that life my sister is with me. She is here for ever. She has all the pretty things she wants. We are so happy.' She sighed. 'This is so tasty, all of it.' And her bosom heaved and trembled again. 'It is like an agony for me to go there, you know? A sweet agony. Well, we can all dream, can't we?'

Then she pulled herself out of the pool of sadness into which she had sunk, gave a coquettish laugh and asked: 'What are your dreams, Stefan?'

Stefan the clown said, as Luli had known he would, that he would like to meet a woman. He described her in lubricious detail and then translated for Helen, toning it down a little. 'She hev to be pleasently plomp wit fine sittink parrts end brreatink parrts. Yonk – twenty few. Beautiful. Culturred. Frrom good femily.'

'English?'

'Of courrse – now I em in Enklend. I hope wit my filty tonk I don't upset it you? You hev to forrgive it my complexes.'

Relaxed by the strong red wine, comforted by the good food and cheered by the warmth and beauty of the fire, the exiles began to talk of how they would like to be in, say, five years' time. Even shy Dimiter was coaxed by Luli into playing the game.

'You don't want to be a little odd-job man all your life! No, Mitko! That's not how you see your future, now is it? You – a qualified doctor!'

'I think I would like to have a restaurant,' said Dimiter after a long pause; but this was no casual fantasy and it showed in the intense careful way in which he spoke. 'A little place, with ten tables maybe – no more. Red tablecloths like this on them. I would make one or two dishes a day only. Spicy – not like the food in this country – and soft, so you couldn't break your teeth. There would be as much wine as people could drink – but not you, Stefan! Yes, I think I would like to be doing this in five years' time.' Then shyly, as if this were not the most important part of the dream at all: 'My mother would be here, of course, helping me.'

Christo said he would like to go into politics, marry into the British aristocracy and own a big estate in Scotland where he would hold grouse shoots. He translated this for Helen with a smile of self-mockery. It wasn't his real dream. That was private. Or maybe it no longer existed.

'Well, Mikhail?' said Luli.

Wary as a cat, Mikhail knew he should not reveal himself to Luli, with her connections. But the relief of discovering that his family were all right combined with the effect of the food and drink to make him say proudly, even arrogantly: 'Well of course I will be established as a poet here. I have no doubt about it at all.'

Helen, watching but not understanding, noted that a curious expression came over the other exiles' faces: a sort of affectionate, understanding pity.

Mikhail looked into the fire. He longed to speak from his heart; and especially tonight when, because Luli had so recently come from there, he could almost smell again the

70

country he had abandoned for ever. 'I have a plan of going back to the Writers' Club for just one day . . .'

Nobody spoke.

'I know how I could get into the country secretly, so no one would find out. I won't tell you how, but I've worked it all out. One day at about a quarter to one I would be there in the Writers' Club – suddenly! Like magic! I would sit down at my table in the corner by the window. I even know what I would order from Rilko, my waiter – the lamb cooked with cabbage. One by one my friends would see me as they came for lunch. They wouldn't believe it at first! Then they would come and join me and we would talk, just as we used to in that place where I would sometimes write my poems on the paper napkins. We'd have a wonderful, wonderful talk. I'd catch up on all the gossip: what people had been saying and doing and thinking of writing. And then, before they realised what had happened, I'd be out again – gone, puff, like smoke! I will do it one day. Really, I'll do it. It's possible. Quite possible.'

'Oh Mikhail!' said Luli, as if vexed beyond endurance.

'Oh please!' begged Helen. 'What did he say? What did he say?' But she might have been a ghost for all the notice that was taken of her.

Luli spoke rapidly, seriously, firmly to Mikhail. She took the newspaper from her bag, unrolled it, licked her fingers, slid them from page to page until she found the one she wanted. She whacked it with her right hand which had been fitted with many gold rings before her trip but was now quite bare. 'Look!' she seemed to be demanding. 'Just look!'

A photograph of Mikhail, a little younger, serious, with much shorter hair, took up perhaps a quarter of a page. There was a headline in thick black capitals and then columns and columns of densely crowded print.

'Please!' Helen implored, this time directly to Christo.

'This is the party newspaper,' Christo told her, peering over Mikhail's shoulder and not wanting to use the spectacles in his top pocket. 'This headline calls Mikhail a traitor.' He

71

screwed up his eyes even more, gave up the struggle, extracted his spectacles and fitted them over his nose and around his ears. 'It says that a special court has sentenced Mikhail *in absentia*. The whole article is a denunciation of him.' Christo looked at a paragraph Luli had jabbed over and over again. 'And here it says – I translate literally – "the arms of justice are longer than the running legs of traitors" . . .'

Helen immediately looked at Mikhail, terrified. But Mikhail was actually smiling.

'And this came out last week?' he was asking Luli. 'While you were there? What did they all say?'

'Mikhail, you are crazy what you say about your friends talking to you,' said Luli. 'No one would dare be seen talking to you now. If you appeared in the Writers' Club – and I have to tell you that this is a crazy sick joke of yours to think it's possible – you would sit like a leper, a spirit. No one would even come near. And I tell you they're not thinking of you as a hero there. No! They say "But he must have been sick, mad, to have given up all the privileges he was awarded – for what? The unknown! Nobody but a madman would do such a thing. Ungrateful as well as mad." *No*, Mikhail! – don't smile at me like that! And as for that silly joke of a poem – they are *furious* about it!'

Mikhail was not at all a frivolous person. One part of him was desperately afraid of the consequences of what he had done, the possible repercussions on those he loved. But another rejoiced that the party had devoted a whole page of its newspaper to him and only him. Since his defection he had found it so hard to come to terms with being unfêted and unknown. Now this massive denunciation, these open threats (which he did not take seriously, by the way) proved that, in his own country at least, he was still talked about. It proved that he still existed as a poet. It was proof that he existed. This was the reason he had smiled.

'I think you must be careful, Mikhail,' said Stefan seriously. 'For a while, at least.'

Careful of whom? Mikhail looked around the circle of

faces. He trusted Helen, of course, and also Stefan, who was far too indiscreet and self-destructive to be any sort of an informer and, anyway, had taken him into his house. He had already formed his own opinion about Luli before Stefan confirmed it. He was less sure about Christo than he was about Dimiter, but he was not entirely sure of Dimiter either because, among these people in exile and separated from their loved ones, you could not be entirely sure of anyone.

'I am always careful,' he said deliberately.

Helen rose, piled the plates, and went to collect her trifle. She felt cross and tearful, as a child might when excluded from an important conversation by grown-ups.

'What am I doing here?' she muttered half-aloud as she opened the old fridge that had been scrubbed out by Mikhail with bicarbonate of soda. 'Why did I have to fall in love with someone I can't even understand?'

Then, appalled, she set the trifle down on the top of the fridge so hard that the glass bowl almost cracked.

When she carried the trifle into the saloon, she looked at Mikhail in a new way: defensively and also with resignation. But he did not notice. They had cleared one end of the trestle table and begun a game of poker.

'Oh darrlink,' said Luli, an observer and therefore not engrossed. She sounded as if it broke her heart to say the words. 'I em soo sorry. I em alrready stoffed.'

Stefan, Dimiter and Christo also rejected the trifle with polite smiles.

Only Mikhail helped himself to a large blob. He dipped his spoon bravely into the pink and yellow mess on his plate as he studied his cards. If Helen had only realised it, this was greater proof of his devotion than a hundred sworn 'I love yous'.

But the trifle was not wasted. When the Irishman came in a little later on, angry at being excluded from the entertainment, he ate the remains at one sitting. There was nothing else left.

73

CHAPTER NINE

'Don't be sorry,' said Caroline. 'We'll give your room to my mother. I've simply been putting the problem off, and Mummy is a problem. I've given her endless pep talks, but it's no good. She's hopeless at coping. Absolutely hopeless. Well, one can't simply pretend the problem doesn't exist, can one?'

The two young women were in the room Stephen and Caroline called 'the drawing-room'. Like Stefan's saloon, it had French windows which gave on to the small neat back garden; but, unlike the saloon's, its shape was long and narrow. In common with every other resident of the street, except Stefan who slept in the front reception, the Johnstons had knocked two rooms into one.

Packed with large dark pieces of inherited furniture and ranks of photographs of relatives – Stephen's father basked in naval medals in one – the room was like most others in the street. There were no bookcases, and only magazines were carefully scattered on the glass coffee table set exactly before the one fireplace which had been retained. There was, however, a superior record-player which was not often used.

Dressed in Bermuda shorts and a frilled shirt, Caroline was on her knees with a hypodermic syringe begged from the local chemist, giving the woodworm in the legs of the Georgian desk near the French windows their annual fix of Rentokil.

'*So* embarrassing!' she said to Helen, as she said to someone every year. 'I'm *sure* he thought I was a secret junkie!'

'So – would a week's notice really be all right?'

'A week?' Strange how any living thing could survive this thorough noxious dousing but, year after year, there were more pin-holes in the furniture. 'Yes, I suppose so.'

Stephen and Caroline had made a point of keeping a distance from Helen: fearful that their privacy might be encroached upon. But now that Helen was going, Caroline felt she could safely ask: 'Like a coffee?'

She got up from the rug which her paternal grandfather had bought in Istanbul. 'What's one to *do* with these pests?'

Helen had been like a wraith in this house: a lodger who never offended by taking too much hot water at the wrong time or making a noise or asking permission (which anyway would have been refused) to invite friends in. Now she would be replaced by Caroline's divorced mother: lonely, garrulous, and a little too reliant on sherry (though one did not acknowledge this). 'And I never knew her,' thought Caroline with a surprising sense of regret. 'Even though she lived in my house for more than a year.'

There had been plenty of chances. Once or twice a week Helen had shared supper with the Johnstons. But the talk had always been circumscribed, with Stephen and Caroline mostly behaving as if Helen were not there. He would tell her about his day at the office, she would tell him about the children. And Helen would sit quietly, eating the meal she had paid extra for and never dreaming that her presence was desirable because, on evenings when she was not there, the Johnstons talked to each other hardly at all.

Every so often Caroline would make a conscious effort to draw Helen into the conversation, almost always asking about her work because she had found that the only interesting aspect of her.

'I feel jolly embarrassed cooking for you, Helen,' she had said often, for something to say. And: 'You *are* brainy to have landed yourself a job like that', meaning 'How did you do it? – you with your looks and your dress sense and your humility?'

'This is delicious,' Helen had always replied (even if, for the fourth time running, it was something overcooked composed of eggs and cheese), with the smile that brought energy and hope to the face that was so often drab and sad in repose, her quality hidden from Caroline, who took people at their own evaluation of themselves.

But having a stranger in one's house meant taking care not to set precedents or to allow dangerous familiarity. It was only now that Caroline felt she could ask a personal question though, once she had made Helen coffee in her kitchen, she proceeded to prepare pastry as if to indicate to her that she was not worth interrupting the day's work for.

'I say, are you absolutely sure you're doing the right thing?'

'Oh yes, Caroline!' That smile again.

'Isn't that new?' Caroline demanded, pointing with a floury hand at the scarlet belted cotton dress Helen wore.

'Yes.' Helen blushed a little. 'Is it too bright? Mikhail made me buy it.'

'Well, it's seriously pretty. Suits you. You look different in bright colours – *and* you've done something to your hair.' Caroline sounded quite cross, as if Helen had let her down by behaving out of character, but it was merely her way. 'Curled it or something. Didn't think that was your sort of thing at all.'

'I'll only be next door,' said Helen shyly, as if aware that only now could they try and establish a friendship.

'James!' Caroline shouted suddenly. 'No darling! Put it down!'

Too late. Crash! Butter and pottery shards lay in a terracotta and yellow composition on the cork floor.

'That's naughty, James,' explained Caroline gently. 'Now Mummy has no butter dish. It's silly too because now James won't be able to help himself to butter from a pretty dish either. Here darling, have a bit of pastry. James make a quiche for Daddy too . . . You were saying?'

'Only that we'll still see each other.'

Caroline viciously punched the slab of pastry into shape. 'There doesn't seem much point in moving.'

'It was a lovely room,' said Helen soothingly. 'I liked being here – in a family.' Then her expression became earnest, even anxious. 'But I want to be with him all the time so I can help him. He needs so much help, Caroline. I'm already giving him English lessons besides the ones he gets at the language school he has to attend once a week. But in that house – well, of course they only ever talk their own language to each other. He'll never learn properly like that.'

'But that house, Helen – well, honestly.'

'You should see all the things Mikhail's done to it.'

'But it's all so dreadfully sordid. I mean, they're all so weird, except yours – I can't pronounce his name. Stephen said he wouldn't go and live there if someone paid him trillions of pounds.'

Helen smiled gently at Caroline. She knew exactly what appealed to her about the house next door. Being in the company of the exiles was like dancing on a brightly coloured rug which had been laid over sad and dreary ground. It was an attitude towards life which made sense to her now. But she couldn't expect Caroline to understand, so all she said was: 'I'm lucky. Really. And it's "Mi-hyle". It's like Michael, you see.'

'Oh, he's the lucky one all right,' said Caroline. 'If you ask me—'

But before she could continue, the telephone started ringing. For the first time since she had taken on the role of breast-feeding counsellor to the neighbourhood, Caroline felt strangely irritated by the obsession and panic of the unknown woman on the other end. 'Why do they all get so frantic?' she caught herself thinking. 'All of them. As if they've failed an exam or something. And why do they all think that I jolly well have nothing else to do?'

Helen, studying the baby, heard Caroline reassure, advise alternate lashings of hot and icy water on the breasts, give the brand name of a reliable emollient cream for cracked

77

nipples. The baby looked sleepy and smug. His hands, cushioned like tiny pink duvets, toyed with a line of woollen chicks strung across the front of his bouncy chair and then, with a sudden unco-ordinated movement, hit them so that they joggled frantically.

'Sorry. Busyness.' Caroline checked that James was happily occupied. He was standing on a chair at the formica-topped counter, smacking his bit of pastry angrily.

'The trouble is,' said Helen, 'there *isn't* anyone to translate his poetry. Not at the moment anyway. So I'm going to try and help him with it myself. If he can translate it into French, then I can turn that into English. We'll get the sense of it like that, if not the style.'

'But your own work, Helen—'

'Oh, there'll be plenty of time for that. It's not so difficult. I'm lucky to be freelance.'

James screamed with rage. He had noticed that his mother was now filling her own pie with a strange lumpy yellow mixture which looked like the stuff that often decorated the front of his brother's jumpers.

'Do you see it as permanent?' asked Caroline as she obediently moved into action, understanding precisely what James wanted though he was unable as yet to speak. She helped him lever his thin grey pastry pancake off the counter and let him spatter a little of her filling on to it before he placed it on a cake tin in imitation of her. Caroline's indulgent attitude towards James's cookery, and the pie which would never be eaten, reminded Helen of something.

'Do you mean am I going to marry him?' Helen had already decided not to tell Caroline that Mikhail had a wife. But now, touched by her interest and out of nervousness, she went on in a rush: 'He's married already, Caroline, and, to tell you the truth, I don't think of that as being important. He never talks about her. He hasn't once. I only know he's married because Stefan told me. What matters now is being with him. I'm only thinking that far ahead.'

'Oh Helen!' Caroline felt much older and wiser even

though they were more or less exactly the same age. 'You've such a lot going for you – a good job . . . Oh, loads of things.'

'I have now.'

'I've seen friends get involved with married men, Helen, and, as far as I'm concerned, it's an absolutely no way situation.'

'His wife's not even in this country, Caroline. He's left for ever. He'll never see her again.'

'But he's not free. It's – different for women, Helen. I mean, it's jolly unfair but it is. We've only got a certain amount of time and you *can't* risk missing out on this – all this.' With a nervous gesture, Caroline embraced the picture before them of the two children: one staring fascinated through the glass panel in the oven door which was exactly at his eye level, the other fast asleep strapped upright in his plastic chair like an astronaut. 'Motherhood's *the* most, well, important experience any woman can have. I mean, I *never* thought I'd hear myself say that. No way! Couldn't stand other people's children before I had my own, believe it or not. Leave Fred alone, darling!' For James was trying to drag the dog by one ear over to the cooker to look at his pie. 'I wouldn't be without them for the world and I'll tell you another thing: I'm not a particularly aggressive character, right? But I'd kill anyone who hurt them, you know? Simply wouldn't think twice about it! Why am I saying all this?' And Caroline scooped the sleeping baby out of its bouncer, pushed up her blouse and put his sprouting teeth to her blue-veined white breast.

'We've never talked before,' said Helen. 'It's strange, isn't it? But I've changed since I met Mikhail. I don't seem so – afraid of things now. Before, it was as if I was asleep.'

'But you can't even talk to him!'

'We communicate very well. I don't understand how myself. It's as if we've always known each other.'

'Now that's simply being romantic,' said Caroline, with a little smile to take away the sting; and she thought: 'I don't know what she means.'

79

'It is romantic,' Helen agreed, her arms wrapped around herself, her eyes soft, remembering. 'The most romantic thing that's ever happened to me.'

'But my dear girl, he has nothing! No proper place to live, no career, no possessions . . .'

Helen cast an unhappy look at Caroline as if to say 'For a moment I believed you were my friend.' Then, carefully, as if thinking about every word, she said: 'All that is true. He has nothing. But he's given me everything I want – that's all I can say. I feel understood for the first time in my life. Also alive and needed – really needed. Before, there wasn't much, Caroline – not really. Well, I didn't know there wasn't – not then. I thought it was all there would *be* – and Mikhail's rescued me, don't you see?' She wanted to add: 'Before, I felt an outsider: I didn't belong', but knew that this would be a mistake. So instead she repeated: 'You do see, don't you?'

'Well then, I'm happy for you, Helen. You must bring him to supper one night. Yes, you must. I'd be absolutely fascinated to meet him properly and hear all about – this simply fascinating country he comes from.'

'I'd like that.'

'Well, we'll fix something sometime. Not this week, though. And next week Stephen's got a mega-project on for the office. Oh, and of course I'll be getting things ready for Mummy.'

'Well, sometime. It doesn't matter.'

'I'm glad we had this talk.'

'Me too. And after all, I'll only be next door.'

'One thing, Helen . . . Oh, this is *so* embarrassing!' Caroline looked down at her baby's large blond head. 'Can you possibly ask whatshisname to do something about whatshisname's singing? We've just about given up complaining ourselves because it seems to lead simply nowhere. Oh, and Stephen's put a trillion notes through his door about the chimney stack. Jack says it's safe for the time being but—'

Then Caroline's sharp eye was caught by a crack – oh surely not a crack! – in the yellow expanse of wall above the beige tiles which flanked the ceramic hob. Caroline screwed up her face in anguish and, baby still clamped leechlike to her breast, leapt up from her chair to investigate.

On her way back to Number 11, Helen met a large balding vicar with baggy black trousers tucked into thick grey socks parking his bike against the Johnstons' beautifully pointed and uncracked garden wall. He was paying his first visit since Caroline had offered to dust his church. He did not glance at the crumbling facade of the house next door.

CHAPTER TEN

'My dearest Mother and Father,' wrote Mikhail in the sloping loopy script all schoolchildren were taught in his native country, 'I hope you are in good health, both of you. I think of you often.'

That was the easy part.

As Mikhail sat at his table thinking, he was not aware that Helen, by his side, had turned to stare at him in surprise. It was so unusual for her to see Mikhail with an unsmiling face. Now, she thought, it looked angry, years older: an abandoned face which had all of a sudden returned. In the short time their affair had lasted, she had become almost accustomed to a man who was invariably in a good mood, unfailingly thoughtful and kind. She did not know that in his previous life Mikhail had sometimes been accused by women of treating them badly. Nor was she aware that behaving towards her with the utmost consideration was just another of his resolutions for his new life.

'Mikhail,' she murmured, concerned, and touched his arm, and immediately the bitter, sad expression was replaced with a smile of almost ferocious amiability.

'Okay?' he asked with enormous enthusiasm. 'You is okay?'

'Are, Mikhail. And it's "Are you okay?" Of course.'

Soothed, she returned to her own task. 'Marinate slices of soft blue cheese in a hot vinaigrette salad dressing', she had scribbled. She gazed into space for a second, then added: 'Serve warm with crunchy bread for a speedy supper.'

'I am very well. You must not worry about me at all.

Everything goes fine. I am learning fast to speak and write in this new language. There is a wonderful girl who is helping me, herself a writer. She has made all the difference. I have no doubt that I will make the literary breakthrough here very soon. I am happy.'

But his pen had not touched the page. Those were the words he wished to write, but he also wanted the letter to reach his parents and so he must be realistic. Had any of the dozen he had already written got through? He had not received a single letter in return and this intensified the illusion that the past did not exist. It was almost as if by stopping letters, threads which bound him to the past, the regime in his old country was deliberately helping the illusion along.

It was an act of faith to put pen to paper. But Mikhail knew he could not say that life had so far been good to him in the West, that he felt himself lucky, destined for new success. No such letter had a chance of getting through.

So – only to be sure of letting his parents know that he was alive – Mikhail wrote: 'It is hard here. Every day is a dreadful struggle. I am starving.'

But maybe even that letter would be stopped. 'And why should I lie?' thought Mikhail. 'Why should I give *them* this false gratification?'

He tore up the letter into little pieces, patted the hand of Helen, who had again looked up in alarm, beamed at her reassuringly, started once more.

If there was to be any hope of his letters getting through and also carrying the messages he wished, then Mikhail knew he had to employ the same subtlety which, particularly towards the end of his time in his native country, had once been an understood part of his art. He was in conflict with a different set of censors now, a far harsher committee, doubly prejudiced and suspicious; and, as before, he would have to trust that the code he employed to get past the censors would later be understood by those for whom it was really intended.

He decided to write about Stefan's garden. What could be more innocent?

'I am growing tomatoes here. Of course the soil is not so rich, the plants not as strong, but they seem to be thriving. I water them each day and a good crop is collecting. It is very encouraging. They are not so sweet as the tomatoes you grow in your garden, my dearest parents. But they have a special flavour of their own . . .'

He thought of his mother and father in the sunny garden full of vines and vegetables and roses where he had played so often as a child in the country he had abandoned. He could not believe that he would not see his family again. The world would change, he thought and knew this was how they thought too. You had to believe in the impossible otherwise there was no point in living. In the meantime, you got on with it and tried not to concern yourself with politics. Life was hard enough as it was and, besides, there was little time to think.

Mikhail closed the writing pad with a snap. He pushed it away. He would finish the letter later.

'Work now?' asked Helen immediately, prepared to abandon what she herself was doing.

They were not like Stefan, who often rose from his bed only in the afternoon. Or the Irishman, whose routine was much the same unless he had money. Or even Dimiter, who got up early but merely tolerated the day. They awoke only a couple of hours later than the children next door and always with fresh hope, as if what had been eroded the day before had been renewed whilst they slept. However much they had earlier agonised over the interpretation and translation of a word, a phrase, crippled by their different limitations, each would think separately 'Today it will be different . . .'

After four months' concentrated tuition from Helen, Mikhail's English was coming along fast; and now, too, when the exiles spoke together in their own language, she found she could make out the sense of much of it. But she and Mikhail did not yet meet on enough common ground to translate his work anywhere near adequately.

When rendered into English, finished, the poems seemed robbed of all grace, metre, poetry itself, their messages crude and naïve. Helen would stare at a result, not daring to confront the hope in Mikhail's eyes, and privately despair of ever achieving success.

'Okay,' she would say briskly in English. 'Not perfect, though. It needs more work.'

If only a proper translator could be found. But where amongst the scattering of Mikhail's countrymen in London? Most were afraid to have anything to do with him. And even if a willing person could be found, there was little spare money to pay for the work.

At the moment, they were trying to translate a poem Mikhail had written last week. It was about a snow rabbit. Like so much of Mikhail's work it was allegorical but to Helen, who could only translate the work from Mikhail's poor French, it appeared like a child's story: simple, meaningless. Slowly the crude sense emerged of the animal whose burrow has been snared by hunters who have tracked its every footprint and now surround it. Presently the snow rabbit must choose, terribly, between making a bid for safety and heading for the unknown or creeping back to familiar and comforting territory but also almost certain death. As always, Helen was struck by the contrast between the cheerfulness Mikhail always showed to the world and the darkness of what he wrote.

Snow rabbit. How could one translate an animal which was unknown?

'We don't have this animal here,' she said in French; and then put it into English for Mikhail's education.

'We don't hev tis enimel in Enklend,' he repeated slowly after her to get the feel of the words. Then he pointed through the window at the golden October day outside. 'Na is no morre hot. *Il fait très très froid*, we hev it snow rrebbit.'

They heard feet climbing the stairs to their room and tried to pretend they had not.

Stefan was beginning to make a habit of interruptions. There was something on his mind and it was causing him to drop in on them most mornings when he got home after a hard night's drinking at Luli's.

'Cen I hev worrd na? Is bed time?'

'It's okay, Stefan. We're stuck anyway.'

He came into the tiny room that was now fitted with packed bookshelves, tripping over a rug Mikhail had found on a skip and Helen had shampooed. He looked into the mirror they had hung above the mantelpiece, peering for his likeness through sprays of yellow carnations and shutting his eyes with revulsion when he found it.

'Milko, I am crippled by this cheap stuff who steals my electricity, who keeps his fire on day and night to spite me. What can I do about this enormous electricity bill I have been sent which he refuses to pay any part of? He laughs when I ask him for his contribution. This Irish peasant is destroying me. I cannot breathe. This terrible vampire is bleeding me dry. What should I do, Milko? What do you think I should do?'

'Throw him out,' Mikhail advised shortly in their language, while thinking what the French word for a particular type of animal snare might be.

'But he has threatened to ruin me. If he tells the social security I have lodgers than I shall go to prison. I will be finished. No, I am in a stranglehold. I cannot move.'

'Well, why don't you sit down?' suggested Helen, who had grasped the bones of what Stefan had said – it was a familiar subject anyway – and could see that Mikhail was getting irritated.

'Tenk you, darrlink.' Stefan had become very fond of Helen and she correctly interpreted his savage black glare as a friendly smile.

Sitting close to Mikhail, she could feel his concentration fight desperately for survival and then crumple before Stefan's

86

self-centred intrusiveness, though she was not aware of his supreme effort to control his temper. He sighed, laid down his pen, and then smiled at Stefan as if he were a much-loved child who couldn't help what he was.

'If something is wrong in your life,' he said gently, 'then you must change it.'

Stefan absorbed this advice, swaying slightly, staring at Mikhail and Helen sitting at their table covered in books and paper and pens with a bleak dour expression which, in anyone else, could only have been construed as extreme hostility. 'Who will change me?' he asked eventually.

Then he went on in English, slurring the words: 'You know, darrlink, tis house werrt lotta cesh na. I em sittink on gold. Is idiotical hevvink tis yuge pless. I tink mebbe I sell end buy it bechelorr flet. Whatcha tink? Dontcha tink is good plen?'

'Well, maybe Stefan. This house is a bit too big for you, it's true. You'd be better off in a flat, I'm sure.' Helen added unwisely: 'But you'd have to spend a lot of money on the house before you could put it up for sale.'

Looking as alarmed and surprised as his drunken state would allow, Stefan asked Helen if she really thought so. He sounded as if this had never occurred to him. He discussed the matter, trying but failing to start an argument with her, for about five minutes. Then he suggested that Helen might care to itemise everything that needed to be done to his house. Look at all what she was doing for Mikhail! He was sure she wouldn't mind.

'Wouldn't you be lonely on your own?' she asked to distract him, realising too late that this was also a mistake.

'Mebbe I don't be elone!' he said triumphantly. He had had it in mind for some time to get married, he went on. Had he mentioned this at all? Actually, this very afternoon a new woman was coming from Computerdate. She had sent a photograph – he was sure it was an ancient production – of herself standing beside a flashy yacht in darked glasses. In return he had posted a picture of himself taken when he was forty few and financially masculine, looking very representative in a suit.

'Well, that'll cheer you up,' she said, trying to remain pleasant.

'Wherre I find it 'oman like you, darrlink? Mikhail is lucky men.'

Helen smiled and cast her eyes down. 'Stefan, hadn't you better get some sleep before she comes? And we've got to work, Mikhail and I, otherwise we'll get nowhere.'

Mikhail, who had understood a little of this, said in their own language to Stefan: 'Of course you must throw this Irishman out. I'll do it for you. He is beginning to destroy my life too because you never talk about anything else and we cannot work, Helen and I. I'll do it tomorrow.' And both Stefan and Helen knew he would: just as he had cleaned up the house and garden and organised everything else here since his arrival.

'But if he tells the social security,' Stefan said doubtfully. 'No, Milko, you cannot do anything. He has me in a trap.'

'He's a bully, that's all. Bullies are easy to deal with. They seldom carry out their threats.' Mikhail added: 'I should know.'

Then, before Stefan could ask about this last rather mystifying comment, Mikhail went on: 'Tomorrow when he goes to collect his social security cheque I shall pack up his possessions and put them in the garden outside the front door. Then I'll change the lock – I'll go and buy one later today with Helen. So now – forget it. Everything's decided.'

'No, this is impossible. Better to leave it like it is.'

'In a minute,' said Mikhail, 'I shall start to think that you need this irritation in your life as a distraction from your real problems.'

Then he bared his even white teeth at Stefan in a smile so sudden and violent it could easily have been mistaken for a snarl. 'Now, Stefan, you must get yourself ready for this poor woman of yours – or rather, Dimiter's – and allow us to continue with our work.'

CHAPTER ELEVEN

When Mikhail opened the front door of Number 11 that evening, an apron wrapped twice around his body, a large dripping spoon in one hand, Hetty Clarke almost burst out laughing. It was all just as Caroline Johnston next door had warned it would be. But, making a great effort, she said: 'I'm your street co-ordinator from Neighbourhood Watch. May I come in for a moment?'

'Plizz,' he urged, opening the door wide. Then he apologised: 'My Enklish is not so fine. One moment is all.' He gave her a ravishing smile and called 'Helen!'

'I've all the time in the world,' said Hetty, smiling back and batting her eyelashes. In fact, both Caroline and Stephen next door had told her she would be wasting it. Who would be interested in burgling Number 11 in the first place? Stephen had asked dismissively. No one was going to keep an eye on the place for them either, such was its reputation; and, as for *their* keeping an eye on the other houses, well they were either in a drunken stupor and sleeping the day through or else eating and drinking or – well, did Hetty know their former lodger had moved in there?

It had added up to an irresistible picture. For an inquisitive person with time to kill (Hetty had been abandoned by her husband and her children no longer needed her), the job of street co-ordinator (though voluntary and unpaid) was perfect. Hetty – who lived way down Shipka Avenue at Number 54 – prided herself on her amusing stories. She would hone unusual experiences into anecdotes for her friends. Even now she was preparing a description of Mikhail in his apron 'like the mother of some enormous and eccentric family'.

A plump fairly ordinary-looking girl with a sweet smile – who could only be the former lodger – emerged from the small kitchen at the end of the hall.

'I'll only take up a minute of your time,' said Hetty regretfully.

'I'm sorry,' said Helen, who had a habit of apologising when there was no need. 'We're cooking and it's all a bit frantic. Won't you – would you mind if we carry on while we talk?'

'Not at all,' said Hetty enthusiastically. She loved food and anything concerning it and, for her, the scene in the aromatic kitchen full of sizzling sounds resembled a kind of paradise.

Mikhail was mixing thick Greek yoghurt with diced peeled cucumber, chopped walnuts, a great deal of garlic and a heavy sprinkling of cayenne pepper. He dipped a spoon in the concoction and then held it to Helen's lips: 'Is okay?' he inquired anxiously. 'Is okay?'

'Delicious, Mikhail. Lovely.'

'May I try?' asked Hetty, who had settled her large bottom clad in a navy jogging suit on to an uncomfortable wooden chair which Mikhail had fetched from the saloon.

'Plizz.' Mikhail immediately ladled out a whole cupful for her.

It was a special soup made in honour of Dimiter's Saint's Day – another good excuse for a feast – and, like so much of the food served here, it was surprising. Several favourite recipes of Number 11 Shipka Avenue had already found their way into the copy for Helen's cookery column, with varying success. The vegetable stew made from courgettes, aubergines, okra, potatoes and tomatoes had been welcomed by her editor for its freshness and originality; as had the chicken stuffed with rice mixed with chopped chicken livers and sultanas and then basted with beer to render it crisp. Two other recipes had not.

'Take a square of sheep's-milk cheese,' Helen had written

a few weeks back, 'sprinkle it thickly with paprika, tie it into a small brown paper parcel with string and pop it into the oven, gas mark 7, for ten minutes. Be sure to set your timer to remind yourself to take it out.' For if one forgot, as Mikhail frequently did, there would be a charred vile-smelling packet which would stink out the whole house, instead of a delicious semi-melted orange-speckled tangy square.

Also: 'Pound the flesh of a roasted peeled aubergine with at least half a dozen big cloves of garlic. Then carry on as if you were making a mayonnaise, dribbling in olive oil (or, if this puts a strain on the family budget, sunflower oil) and, finally, a squeeze of lemon juice, salt and freshly ground black pepper. It makes an excitingly different starter.'

'Impractical and bizarre – really Helen, I'm astonished', the home editor had written on the first bit of copy; and, on the second, 'Quite unsuitable for our readership – remember they're mostly newly married young women.'

'Mmm, this is so *good*!' exclaimed Hetty Clarke.

'Hev it brread wit,' suggested Mikhail, cutting a fat wedge off a crusty white loaf. Without even asking if she wanted one, he poured her a large glass of red wine. It all contrasted happily with her reception at Number 9 (and all the other houses in the street she had so far visited this evening, come to that) where she had not even been offered a cup of tea.

'If I could explain about Neighbourhood Watch,' said Hetty between mouthfuls while Mikhail chopped parsley precisely on a wooden board and Helen rolled out pastry for an apple pie. She and Mikhail appeared to be having some sort of friendly argument about the pie, mixed with talk concerning a film they had been to that afternoon. Unable to resume their concentration after Stefan's interruption, they had decided to visit the cinema. Helen had maintained this was not a waste of time since there was no better way to learn a language than to hear it spoken while watching action which should explain the words. But the action had been slow and Mikhail had not enjoyed the film, which had centred upon two rich, middle-aged and bored American couples going on holiday together to Florida.

'Is not *interressant, rrelevant.*' As usual, Mikhail talked in a mixture of French and English whilst Helen tried to force him to speak English, enunciating her own words slowly and deliberately. 'Why I should cerr?'

'Interesting, Mikhail. Relevant is the same, I think. And it's "should I care" – you know that. Cooking's my job. I'm making the pudding tonight and I want you all at least to try it for a change.'

'*Demain, demain.* Why pipple want *see* it tis rrobbish?'

'Tomorrow, Mikhail. Tomorrow is what you always say. You always eat your own food – all of you. You're in England now.'

'But is so tasty, ourr food – *délicieux.* Why I should cerr of tis pipple? Is mysterrous. Tis is proplem wit Enklish culturre . . .'

'Mysterious, Mikhail. So is English food, if you'd only give it a chance. And it's delicious, Mikhail, delicious.'

'I should say so,' said Hetty, who had been following this exchange with keen interest. 'Steamed treacle sponge, Yorkshire pudding, Irish stew,' she went on with dreamy lust. 'Yum!'

They both turned to smile at her. They seemed to have forgotten her existence – or had they? Now she thought about it, it was more likely Mikhail had been playing to the gallery, displaying a cosy relationship complete with affectionate grumbling. She wasn't convinced by their happiness and she prided herself on her intuition. There was something desperately tentative about the girl, for all her attempts to show the equality of the relationship; something artificial about him. No man was that nice, as Hetty well knew. Interesting. What a dish! – and what on earth was he doing with her, sweet though she was?

'You're not the owner of the house, are you?' she asked Mikhail, knowing he was not. Caroline had filled her in on Stefan too.

'No,' Helen answered. 'But he's around.'

Stefan had been closeted with his new woman for the past couple of hours in his dark nicotine-steeped bedroom with its looming old wardrobe, the doors of which perpetually swung open, and its hard high double bed. No one else had met her yet, though. Stefan had told Mikhail she would be staying for supper. He was taking a calculated risk in inviting her when Dimiter would be present. She would probably call Stefan Dimiter, like her predecessor. But what was life without a flavouring of risk? as Stefan had commented to Mikhail. Besides, he had added, these women were all hens.

'I know it sounds a little bit like "Big Brother is watching you",' said Hetty, coming out with her usual patter. 'I don't want you to get the wrong idea. It's a way of helping each other – and it works. Oh yes, I assure you it works.'

Stefan appeared in the doorway of the kitchen: spruce and cheerful, his brown shoes shimmering. 'I em starrvink to det. Tis is epple, Helen? I em sorrry but you arre eatink in solitarry, darrlink. I em not intendink it offence.'

'This is Hetty, Stefan. She's come about the Neighbour-hood Watch.'

Stefan looked first puzzled and then enormously touched. He took Hetty's plump ringless hand and kissed it, his usually rough chin quite smooth on her flesh from three separate shaves earlier. This was very kind, he told her. Very very kind. But actually Mikhail had taken over all this idiotical business with the laundry (which Stefan pronounced 'lan-drry'). Mikhail enjoyed looking after them. He showed off his clean shirt with pride. See, he was a new man now. Very representative.

'No, no, no!' But Hetty couldn't explain the misunder-standing – though she tried embarking on it several times – because no one was listening. Helen was preoccupied with resolutely crimping all round the lid of her apple pie and cutting out pastry leaves and flowers to adorn it; Stefan was talking to her about some friend of his whom they would meet in a minute. She was doing repairs on the bodywork in

93

the bathroom, he told Helen. He had said to her that now she would have some real food. He meant the soup, of course, and the lamb which would follow.

'What's her name?' asked Helen.

'Mevis. She is not yonk, you know. Nottink special. But in good condition wit all the parrts worrkink end so end so.'

Hetty would have been outraged by this under normal circumstances, but it was hard to take seriously – particularly when more and more outlandish characters kept materialising.

Now entered an extraordinary woman old enough to be Helen's mother, all viscose pleats and floppy neck-tie, with a stiff and brassy coiffure looking more like metal than hair. Hovering quietly somewhere in her sweetly perfumed wake was a small sad man who would not meet Hetty's eye or anyone else's.

Hetty was enjoying herself so much that she eagerly accepted when Stefan – who appeared to regard her with the greatest goodwill – invited her to stay to supper. 'What can I do to help?' she asked, easing her bottom off the chair. 'Shall I lay the table? Let's see . . . how many are we?'

Helen said that, if she was sure, could she lay seven places at the trestle table in the saloon? She explained that, even though there were six of them, extra people nearly always turned up. Although the Irishman was never invited, he often came; and so did Luli and Christo.

Mavis said she would give Hetty a hand, seizing the chance for a private chat with a fellow countrywoman. 'Funny set-up, isn't it? I've never heard of this country Dimiter comes from, have you? I've never been out with a foreigner before. Funny how they're all called Dimiter, isn't it? I s'pose it's like John here.' Then she said with a giggle: 'It's not quite the Ritz, is it?'

There was simply no point in going on trying to explain about the Neighbourhood Watch, thought Hetty, taking a good look round the saloon. Stephen Johnston was right: no one would ever try to break in here. True, some sort of effort

94

had been made to cheer the place up, but everything was of the very cheapest quality. She moved to the French windows and peered through the gleaming glass into the dark garden beyond. Christ what a jungle! – though, again, an attempt had been made to restrain it. Just as her eyes were becoming accustomed to the darkness outside, she felt Mikhail touch her gently on the shoulder.

'Excuse,' he said, 'excuse.'

'Of course.' She moved away and watched in surprise as he climbed on to a chair and proceeded to drape a heavy hairy blanket from the unused curtain rail and secure it with three big safety pins. Hetty didn't know it but he had taken to doing this over the past week. Helen thought it very practical, since the nights were getting colder, but Mikhail had another reason which he kept to himself.

Just as they had started the soup (Hetty enthusiastically accepting what was, for her, a second helping) the front door slammed and the house shook. It was the Irishman, who never brought any sort of contribution. But this night would be his last at Number 11. Though he did not know it, they were celebrating that as well as Dimiter's Saint's Day.

Everything about the Irishman was large and round, from his rosy bulbous nose to his protruding brown eyes and his belly which had grown that way because of his fondness for beer. 'Is it lamb again?' he grumbled as he sat down at the empty place at the trestle table. 'Have they heard of no other meat?' He always referred to the exiles as 'they', in the same way that they themselves referred to the authorities back in their old country. 'I'll have some of that' – and he flicked his fingers at Dimiter, who had that moment opened a bottle of red wine.

There was no real mixing amongst those at the table: like an unsuccessful mayonnaise, they quickly separated into two distinct groups, though Helen sat close to Mikhail.

Mavis talked to Helen and Hetty as if the others did not exist, whilst the exiles' conversation – a flat jumble of incomprehensible sounds – flowed back and forth across the laden table like a troubled sea.

'Well, you meet all sorts. I expect he's told you how we met.'

'No, do tell!' urged Hetty warmly.

But Helen said hastily: 'Yes, oh yes, he has.' For Dimiter sat opposite and surely couldn't be quite as detached and passive as he appeared.

'When they sent me his name and 'phone number,' Mavis went on, 'I realised he was a foreigner of course and I thought "No, I'll give this one a miss." Oh, call this soup! Can't eat this! They've ruined this, they have! Now if they'd've put in sugar instead of all this garlic and left off of all this red pepper, it might've made a nice sweet . . . I'm in the wrong age bracket, see? That's what they told me. They said "You're going to have a problem finding men who want women your sort of age." Well it seems this one particularly specified he wanted a mature type of woman – thirty-five to fifty he put on the application form. Usually they want nothing over thirty-five. Well, you can't look a gift horse in the mouth. Beggars can't be choosers. I expect he wants a bit of mothering and he makes me laugh. I'll say that for him.'

Rat-a-tat-tat at the panes of glass in the front door. It was Luli, who often announced her arrival in this way.

She was in all her finery tonight: hair snaking over plump shoulders in fat black ringlets, metal beads clanking on her bosom upholstered in purple lurex, little feet neat in black patent leather high-heeled mules. She was gleaming with excitement, radiant with a secret she longed to reveal.

'She is coming! They are letting my Ivanka come to me for one month!' Then – to the astonishment of Mavis and the amusement of Hetty – she sank into the chair Mikhail had fetched for her, put her head in her hands and laughed and cried at the same time, black coils of hair sweeping the clumps of crumbs on the table.

'Ah, Luli!' There was longing, not envy, in the way Mikhail

96

and Dimiter said it; and Stefan added with a lecherous wink: 'I hope you have warned her about me!'

'Do they always carry on like this?' Mavis asked Helen.

'*Always*,' replied the Irishman.

'It's her sister,' Helen translated for those who had not understood a word. 'She's being allowed to come to England on a visit. Luli's waited, oh, ages for this.'

'But can't their relatives come whenever they want?' asked Mavis in surprise. 'And don't *they* go back regularly for holidays?'

'She is arriving next month,' Luli was saying. 'Oh, I can't believe it! She is coming at last! Oh, how I shall spoil her! I shall take her everywhere! My baby!'

'The time will be gone just like that,' said Stefan, who quite enjoyed putting a damper on things.

'Ah, but I have a plan.' Luli looked mysterious and sly. 'I thought of it only now – on my way here. I don't know why I didn't before. It's so obvious.'

Desperately trying to remember every look, every action – though understanding not one single word – Hetty observed something rather strange. She noticed that, since Luli's arrival, Mikhail kept one hand over his glass of wine rather like a child guarding a precious possession he feared might be snatched by another. He ate with a fork in his right hand while his left lay across the wine glass until he wanted to drink, when he would remove it. It looked as though he intended to prevent the others from refilling his glass. But no, it was Mikhail himself who refilled the glasses every time, keeping hold of his own as he moved around the table with bottle after bottle, always replenishing it himself.

'She must marry!' announced Luli triumphantly. 'I told you this was obvious. If she marries while she is here, then she can stay. For ever. This is the law.'

'It is not so simple,' said Stefan.

Breaking his usual silence, Dimiter asked: 'Who?'

'Well, I thought we should discuss this tonight,' said Luli.

'Oh!' – trying her soup – 'I remember this. My grandma used to make it! So tasty! Is this your work, Mikhail?'

'She's a friend, is she?' Mavis asked Helen. 'Can you understand a word of it?'

'A little.'

'Oh you are clever,' said Hetty. 'Is it difficult? Could I learn?'

'You are out, Mikhail,' said Luli. 'One of the reasons is you can't apply for naturalisation until you've spent five years in Britain, and I'm assuming you're going to be allowed to stay until then. But Mitko is a British citizen and so is Christo.'

'So is Stefan,' said Mikhail with a private smile.

'Yes, but I am not thinking of Stefan,' said Luli, without explaining why. 'Now, you would do this thing, this act of friendship, for me, my Mitko, wouldn't you? So that I can keep my baby here with me for ever?'

Dimiter looked up from under his thick fringe like a shy animal peeping from beneath a hedge. He drank more wine. 'If I marry her,' he said after a long pause, 'it means I cannot marry anyone else, doesn't it?'

'Well, yes, darling – but only for a while. You can always get a divorce. But you don't want to marry seriously, Mitko! No, I can't believe this! Why should you want to marry? You're happy with all of us, aren't you? You don't want to marry a joke like this, do you? Or this?' Bestowing her luscious smile on them, stunning them with her charm, Luli flicked a long scarlet nail first at Mavis and then at Hetty.

Dimiter was too gentle and also too courteous to agree. He merely gave a little smile and said: 'There are others.'

'Where?' Luli's black-rimmed black eyes looked right through Helen. 'I don't see them.' Then her top lip curled up over her snowy front teeth and a tender husky note came into her voice. 'Mitko darling, you are my friend, aren't you? Yes. We know we are friends, good friends, and friends do favours for one another as we well know, you and I. So – you'll do this thing for me? Such a little thing!'

'I think it's ever so rude of them to carry on like this when we can't understand a word,' said Mavis.

'They gabble,' said the Irishman. 'Gabble, gabble, gabble. It's all they ever do. Will you pass me the bread, Helen?'

'No,' said Dimiter softly but firmly. 'I'm sorry Luli, but it's impossible. I can't tie myself up like this. I am your friend but I cannot do it.'

Tears sprang into Luli's eyes, clotting the mascara on her eyelashes. How could Dimiter hold out against such obvious distress? But he did.

'There is Christo,' he said.

'Christo will take the same line as you,' said Stefan. 'We all know our Christo – he enjoys making problems for people, this is his amusement. No, Christo won't help and there's no point in asking him. No' – and suddenly Stefan looked both important and triumphant – 'I think you must find an Englishman for this, Luli. You will have to pay. But many people do this. It's no big problem.'

'Wish I knew what they were saying,' Hetty whispered encouragingly to Helen. Then when there was no response: 'Lots of drama going on obviously. They're very emotional, aren't they?'

'But I don't *know* any Englishman who will do this! Oh, I am finished! I will never have my baby with me for ever now! And I believed you were my friends – all of you! I was wrong! Ah, how could you do this to me! Look at all the favours I've done for you!' And, for the second time that evening, Luli put her head on the table and wept, but this time there was no laughter mixed in with the tears.

'I wonder she's not exhausted,' said Mavis, 'if she always carries on like this. How old is she? Forty five if she's a day. I'll say this for her, though, she carries it well.'

'But you do know someone who would do it,' said Dimiter. 'We all do. He'd do anything for money. I know he would do it' – and he darted a sidelong glance at the Irishman.

'Oh no!' bellowed Stefan suddenly, and both Mavis and Hetty jumped on their uncomfortable wooden chairs. 'This is totally impossible! No! This cheap stuff is getting out tomorrow – it's all arranged. Mikhail's promised to throw him out for me. No Luli, if he marries your sister this peasant will be a member of the family and I will never be rid of him. Oh no! Think of someone else. I am not having this!'

'But it's a wonderful idea!' said Luli, her wide red smile returned and the only trace of the tears black stains of mascara on her cheeks which she carefully blotted with a green paper napkin. 'He's not so bad after all, and I should know.' (She gave a look which, on anyone else, might have been coy: remembering an occasion long ago when, after a night of drinking, the Irishman had shared her bed.) 'But it will be a business arrangement, that's all. Many people do this. Oh this was a brainwave of yours, Mitko! A brainwave! And you are my darling boy!'

'I think it will cost you a lot,' said Mikhail. 'He is cunning – and also mean. And he knows you are desperate.'

'Well,' said Luli, 'I have a friend who will help me, I am sure.' This time she did look coy.

'Are you still having something with that Arab?' asked Stefan curiously. 'Well, yes, this cash dispenser can afford to help you, I suppose . . .' He himself took on the sort of look Christo had when he got out his pens and squares of paper to calculate his precise finances. 'It may cost anything up to a thousand,' he said. Then an idea struck him. 'If this cheap stuff gets some money then he can pay me all the rent he owes me. There'll be no excuse. I'll know he has it . . .'

'So, you see, this arrangement will benefit all of us!' exclaimed Luli joyfully. 'Oh, this is a lucky night! Your Saint must be blessing us all, Mitko dear. So – let us drink to it!' She raised her glass.

'Oh,' said Mavis. 'This is one of their customs, is it? Are they going to smash the glasses after? I s'pose I should drink to my relationship with Dimiter.' There was sadness in her small brown eyes, magnified by the thick lenses in her spectacles. 'I'd like to get married again. You miss having a man around. A man's a man, whatever he's like. Since my husband died I've been ever so lonely even though my marriage wasn't what you'd describe as ideal. Dimiter does make me laugh. I'll say that for him.'

'Are we drinking to the arrival of the second course?' asked the Irishman with his usual sarcasm. Hetty watched, baffled, as four amused pairs of slanting eyes were immediately levelled at him. She'd had enough for one night, she decided, and besides there was still time to visit a couple more houses. They certainly weren't mean with the wine here; and probably that was why, without explanation, Hetty handed a large bunch of Neighbourhood Watch stickers to Mikhail as a parting gift.

Chapter Twelve

'You're always so grateful,' Helen had been told by a previous lover, a man who specialised in making faults out of what were generally considered virtues. She didn't know why she thought of it one morning as she placed a cup of hot coffee mixed with three spoonfuls of white sugar before Mikhail and checked there was enough paper on the table for the day's work. In the end, Mikhail's predecessor had drawn up quite a catalogue of her faults, each worse than the last. She was humble, she had a low opinion of herself, she was too loving; and he had concluded the list (and the relationship) with the helpful suggestion that it was time Helen learnt the rules of the game.

Whatever that meant. She couldn't imagine receiving this sort of sadistic advice from Mikhail, even if his English were up to it. This wasn't only because he seemed to be kinder than anyone she had ever been involved with before; he also had a greater sense of purpose and his own destiny. There was no energy to spare for cross-examination either of himself or others; no gaps in the timetable he had drawn up. There was learning English, working on his poetry, dealing with the assorted problems of Number 11. Finally there was love. Helen sometimes thought wistfully that another man working alone all day with his girlfriend in what was also their bedroom might have been tempted outside the confines of the timetable. Not Mikhail, who anyway believed that Englishmen only made love at night. Love was for the very end of the day but, as with everything else, Mikhail then gave his full attention to it.

There was an explosion of paper through the letterbox, two floors below. Each day Mikhail was aware of the post. It was one of the new rituals already set up in this new life, like fancying he could only write his poetry with a black Biro on the ruled paper Helen bought from the stationery shop near the tube. 'Letterrs?' he would ask eagerly, as if certain that day would bring a message from his family at last.

It was Helen who always ran down the stairs to sort through the circulars, the proofs of her cookery column, the giro cheques from the Department of Health and Social Security and the red-printed bills for Stefan marked 'final notice'. To her astonishment, there were two letters for Mikhail that day. One gave her a thrill of pleasure and also gratitude – 'Thank you' she whispered to some invisible presence as she touched the top right-hand corner of the envelope – the other was a mystery, though she noticed there were similar envelopes for Stefan and Dimiter.

'Sometink?' Mikhail asked, looking up from the dictionary.

'Something,' Helen agreed. She gave him the less interesting letter first, hiding the other behind her back as a treat to be saved.

But once Mikhail had ascertained that the letter – almost the first proper one he had ever received in this country – was not from his family, he looked anxious rather than pleased. First he shook it, then he held it to his ear; he even sniffed it.

'Oh Mikhail!'

'Why perrson send it me letterr?'

'Open it, Mikhail! Then you'll find out!'

Mikhail took the envelope to the window, held it up to the wintry early morning sun, and only then – when he was sure all it contained was a sheet of paper – did he open it, though he held the sheet delicately by its edges.

It was an invitation to a meeting. The pleasure of Mikhail's company was requested by a group calling itself 'Freedom Fighters in Exile' that had originally hailed from a country which bordered on his own native one. The meeting would be addressed by an Englishman described as 'a professor in the Oxford University' and the subject was to be 'Dramatic Frontiers – the Leaping Capabilities of Direct Broadcasting by Satellite and How They Can be Harvested to Freedom's Cause'. Mikhail was touched when Helen explained what it was about. Yes, this was interesting. If he had more time to spare, he might go.

He did not yet know that all the exiles regularly received invitations of this kind. The meetings organised by different groups were often held in the same yawning dusty hall near Blackfriars Bridge which was not too costly to book. Nearly always present were the same cast of dubious characters: those known to have links with the embassies. Sometimes there was a politician or two who reckoned that lending their names to any sort of cause connected with human rights could do them no harm. Also, frequently, there was the same bald stocky Georgian, deaf in one ear, whose English was not perfect and who asked question after irrelevant question and became progressively more aggressive if asked to shut up. There was always the same unbridgeable barrier between those who knew and understood and those (always English) who presumed to speak with authority but did not know or understand. Stefan attended the meetings quite often because of the free wine afterwards, because he enjoyed riling the Georgian, and because it was always interesting to see who turned up. But on the last occasion he had been so incensed by what he described as the babyish spurtings of a so-called expert on the Eastern bloc – an Englishman who lived like a bloody lord on the profits, said Stefan – that he vowed never to go again, though he himself knew better than anyone that he would most certainly relent.

'Surprise!' Helen produced the next letter.

Mikhail shook his head in puzzlement and wonder. He was unprepared for the generosity of the day.

'Don't go through the shaking and sniffing routine, Mikhail. It's from the *Literary Journal* – see?' And she showed him the name and address of this prestigious magazine which reared gently in shiny black from a thick cream background.

'It's about your poems, Mikhail.'

'Is nottink mebbe.' But he could not hide the hope which had suddenly lit his eyes.

'Look, Mikhail, they can't have returned them – not in this sort of envelope.' For she had carefully packed the unfolded sheets of immaculately typed paper in a quarto-sized envelope backed with cardboard for protection. This envelope was long and narrow. It could only contain a letter.

'Mikhail, I think we've cracked it!'

'Crrecktit?' He held the envelope as if it was precious now, staring at his own name printed there. It was like receiving proof of his existence.

'Beaten it. Made the breakthrough. Succeeded!'

In the letter which had accompanied the half-dozen poems on their trip to the *Literary Journal* three weeks ago, Helen had written truthfully but modestly, as from Mikhail, that he had been a major poet before his defection. She had said that several of his collected works had been published in the Soviet Union also, and listed their titles. She had enclosed excellent reviews of his work, which she herself had translated into English. In the end, it had been a letter of some length. It was important to explain Mikhail.

Why did they not open the envelope straight away? Rip along its flap and tear out the letter? It was as if they had an unspoken agreement to savour this moment: to sit side by side at the table they had learnt not to lean too hard on because it wobbled, and only stare.

Perhaps, Helen thought, they would remember this silence for the rest of their lives. Whatever happened in the future between Mikhail and herself, perhaps this bare little room and even the impatience and anguish involved in getting those first poems as perfect as possible would be fixed tenderly in their joint memory. In years to come, they might recall sitting close to each other and staring mute at the envelope as the moment when it all changed. Mikhail had been right. Provided you had sufficient determination and industry, you could achieve anything you wanted – anything. There were no frontiers for talent. Of course, luck – often so capricious – had to play its part too. But then suddenly it touched you on the shoulder, singled you out from the rest. All you had to do, thought Helen, was go along with it and behave as if you believed it would last for ever.

Finally she said: 'Well?'

Taking up his lucky black Biro, Mikhail inserted it into a small gap between the envelope and its flap and levered it open neatly. He smiled at Helen before he pulled out the folded paper inside.

'Ohh!' Helen sounded as if she were sighing. For the envelope contained the poems, all bundled up any old how.

Mikhail unfolded them and revealed a printed slip pinned to their top.

'The Editor regrets that it is not possible to make use of the enclosed contribution, which is returned with thanks. He expresses all good wishes for your future career.'

'Well,' Helen went on after just a moment's recovery, 'this was only the first magazine we sent them to.' She would not even acknowledge the spectres of disappointment and discouragement. 'Look! They wish you luck. Well, they wouldn't say that unless they could see the poems had real merit. They're just not right for them – that's all it is.' As she spoke, quickly and brightly, she smoothed the poems as if it were possible to rid them of the creases they had been dealt with such casual indifference.

Mikhail put an arm around her shoulders, kissed her cheek, stroked her lips with one finger. 'My Helen,' he said.

He went on to say that this happened. It was part of the game. He spoke in the same confident tone she had. He compared being a writer with being a butcher. One must put much meat in the window, he told Helen, not only one or two legs of lamb. Then one had more chance of selling. Sooner or later somebody would buy. It was bound to be hard to begin with. He expected it.

And now – shouldn't they get on with this new poem? Send off those ones which had been returned to another magazine? Yes, he agreed, it might be a good idea to retype them on fresh paper. The time was moving fast, he said. Always there was too little of it. One must use it well.

CHAPTER THIRTEEN

'But I'm sure there's something I can do to help,' said Caroline Johnston's mother, sitting at the table and sipping the cup of coffee which had just been given her.

'Nothing,' said Caroline. 'Except get out of my hair,' she thought. 'Surely there's something else you want to do besides sit in my kitchen telling me the stories of my early childhood I've heard so often that they've become my memories too, making the children behave impossibly because they no longer have my entire attention?'

'Nothing,' she repeated. 'Everything's under control.'

Except that, as usual, the telephone rang constantly, James tried to torture the dog which cowered under the clothes-drier and Jack and Bill should have arrived half an hour ago to assess the crack which now seemed to Caroline like a small crevasse in the kitchen wall above the hob.

In Caroline's house, her mother had become an extra child: someone Caroline was expected to talk to, feed, kiss good-night at the end of the day. She was a part of the household and not an adult living in the spare room, Helen's old room, leading her own life. She was a fourth person for Stephen to come home to and, in the weeks since she had arrived, he had returned from his office progressively later. Strange how often Caroline had nostalgic thoughts of her former lodger.

'Can't I do the veg for you, Caro? Or iron the napkins – I see you haven't had time yet.'

'No really, Mummy. Anyway the napkins are *perfectly* all right. You sit there and relax. Read the paper. I don't *believe* this!' Because, for the fourth time in the last half-hour, the telephone had started to ring.

This time it was somebody making an appointment to be fitted with one of the nursing brassieres which were kept in a stiff, brilliantly white pile behind the sofa in the drawing-room where James could not discover them. For these garments with thick insets of elastic, their large cups encircled by stitches, their tapes and buttons, held a strange fascination for him. Twice Caroline had found the brassieres in odd corners of the house and garden: once in the sandpit, cups packed with wet sand; once knotted around a toy badger.

'You take on too much, Caro. You do, darling. Now – let me take the boys for a walk on the common this afternoon. Then you can get on with preparing for your party in peace.'

'Mummy!' said Caroline with a dangerously high note in her voice; and, recognising it, her mother said placidly: 'Well then, I'll see if I've won a fortune' – as she said each morning – and began to do her *Times* portfolio.

Caroline knew a great deal more about the house next door now because, since Helen had left, a kind of friendship had formed between them. Caroline had met Mikhail too. Helen had brought him one afternoon when she was alone in the house with the children. Mikhail had said not a word while the two talked. But he had smiled at Caroline in a friendly way and played with the children. He had built a fortress out of bricks for James, who had not knocked it down straight away, then he had picked up the baby and rocked it in his arms, crooning a phrase in his native language that sounded like 'ooshi mooshi, ooshi mooshi' over and over again while the baby goggled at him entranced. The only one ignored had been the dog.

'He's jolly attractive, Helen,' Caroline had said on a later occasion when they were alone, as if it cost her to utter the words.

Helen was glad of Caroline's friendship. Because Caroline was next door, she felt she understood her situation better

109

than any outsider. As for Caroline, Helen had become a cause like her breast-feeding counselling.

Number 11 held a perverse charm, besides. When she was in her back garden, weeding and trimming, Caroline would peer through the tangles of creeper or look covertly up at the battered bulk of the house for signs of life. Since meeting those odd people, Helen had changed so much, mystifyingly become so happy. Caroline wanted to touch that happiness which fed on so little: find out its source and its nature.

The two houses joined together were like a complete fruit, one half of which was firm and sweet, the other soft and discoloured. But like a wasp, Caroline was attracted by the sharp richness of the rotting part, bored by the blandness of the other. She wanted to hover at a distance, inhaling its scent of decay. She and Helen sought one another out: each taking something different from the friendship.

So when the doorbell rang this morning, it was no great surprise to find Helen on the doorstep and not Jack and Bill.

'Can you spare a lemon, Caroline?' Helen always sounded breathless, thought Caroline: as if she even lacked confidence about speaking. 'We've got a feast tonight and I want to astound them with a lemon meringue pie and I've only got two lemons.'

'Another feast! You're always eating over there! Eating and – well, eating.'

'This is special.' Helen followed Caroline into the kitchen and greeted her mother, whom she knew only slightly. 'Luli's sister's just arrived. Luli's bringing her over tonight.'

'Actually, I can't talk because we're having a dinner party too' – Caroline waved a hand at the kippers which would go into the blender and emerge as kipper pâté, the chicken to be turned into *coq au vin*, the oranges for the sorbet. She didn't add that it was stories of evenings at Number 11 which had prompted the idea of a dinner party, their first since William had been born.

Caroline's mother was looking at Helen, of whom she had

heard much, with interest. Now perhaps there would be a chance at last to hear of this bizarre set-up next door. Maybe she could even ask Helen (who seemed a perfectly decently brought-up, nice enough girl) what on earth had possessed her to go and live there.

'Mummy,' said Caroline, 'you *could* do something for me. Could you possibly change William? I can smell him from here.'

'Of course, darling.' Caroline's mother heaved the heavy baby on to the hip that was not arthritic, saying to Helen with a smile: 'Caro won't let me help her usually.'

When she had gone slowly upstairs, feet thumping the treads, bannisters creaking as she grasped them, Caroline asked: 'Everything all right?'

'Well – just about.' Which, from Helen, meant it was badly wrong.

'Stefan has yet another Computerdate contact there,' she went on, trying to sound flippant and knowing how much this sort of story interested Caroline. 'This one owns kennels in Stockbridge.'

'And whatshisname—?' Caroline kept her fascinated stare on Helen as she gently removed a kipper from James's sticky hand.

'Dimiter still hasn't cottoned on to what's happening. He looks a bit puzzled every so often as if he can't understand why no one ever contacts him from Computerdate. And I think he's mystified as to how Stefan suddenly has all these women who call him Dimiter too.'

'What a hoot, Helen!'

'Except that they always want to talk to me, for some reason. Breakfast was a strain.'

'I'm sure.' A pause while Caroline checked that James was only hurling a plastic colander at the dog. Then: 'How's Michael?'

An expression of sadness – no, perhaps pain – crossed Helen's plump face with its candid blue eyes that so easily

111

registered hurt and its sweet full mouth. 'Not – terribly good, Caroline.'

'But I thought things were going so well!'

'Oh well,' said Helen. 'It's bound to be hard trying to make the literary breakthrough here. He's so good about it, too. But then, this business with Luli's sister has depressed everyone else as well.'

Dimiter, who had tried over and over again without success, and was still trying to get his old mother out on a visit, had crept about like a ghost these last few weeks since they had heard Luli's sister was coming.

But he at least received letters from his mother, even though they were always clumsily sellotaped together after they had been opened and read en route. Mikhail, of course, got none.

Since Luli had heard that her sister was coming, she had been self-centred in her happiness, so obsessed by the coming event that, like a delighted newly pregnant woman talking to barren ones, she had discussed nothing else with the other exiles. What would Ivanka like to do? To eat? To drink? Would Luli's bed be comfortable enough for her? – for of course she herself would be sleeping on the sofa. Nothing but the best for her Vanya, her baby, the light of her life.

'It's hard,' said Helen.

'But can't Michael 'phone?' asked Caroline. 'I mean, if he's worried about his family, why doesn't he simply pick up the 'phone?'

Helen sighed. Then thought: 'Well, I knew nothing about it either before I met Mikhail.'

It was only Luli who could pick up the telephone, book a call an hour or so in advance (for there was no direct dialling to their country) and be sure that the operators at the other end would put her through every time. (And Luli rang often from the hotel where she worked, leaving her employers to pay the bill.) Sometimes Christo and Dimiter were put through, Mikhail never. As for Stefan, he did not even try.

'They say the line is occupied,' Helen explained to Caroline. 'Or that there's no answer. Even though Mikhail knows that at six o'clock in the evening they're always there. He's never managed to talk to them, never. Once an operator at the other end laughed down the 'phone – she actually laughed as if she was mocking him.'

'So he doesn't know how they are? Not at all?'

'No. Luli sometimes tells him things she's heard. But none of them trusts Luli much.'

'Riveting.' Hearing what went on in that house was like having a secret affair, particularly as Stephen disapproved of them all so vehemently.

'Mikhail's so jumpy,' said Helen, at last mentioning the real cause of her unhappiness but sounding much the same as before. 'He doesn't sleep. Often he has terrible nightmares. Last night, we sat up for most of it talking.'

'Oh.' Caroline thought of Helen next to Mikhail's slender strong body at night. 'I suppose he's beginning to regret leaving,' she said. 'I mean, well, gosh it's jolly tough for him, isn't it?'

'Never!' Now Helen sounded exactly like Mikhail. 'He says he never never regrets leaving – though once he said that if he'd been braver he would have stayed. But he had no choice. If he'd stayed, Caroline, he'd have been in prison by now. They were beginning to close in on him. He also says' – Helen's voice trembled and her eyes glistened slightly – 'that he couldn't bear the person he was becoming. He had to leave or he would have gone mad.'

'Poor old you,' said Caroline. 'It's *the* most appalling strain on you too.'

'Oh I can manage.' Helen tried to smile. 'It's only that I feel Mikhail's worried about something else and he won't tell me. I have this feeling—'

'All sweet and dry,' said Caroline's mother, returning with the baby wobbling passively on her hip, its incurious gaze sweeping the room. 'Is that a cup of coffee I see, Caro?'

'Well, it's not sherry,' said Caroline tartly.

'Now, Helen – you live next door in the Hungarian house?'

'Not *Hungarian*, Mummy! I've told you a hundred times! Oh, there are the builders.'

So instead of talking to Helen, who slipped back to Number 11, Caroline's mother had to talk to Jack instead: or rather listen, while he told her about the soft way the country was governed. And while this conversation was taking place, Caroline went upstairs to her bedroom to make a telephone call. 'Mummy's simply longing to come and see you,' she told an old friend of her mother's, 'and I happen to know she's at a loose end tonight . . .'

CHAPTER FOURTEEN

There was always enough food at Number 11 Shipka Avenue, but never quite enough wine. All the exiles were familiar with the off-licence on the corner of the main road. At least once in an evening they made their way there.

This time it was Mikhail, who had won at poker the night before, who volunteered to go. In the end, money spread itself evenly between the exiles. Christo and Dimiter, who both earned moderately well, had more to start with but Stefan and, particularly, Mikhail were better poker players.

'I'll come too,' said Helen, already jumping up.

'No swithearrt. You stay. One moment is all. Stay' – and he put his hands on her shoulders, pressing her back into her chair.

Mikhail badly needed to be alone. He wanted to escape from the stuffy noisy saloon with its echoes of the past: get away from the blatant happiness of Luli and the disturbing presence of her sister Ivanka and try to repair his mood. So it was a relief to have an excuse.

Cold wind swirled about his naked ears and throat as he shut the front door behind him. In another month it would be Christmas.

'Have I really been away for almost six months?' thought Mikhail. And then: 'Why do I think of it as "away"? In a moment I shall start to think that I am missing that place' – and he smiled to himself at the craziness of the notion.

The street was not dark by the standard of those in his native land, where all lighting was kept to the minimum to save energy but, being less central, was darker than some.

There was no neon here: only soft golden light radiating from old-fashioned green-painted lamp-posts which picked out the pastel fronts of the houses opposite, the yellow blotches on the dark wide leaves of the laurel tree in the garden of the house next door which Mikhail always thought of as 'the children's house'.

A car drew up outside the Johnstons'. Out climbed a young couple who carefully unloaded a carrycot from the back seat and then, baby swinging between them, pushed through the wrought-iron gate and up the neat path to the front door. There was a loud burst of speech as the door opened – 'They sound like the ducks on the pond,' thought Mikhail – and then silence after it had closed behind them.

At this time of day, the curtains were drawn and the blinds unfurled in looping flowery swags. The inhabitants of Shipka Avenue had taken a mass vote on privacy and one could only guess what went on behind the cream linings. But sometimes, through a careless gap, one could see the flash of a television illuminating a darkened room like blue lightning. Just one living-room was still on show for the spectators outside. Around a long pine table sat a family of five – mother, father, and three little children. Just an ordinary family eating the evening meal with the usual attendant bad behaviour and arguments. But Mikhail gasped as he stood gazing at this theatre of family life. He felt as if he had been punched hard in the chest. He could not move. But then the father of the family became aware of an observer in the gloom outside, came to the window, peered through it with angry mistrust, then twitched the curtains together.

Mikhail wrapped his mackintosh more tightly around his thin body and continued down the street. If someone had looked out from the hidden windows of those houses they might well have wondered: 'Why does he not walk along the pavements? Why does he, instead, walk in the middle of the road where he is so vulnerable to passing cars?'

Now Mikhail walked fast and he himself thought: 'Why did I volunteer to come? Why do I always believe that I am

116

protected?' For behind him, distinctly now, he could hear footsteps. He stopped, turned, studied the avenue unrolled before him.

There was no movement; just stillness in that dark street bleached of life, the houses fringing it like pale shut boxes.

Then suddenly, in an alleyway beside him, there was a crash of metal and Mikhail shuddered violently. But it was only a cat scrabbling for chicken bones in a dustbin, the cover of which it had knocked off.

'Wretched creature,' said Mikhail out loud. 'So many cats here', and he resumed his walk up the middle of the street.

Now he heard them again: not clipped, brisk, but stealthy and soft. This time Mikhail did not turn. The main road, much better lit, was within a few yards. So, walking quickly but taking care not to run, Mikhail continued on his way as if thinking only of getting to the off-licence.

Mikhail was proud that he could now shop properly: convey what he wanted, sort out the correct money, then check that he had not been cheated. It was a new pleasure. It even applied in the off-licence which was not really like a shop at all but more like a high security prison where the owners and their wares sat behind thick glass and one could only point to what one wanted, not touch. A large Alsatian with a hairy black ruff lay on the floor, its pointed ears twitching, paws stretched before it in dark grey and cream parallel lines.

'Tis is good?' Mikhail knew the wine was good, but longed for the comfort of contact with another human being.

'We sell plenty of it.'

Mikhail said he thought the wine improved with warming – he used Stefan's favourite French term, *chambré*.

'Pardon?'

'Nottink is imporrtent.'

He received three bottles of the wine, wrapped in purple tissue paper, through a narrow gap in the glass barrier. 'Tenk you. Goodnight.'

117

There was no reply. They appeared incurious and glad to see him go.

When Mikhail looked down Shipka Avenue, as seemingly empty as when he had come up it a few minutes ago, he could not bring himself to start home. What should he do? He wished he could telephone Dimiter from the kiosk near the tube station and ask him to come and help carry the bottles, but it would sound absurd. Should he perhaps skirt around Shipka Avenue and approach it from the other end? He was hesitating, wondering what to do, when suddenly he felt a hand clap him on the shoulder.

'Ohhh!'

'Jesus you're nervous!' said the Irishman. ''Tis only the bridegroom on his way to meet his intended.'

'Oh, he's jolly well got bags of energy,' said Caroline, passing around her kipper pâté for the second time. It was a little too salty. She noticed that the wine glasses were empty and, catching her eye, Stephen half-filled them again. 'He just doesn't want to put any of it into his house.' She was flushed with the excitement of giving a party, anxious not to be boring: dangerously primed for indiscretions.

'How absolutely priceless,' said the rosy-cheeked blonde Mikhail had seen arrive at the house earlier. 'And where does the woman with hair like a bus conductress come in?'

'He talks like this,' said Stephen and, lips pouted to mock Stefan's slack-mouthed sullenness when drunk, he gave a passable imitation of him arriving home in the morning after a night's carousing at Luli's.

There was a comforting feel of solidarity about the evening. The two couples invited to sit at the table which had been laid with a lace cloth and pale blue candles appreciated the show: knowing full well that, only a little earlier, the kitchen had been littered with toys and books because their kitchens were like that too. They knew the problems of raising the young in this uncertain world. They knew, too, who they were. They were on the way up: passing swiftly through this stage when money was still tight. In the future they would look back with nostalgia to the time spent in these houses that would have been prettier had they been Georgian rather than late Victorian; that never had quite enough bedrooms and should have had bigger gardens, and were in areas which would be fashionable but were not quite yet. Later on in the evening, they would discuss serious topics like the lack of good free primary schools south of the river. Now they could be frivolous and even Stephen could put up a pretence that the state of Number 11 next door was a joke rather than a permanent worry.

'Extraordinary to live *here* of all places!'

'Well, it makes a change. I mean, we've got the same thing only different in Peckham, if you see what I mean.' (They called it Peckham or Camberwell or Myatts Field, never Brixton.) 'Oh gosh . . . I am a pig . . . This is seriously good, Caro.'

'Where is this country exactly?'

'Actually, we may laugh,' said Stephen, sombre now. 'But it's no joke living next door to them, I assure you. Value of our house must have dropped by twenty per cent, I estimate.'

'Oh no, surely not, darling!'

'And has Caro told you about our lodger?'

'I didn't know you had one any more. I thought your mother . . . Where *is* your mother by the way, Caro?'

'Out, thank God. D'you think I'm awful? I adore my mother of course but you can't imagine how heavenly it is to have the place to ourselves for the evening. No – toast Simon? – you won't believe this but our perfectly good lodger's gone to live next door. She's moved in with one of *them*!'

'It can't be the pathetic little one,' said the third girl present – fashionably red-haired, married to an insurance broker who sat, pink and shining, on Caroline's right. 'Not the greasy one who tries to talk like us? *Not* the drunk one who keeps you awake at night with his singing and pinches all the pathetic little man's girlfriends!'

'There's another one,' said Caroline. She had gone too far now to retreat and, feeling disloyal, she rose and started to collect the plates. 'Quite attractive, actually. He was once a famous poet apparently. But all the same . . .'

'You couldn't imagine a more unlikely girl,' said Stephen. 'Quiet. Oh, perfectly nice. But shy. Didn't even think she liked men much. Bit of a feminist, you know – never bothers with herself at all . . .'

'They're *always* the worst!'

'You haven't seen her lately, Stephen,' said Caroline.

'I think I can speak with some authority. Anyway, she's chucked her oar in with this character who has no job, no money, no prospects, can't even speak a word of English (no, he can't, Caro – that's not English) and has nowhere to live but the tip and knocking shop next door. Well, it can only end in disaster and I for one won't be around to pick up the pieces.'

'Well, he is *using* her,' said Caroline. 'I mean, that girl does literally everything for him. People jolly well don't know when they're well off, do they?'

'What's the – no, seriously, what's the attraction?'

'She says she loves him.' Turning her back on her four guests, Caroline took her overcooked *coq au vin* out of the oven.

'Isn't she beautiful?' Luli demanded of the Irishman, her proud caressing glance never leaving her sister. 'Isn't she feshion plet? Isn't she picturre?'

'Gorgeous,' said the Irishman and, as always, it was impossible to tell whether he was sincere.

Ivanka's smooth passive face registered faintly amused agreement. She accepted the tribute.

'End she spikkink good Enklish. Vanya learrnink good et school end she brrushink up in clesses wit frriend livink in nearr house what spik good Enklish. My Vanya always she plennink she comink to West.'

Ivanka was smaller than Luli, as blonde as she was dark, but just as shapely. Tonight she wore the sequined green cocktail dress Luli had taken on her trip home the time before last. She wore Luli's jewellery too and, on her feet, Luli's little arched black satin shoes with four-inch heels and bows on the toes.

'Don't she hev beautiful skin?' Luli went on, touching it with a finger. Her Vanya took good care of it. Every morning she gave herself a face pack. This morning she had made one from avocado pear and egg white. Was like a peach, this skin.

'Very nice,' said the Irishman. 'Very nice indeed.'

Ivanka's gaze between lashes burdened by many coatings of green mascara flickered over the saloon. This was not what she had been led to expect of life in the West. Where was the three-piece suite? The video recorder attached to a colour television with a twenty-eight-inch screen? (There was not even a black and white set in this house.) The Wedgwood and Royal Worcester china?

She did not feel at home here.

For one thing, there was Mikhail. Ivanka knew all about Mikhail. He had been one of the charmed ones at home. His wife was a famous beauty: Ivanka had seen pictures of her once in a magazine. He had had a Mercedes, two beautiful homes, friendship with the President. And yet here he sat in this bare unluxurious room whose attempt at cheerfulness Ivanka entirely missed: subdued, pale, cheaply dressed, in the company of a plump and unfashionable English girl. He was a fool. How otherwise could she view him, since everyone else saw him thus?

Amongst her luggage, Ivanka had a newspaper cutting all about Mikhail which, sooner or later, she intended to show him. The great poet, it said, was now living in penury and squalor in the West, his talent unrecognised, shunned even by his fellow countrymen in exile. This was what happened, the article warned, when an indulged artist turned traitor: this was the sort of reception to expect.

Or maybe she wouldn't show the cutting to Mikhail. There was just enough truth in it to invite speculation as to how the author of it had obtained his information. Luli's sister knew the answer to that question. It was part of the price of the exit stamp on her passport. Better perhaps that the cutting remain hidden in the suitcase. But she conveyed her contempt for Mikhail each time the general conversation forced her to talk directly to him.

But anyway, where was the life in them all? Dimiter was a miserable-looking and silent specimen. Christo said only slightly more. Stefan alone sparkled. He was invigorated by Ivanka, full of extravagant compliments and saucy anecdotes.

'Put some of this between your juicy lips,' he said to her. 'This is chicken soup made like my mother used to make it, God bless her. Nourishing. Sweet. It won't make you fat. Has Luli told you the story of the gorgeous blonde nurse who used to feed me chicken soup when I was in the infirmary with the pleurisy?'

'My Vanya cen it anytink witout she get fet,' said Luli to the Irishman. 'Don't she hev beautiful figurre? Don't she hev merrvellous legs?'

'Only me,' said Caroline's mother as she came into the kitchen, all softened by candlelight like the saloon in the house next door. 'Hope I haven't missed all the fun.' And, as the men rose like water splashing out of a puddle when a stone is thrown into it, she said: 'I came home just as soon as I possibly could. Any of that heavenly pud left, Caro?'

CHAPTER FIFTEEN

Dimiter learnt of his mother's death the week before Christmas and told no one.

He had known bad news was on the way as soon as he heard the familiar accent of the telephone operator, a click, and then the faint voice of his aunt Anka. A telephone call from his old country was like a telegram: it spelt death. It was very difficult to telephone from there, it was far too expensive for ordinary folk, it was not at all private. It was better to write.

'She is no longer with us,' Dimiter's aunt told him, her voice trembling with grief and drama and age and also relief at getting through. 'She did not suffer, thank the Lord. She spoke of coming to you right until the end, Mitko dear. Let us pray that she has gone to a better place.'

No one knew of the telephone call, which came just after eight o'clock one morning as Dimiter was preparing to go to Number 4 Shipka Avenue to put up some bookshelves. It was too early for Stefan, who had seemed keen lately to answer all telephone calls, and also for the Irishman. Mikhail and Helen were already working over cups of coffee in their room.

'Freedom for her dust,' Dimiter whispered with a sob as he sank on to the divan bed in the saloon, his head in his hands.

He did not turn up to do the shelves and did not tell the owners of Number 4 he would not be coming. ('Hopeless!' they would tell each other later. 'One makes a point of staying in. Why on earth can't they let one know?') He drew the unlined curtains of his room and, like Stefan and the

Irishman, stayed in bed for the rest of the day, blankets pulled up over his head and the scarf he always wore to protect him from chills, even in the hottest weather, knotted around his neck.

But unlike those two, he was not still doped by alcohol, suspended in a sluggish world, half-asleep, half-awake. He was in the past, in another place, and painfully alive.

It was agony to remember, but he wished to record each proof of love from the one person in the world who had truly loved him. So, curled up under the hairy weight of the old blankets on his bed, chilled by shock and grief, Dimiter relived his life until the time when he had defected, as if it had ceased to have meaning after that.

It was his mother who had brought him up, his father having died of tuberculosis when he was just three. He had a photograph of her taken at that time, but thought he could clearly remember her slenderness and dark radiance. However, maybe he only thought he could remember: the way he thought he could remember his father because his mother had told him so often how his father used to carry him on his shoulder to the baker to buy bread; how he used to dance to the music of the wireless, his little son held high in his arms. But Dimiter had a clear recollection of events two years later. There had been a man around his mother then: a second cousin of an old schoolfriend attracted by her sweetness and gaiety. As an only child used to having all his mother's attention, Dimiter had resented that man and now, with awful remorse, he remembered how he had deliberately broken up the budding love affair. He had blitzed it by behaving badly whenever the man was present.

There was an occasion when, for a special weekend treat, the three of them had visited a zoo some distance away. Dimiter, who had never seen a giraffe or a rhinoceros before, had declined even to glance at them, keeping his chin tucked against his chest inside the big collar of the dark blue jacket his mother had made him. He clearly remembered the yellow gravel everywhere, puddled with recent rain. Later, when they had tea in a café, he had refused to sit next to the man or to eat the sugared cakes which had been ordered. His mother had worn a white dress with tiny red flowers on it. He remembered her excitement as they set out on the expedition; the rage in his heart when he saw how she laughed and chatted with the man; and, later, her instant forgiveness of his own monstrous behaviour. He must be ill, she had said, worrying about him and not the way the day had been ruined. There had never been another like it. The man well understood why the child had behaved so badly, even if the mother did not. There were no more chances to remarry.

She had grown old. As a widow, she had taken to wearing black – but for ever. She had allowed her hair to grow grey. She had put most of her energy into her garden. Her cheeks, which were left unrouged, acquired deep creases. Only her neck and bosom stayed white and smooth. Hidden beneath her loose black clothes, they were her sole vanities. Occasionally she patted them with cotton wool soaked in rosewater and in summer sometimes inadvertently allowed small glimpses of them.

She had been almost sixty when Dimiter decided to defect. She was anxious to see him settled with a girl who would care for him, longing for grandchildren to spoil. Yet she never told him not to go, never let him see her great sadness at the prospect of no longer having him near her. 'If you feel it is right, my dearest, if it will make you happy,' she had said to him, 'then of course you must leave – and you are right to want to turn your back on this cruel system which has made you suffer so, and create a new life for yourself in a free country.'

But of course she had never believed she would not see him again. Through the lonely years which followed, she lived with the dream of being allowed to visit him in the West, unable to understand why this was impossible. After all, she did not want to emigrate also: she was too old to start again and she wished to be buried beside her husband in the land where she had been born. But oh how she ached to see her only child again!

She sent Dimiter one of the passport photographs she had had taken in the hope of coming. She confronted the camera in her black blouse, her eyes fierce and longing in the face which, in old age, had become so like his face. It was as if, in this photograph, she defied the authorities in her country to tell her why she could not come, why she should be denied this most elementary of human rights.

'Why didn't I write to her more?' Dimiter thought now in agony – even though he had written to her often, thought of her every day, sent gifts with Luli each time she went back. Had he not taken that love for granted? Believed it would always be there for him? Even, sometimes, felt impatience with it? Tested it? And then: 'Why did I leave? Why did I do it?'

When she had written to him, she always began by asking whether he was happy and in good health. Then, if something had gone wrong in her life, she would say: 'Now I will tell you a little about myself.' So casually she would pass off a broken leg (two years ago), a bad bout of arthritis which made gardening difficult, an attack of bronchitis brought on by the harsh winters.

He saw her as she must be now: prepared for the black nothingness of the grave. Dimiter had seen dead bodies often: at home it was considered normal to view a corpse to pay one's last respects before it was put away for good. Once, as a child, he had forced himself to follow his mother's example and kiss the marblelike forehead of a great aunt as she lay uncannily small in a room smelling of dust and sugar. This old woman, so energetic and malicious in life, had not looked peaceful – as his relatives murmured to each other. She was not there at all. His mother told him afterwards for comfort that casting off the body was only like throwing away an old shoe. The soul had outworn it. It was nothing, the body at the end, only an old leather envelope no good to anyone.

But now when he thought of his mother – dead – he

remembered those other shrunken cold bodies and could not bear to picture her veined eyelids folded over empty eyes, her wrinkled stiff hands crossed over her motionless chest. 'Always remember I am with you,' had been one of the last things she told him. But he would never again hear her soft sweet voice – so touchingly feminine in a woman of her age; never again be able to say to himself at intervals during cold rainy London days 'Now she will be out in the garden, tending her fruit and vegetables', 'Now she will be standing before the stove turning them into jams and pickles'; or know that promptly at one thirty in the afternoon this industrious and disciplined person would go to sleep for one hour, her outer garments removed and laid across the end of her bed, a woollen shawl wrapped around her head if it was winter.

Just as Dimiter heard the echo of her voice and her laugh and believed he was going mad, there came a soft tap at his door.

'Dimiter,' called Helen from outside. 'Dimiter, are you all right?'

Silence.

'Dimiter, I've brought you a cup of tea. Can I come in?'

Dimiter scrambled out of his bed, smoothed his hair and his clothes, and opened the door.

'Dimiter, are you ill? We heard the door of your room shut.'

'I'm okay.' He longed to tell Helen, who was kind, what had happened. But he did not. He accepted the tea, which he disliked. 'A little influenza, I tink.' And he touched the scarf at his neck, pulled it a little tighter.

'Well, I won't ask you if you'd like me to get you a doctor,' she said, making a joke out of the fact that he, who had qualified in medicine, would certainly know what treatment was required.

'It's okay, Helen. Tenk you.'

'You're sure you're all right?'

He looked into her round blue eyes, so concerned for him. Why could he not tell her, of all people? Afterwards, of course, he would wish that he had. But living in the West had taught him stoicism about all things. In that respect, he was quite like the Johnstons next door. Only they called it 'keeping a stiff upper lip'.

Chapter Sixteen

Two days before Christmas, Caroline Johnston was unloading carrier bags from the car outside her house one lunchtime when she saw Ivanka.

She knew it was Ivanka because of Helen's minute description. She recognised the long curled bleached hair, the unsmiling thickly made-up face, the way she hobbled slowly along the pavement on her four-inch heels. Caroline also recognised the scarlet jacket she had seen Luli wearing once. There was no one else it could possibly be.

'Good morning,' she said pleasantly.

Ivanka's response was suspicious, even hostile. Why was this rosy-cheeked young woman with hair like a dark mop who resembled a milkmaid and was dressed in a fattening green quilted waistcoat addressing her as if she knew her? There was no reason to reply.

Throwing Caroline a wary glance over her shoulder, Ivanka pushed open the gate of Number 11. It did not shut properly, she noticed, not realising that once the neatly clipped hedge had grown right across the gate like a pair of bushy eyebrows meeting over the bridge of a nose.

'This house is a disgrace,' she thought; and, as she bad-temperedly banged on its scratched but polished brass knocker, ignoring the bell, she was unaware too that, only a month ago, Mikhail had carefully repainted the front door shiny black.

Ivanka was paying a call on her bridegroom: ostensibly to check arrangements but really to make sure he was still amenable. Luli had suggested it. 'But don't go too early,' she had cautioned. 'This pig sleeps late.' However, there was nothing else to do at Luli's bedsitter when Luli was out at work except watch television. This morning there had only been a children's programme so Ivanka had decided to come anyway.

As Caroline let herself into her own house next door, saying to her mother, who immediately appeared from the kitchen, 'It's all *right*, Mummy, I can manage', she thought 'What's going on over there now?'

'Shall I get the boys out of the car for you, darling?'

'It's all *right*, Mummy, I can perfectly well get them out myself. Anyway, they're both asleep so I thought I'd leave them there. Anything for a bit of peace – and I don't want them to see these presents. I had a ghastly job buying them in the shop without their seeing them.'

'Well, all right darling. Do you know, when you were a little scrap Daddy and I used to have to take you for a drive in the car in your Moses basket sometimes to get you off to sleep. You were a dreadful sleeper. Dreadful. *Just* like the boys. *So* amusing. I remember once . . .'

'Mummy!' And Caroline slapped the hand that had started to unpack the contents of one of the plastic bags.

So Caroline's mother sat down at the table to do her *Times* portfolio as usual while Caroline unpacked her shopping alone.

She had spent much too much money although Stephen had warned only this morning: 'Steady on, Caro. Don't overdo it this year, will you?'

But what was Christmas without an oversized turkey which even the dog would have a slice of? Christmas pudding decorated with a sprig of holly pinched from the bush on the common only to be incinerated? Stockings packed with presents? Crates of drink to entertain their friends?

Stephen had been odd lately: short-tempered even with the children. But Caroline did not think about that now. She was still wondering what Ivanka was doing next door.

Helen did not tell Caroline everything. She had not told

her about the forthcoming marriage between Ivanka and the Irishman. Caroline would be shocked, perhaps even out-raged. Helen was a little outraged herself that it had all been so easy for Ivanka.

She was making a cup of coffee in the kitchen when Ivanka knocked on the front door. Mikhail was shopping, Dimiter was out on a job, Stefan and the Irishman were in bed.

'Good day. Kevin is heerre?'

'Still asleep, I'm afraid. I've just made some coffee. Would you like some?'

'I like.'

Something about Ivanka upset Helen. Was it her supreme self-confidence? Or the way she accepted Luli's loving care as if it were only her due? Or the fact that Helen had no idea what sort of person lurked behind the mask of beige paint, the brown eyes which peered out between stiff lashes beaded with mascara? Ivanka never smiled. Only her eyes moved occasionally. Perhaps she had read that smiling gave you wrinkles? Or maybe she had spent so many hours encased in face packs that she had got used to a certain immobility of expression?

Helen managed to ask pleasantly: 'How are you enjoying England?'

'Oh, I like.' Ivanka sounded almost enthusiastic. 'Luli tek me to Herrrods forr the shoppink. Was merrvellous.' Then her glossy pink lips drooped a little more. 'But heerre is not nice. The strrits is so filty. Is no life. I like it Luli hev flet in centrre. Is betterr.'

Helen handed her a cup. 'I think Luli likes being near the others. I think they need to be together. One must miss speaking one's own language. I know *I* would if I was in a strange country.'

No reply. Ivanka just gave Helen a look as if to say 'I know something you don't.' She was staring at Helen's simple clothes, her unmade-up face and straight uncoiffeured hair almost with disbelief. Her little brown eyes travelled over her inch by inch as if to try to discover what on earth could have bound Mikhail to her.

'Wherre Mikhail?'

'Mikhail's out shopping.' Helen added with a shy smile, feeling defensive: 'He's being very secretive. I think he's buying me a present.'

'You arre loffink Mikhail?'

'We're very happy.' Helen looked away into the garden, now almost bare of greenery, the creeping vine quiescent, a mass of brown twigs.

'Mikhail hev wife,' said Ivanka. She was a very beautiful woman, she told Helen with enjoyment. Very fashionable. She was waiting for Mikhail even now. Ivanka said she thought Mikhail had never wanted to leave this woman. He wouldn't be staying away from her for long . . .

Helen stood as if turned to stone, while everything Ivanka wanted to say to Mikhail but did not dare came pouring out.

He had gone mad. This was the only explanation. Why had he left this Mercedes? And he had beautiful villa outside of town, elegant furniture, a wardrobe of fine clothes. They were saying in the newspapers that he was mad. He had done awful things, awful – like writing that shocking poem about the President. But was only because he went mad. She thought Mikhail was very unhappy now. He had made big mistake and he knew it. He had nothing – nothing at all. He was living in this awful house with person like Stefan who she, Ivanka, wouldn't like even to be in same room with if she met him normal. He was peasant. A drunk. Nothing. What was Mikhail doing here? He had been top person there. But Ivanka said she thought that in her country they understood he had gone mad. They wouldn't punish him when he went back. They would forgive. She was sure of this.

'Who told you to say this?' Helen was trembling with terror and also revulsion.

'No perrson tellink me nottink.' Ivanka helped herself to one of the macaroons Helen had made yesterday, grimaced after the first bite, pushed it away from her, touched her lips carefully with a sheet of kitchen roll. 'You arre helpink Mikhail wit his worrk?'

'Yes. You know that.'

Ivanka said she thought Helen was very useful for Mikhail and that was all. She believed he needed Helen's help very much. She thought Helen was giving Mikhail money also. Luli had told her Helen had a very good job.

And then the bell rang.

It was Caroline, overwhelmed by curiosity and also desperate to escape from her mother.

When Helen opened the front door, Caroline exclaimed immediately: 'Helen! What is it?'

Helen looked as she had before she met Mikhail. All her new-found confidence had gone. She slouched. Her eyes shifted miserably from Caroline's. Even her hair suddenly seemed lank and lifeless. It was as if the self Mikhail had brought into being had been called away.

'What's happened, Helen?' Caroline put an arm around her shoulders. 'Tell me.'

Helen pulled away – though glad, as always, of Caroline's friendship. Fears became more real when articulated. So all she said was: 'I'm fine. Come into the kitchen.' Then: 'Do you know Ivanka?'

'Yes, we just saw each other in the street.'

Now it was Caroline who got the inch by inch scrutiny: Ivanka staring at her as she might an alien from outer space. Caroline had expensive shoes with little gold chains around their heels, she noticed; the sweater she wore over a disastrously plain pleated skirt was of good quality, as were the pearls looped over it. Ivanka was mystified although, as usual, her face did not register it. As if for reassurance, she glanced down at the purple looped crepe wool dress with diamanté swags on the shoulders she wore under Luli's scarlet jacket.

'I'm sure Kevin wants to see you,' said Helen faintly, looking away because she felt bad about saying it. But she also felt she could not bear to be near Ivanka for a moment longer. 'He's upstairs. On the second floor. The room on the left. Why don't you go up?'

Helen had caught a glimpse of the Irishman's room once: seen its permanently un-made bed with tangled sheets that were seldom changed, its floor crowded with piles of dirty clothes, and smelt its mixture of old socks and sweat. The Irishman would be asleep, she knew. He had had a heavy evening yesterday, having just received his social security giro cheque. But knowing him, he would be pleased to see Ivanka – and, after all, she would soon be taking him for better or for worse.

'Okay, I go find him', and with a last puzzled stare at Caroline, Ivanka edged out of the room on her high heels and tottered up the stairs.

'Kevin?'

'Stefan's Irish lodger.'

'Uh??'

'Can't explain now, Caroline.'

'Helen, what is it? Something *is* dreadfully wrong. Now don't con me. I can see it in your face. Is it Michael?'

'It's nothing, Caroline,' insisted Helen, misery and defeat still clinging around her like a shroud. 'Have some coffee. Have one of these macaroons I made.'

When Mikhail returned, a little later, Caroline was struck, as always, by the energy which radiated from him. He was always cheerful. His white smile flashed on and off, embracing all around him. It lifted the spirits just to look at him. 'If he was English,' thought Caroline, the idea skittering across her consciousness, barely registering, 'he'd be just about the most attractive man I've ever met.'

'How you arre, Cerrolin?'

'Oh – all right thank you, Michael.'

'End the kids? How is the kids?' He put his arm round Helen and hugged her to him as he spoke.

'Fine. Well, you know, bags of energy. The whole Xmas bit is absolutely too much, isn't it?'

134

When Mikhail could not understand what someone had said, he never revealed it out of pride. He started to unpack a plastic carrier bag full of food. This was halva. Did Caroline know it? It was sweet. Kids liked it. He urged her to take it for her kids – take it all. He could buy more.

'Oh no, I couldn't possibly!'

'Why? Kids don't like?'

'Oh well, yes. Gosh, I'm sure they'd love it. But I couldn't possibly . . .'

'Plizz.' He pushed it into her hands. Now he was going to make lunch. Was Caroline staying?

'No, I really must get back. Oh gosh how frightful – the children are still in the car!' and Caroline rushed distractedly from the house.

CHAPTER SEVENTEEN

Christmas passed almost unremarked at Number 11 Shipka Avenue.

No wreath of holly picked from the sparse bush on the common was hung from the house's scratched door knocker; no paper-chains festooned its bare hall; and there was no miniature fir tree studded with lights to send out a twinkling message of goodwill by night from the window of the saloon. In contrast to the other houses on the street, Number 11 was dark and sad.

It was as if the exiles, who usually seized on any excuse for a celebration, could not bear to admit that Christmas was happening because it provoked too many painful memories. By common consent, they behaved as if the Christmas holiday was Sunday: dreary and empty, best slept away. They knew they would feel better once New Year had gone by.

Stefan, Dimiter and the Irishman all retired to bed: Stefan and the Irishman with bottles of whisky, Dimiter still clutching his misery to himself. They heard afterwards that Christo had accepted an invitation to family lunch from his English assistant in the carpet shop he ran, and that Luli and Ivanka had gone to a smart hotel in Mayfair where they drank cocktails called piledrivers.

As for Mikhail and Helen, they made a simple meal for themselves, exchanged presents, and, enjoying this licensed laziness, talked of the past as people often do in order to explain who they are now.

'I never had a Christmas like this before, Mikhail.'

'Tell me what is, swithearrt.'

136

What is, or what was? In Helen's immediate past lay duty Christmases with distant relatives: Christmas with people who resented the money and the trouble involved and didn't hide it – where, year following year, the same conversations were replayed. But Christmases past – that was a different matter. So, sitting before a fire in the saloon of Number 11 Shipka Avenue, her chin resting on her crossed arms propped on her knees, Helen described the Christmases of her child-hood in the remote cottage in the West of England where she had been brought up, exaggerating a little to amuse Mikhail, and all the time telling him another story. She had been the only child of a marriage that was more like a love affair, then lost both parents in her early teens in a car-crash that was not their fault.

'My parents were very happy together. They died when I was fifteen,' she had already told Mikhail, saying beneath the surface of that brief statement 'I learnt how to love by example, and then the example was torn away from me when I was at my most vulnerable.'

She told him about lying in bed and listening to her parents laughing in a room below as they packed her stocking; pretending to be asleep when they tiptoed tipsily upstairs with it all hard and distended with presents; emptying it feverishly the moment they had gone, so tired with forcing her eyes to stay open that she hardly noticed what was inside; and thinking tearfully afterwards when the orgy was over and the stocking lay flat and empty and torn wrapping paper scattered her whole bed 'Now I have nothing for tomorrow.'

As he listened, Mikhail looked first cunning, then wildly excited; finally disappointed, self-pitying, heart-broken in sympathy like a child himself.

'Are you sure you like your present, Mikhail?' Helen had asked him this question at least three times already.

'Oh, is rrill fine, Helen. Rrrilly is hot also.'

'We say warm, Mikhail. I can always take it back if you don't like the colour. It's no problem. Just say. I won't be offended, I promise.'

Looking at him, so handsome in the dark green sweater, she no longer thought in wonderment 'Why did he choose me?' Since the conversation with Ivanka she understood, and despised her own naïveté in not realising it before. Now she knew with certainty that this time with Mikhail could not last and surmised fearfully why he treated her with a special tenderness, not knowing that each time she looked at him she betrayed herself.

'End?' he said. 'End?'

'And we'd go to church, Mikhail.' Earlier they had seen the Johnstons from next door setting off for the morning service: Stephen abstracted and short-tempered, Caroline clutching her two boys, her mother wearing too much powder and an unsuitably crimson velvet beret which needed brushing as well as, of course, her habitual bright interested smile. 'It was one of those family services where the vicar would involve everyone. All the children came along with their best presents and he'd invite them up to the front so everyone could get a look.' She had lost a doll's silver high-heeled shoe once in the hurry to display it and still remembered the anguish. 'He was lovely, that vicar: so good and straightforward. And he told you the truth always insofar as he could.'

It was the same vicar who later buried her parents on a foggy day when hidden rooks cawed around the awesomely deep double grave which had been dug in the churchyard. 'Why do you believe there's a life after death?' she had asked him, clutching a wet handkerchief, on one of the many visits he paid her afterwards. 'Because He said so,' he replied. This simple truth was enough for him. Because it was obvious, she was comforted a little.

She told Mikhail none of this. The last thing she wanted him to do was feel sorry for her. Besides, the more you hid your true feelings, the harder it was to show them. Her parents' sudden death and the unsuccessful love-affairs which shouldn't have followed but had – partly because she was too desperate to replace the loving security she had lost,

138

partly because she chose unwisely – had finally defeated her. It had ended in a wish not to be noticed, and consequently hurt, ever again – and that was the exact point when she had met Mikhail. Sometimes when she looked into his grey eyes she fancied he understood all this.

She touched the necklace of deep red glass beads he had given her and asked: 'Do they go to church where you come from, Mikhail?'

'Ohh! Is no Chrristmas witout.'

Christmas was not such an important festival as Easter, however. Easter was the holiest day of the year for the Orthodox Church and, coaxed and aided by Helen, he painted a picture of the spectacle. He described the old women in black headscarves – the most fervent believers – who remembered how it had been before it all changed, who always arrived early to be sure of getting the best seats whilst, outside, cordons of police turned the young people away. They didn't like the young people attending church, said Mikhail, although in theory they allowed religious ceremonies and observances – though forbade religious teaching. But strangely, more and more people, young and old, wanted to go to church; and he described the elaborate rituals of the priests and the beautiful singing of the choirs. (Luli had given Stefan a record: if Stefan had a record-player, which he did not, she could judge for herself.) Mikhail said some people thought the young people only wanted to go to church because it was their sole means of protesting against the regime, but he himself believed there was more to it than that.

Helen thought of Caroline's mother sitting in the cold church on the common, probably allowed to keep the children under control whilst Stephen and Caroline took holy communion with other young parents under the watchful calculating eye of the vicar. That church would be packed too.

Then she wondered if the landscape in Mikhail's old country was now masked by thick snow. Stefan often spoke of its great beauty. What sort of childhood had Mikhail had? What sort of adolescence? Those questions did not belong in the category of subjects, like his wife, which must never be mentioned.

But when Helen asked Mikhail, he told her instead about another person and another life. Mikhail had not yet reached the state of struggling to exhume the past: scrabbling over and over at the same patch of ground to unearth the truth whilst, all the time, the truth sank a little further from him. Now, he did not understand why, it afforded him a strange relief to concoct a false past. He had been a lonely child, he said, not smart; and the cleverest and most popular child in his class described to Helen how he had once been humiliated by a teacher before his fellow pupils. Telling the story, Mikhail acted out all the different roles: playing the stern teacher, the tearful boy, the jeering classmates. At the end, his eyes glistened a little, though another part of him was appalled and bewildered by the untruths. What was happening to him? This morning when he had gone for a short walk, he had looked up and seen the famous mountain that dominated the city he had lived in nearly all his life. He had taken a dreamy pleasure in its purple curves and thought 'The mountain looks good this morning.' Then with a shock he realised it was a low cloud and that was all. How could he have believed even for a split second that he had seen the mountain, rearing over a frosty litter-strewn common in south-west London?

The sad tale about Mikhail's schooldays touched Helen. She felt grateful that he had shared the experience with her, but cursed her thoughtlessness in asking him anything – today of all days – about the country he had left. She should, instead, have tried to distract him.

'Mikhail, I've an idea! Let's give a party to make up for not having one today.'

Mikhail apologised for the boredom of the day. This must be very different from her other Christmases.

'Oh no, this was one of the best. But let's give a party!' It would cheer everyone up: banish this thick mantle of gloom which had settled on the house. 'Let's give one for New Year. Oh let's, Mikhail!'

Maybe after New Year would be a better idea, he said.

'Yes, well maybe New Year isn't such a good idea,' she agreed immediately.

'Ivanka gettink merrried . . .' Mikhail said slowly. After all, there had to be a reason for a party.

'So soon?' Helen tried to sound as enthusiastic as before. 'Well, perhaps . . .'

So it was that Ivanka's unromantic marriage turned into an occasion for celebration to which even the Johnstons from next door were invited. You couldn't have a wedding without a party, even if you had no great fondness for either of the couple involved. But they decided to wait until afterwards. Better that the odd alliance should remain a secret until it had been safely effected.

CHAPTER EIGHTEEN

The local Neighbourhood Watch scheme which had been set up was not, as yet, working too well. In the ten days that followed Ivanka's hasty and secret marriage, there were a dozen burglaries, fifteen muggings and twenty-five cases of what the police described as 'autotheft' in the network of streets surrounding Shipka Avenue. A concrete mixer was stolen, in bright daylight, from the front garden of Number 62; a BMW belonging to the family at Number 16 had all four wheels removed on the night of 8 January, but the thieves thoughtfully propped the car up on piles of bricks pinched from the garden of Number 43.

As she was required to do, Ivanka had registered her marriage immediately at the local police station. But such was the pressure of work that the police might have set investigation of the case aside for the moment had it not been time for a routine call on Mikhail. So Police Constable John Baines walked slowly round to Number 11 one cold and rainy morning on a double mission.

As he pushed open the gate, his professional eye took in the absence of a mortice lock on the front door, which had no protective mesh grille either. There was nothing to prevent a thief (who would be well hidden from view by the over-grown privet hedge) from smashing the pane of patterned glass inset in the front door then putting his hand through and turning the knob of the Yale lock. Alternatively, he could simply slip the lock with a plastic credit card before looking for more inside. But PC Baines was not here to point this out: it would be the job of the officer at the station assigned to Crime Prevention who, like a guest, had to be invited. Besides, PC Baines was not in a mood to be helpful. He had strong views on Ivanka's marriage. It was a scandal. He had said so over coffee in the police station that morning.

Luli's solution to keeping her sister with her was not original. In fact, anyone in Ivanka's position could obtain a special licence to be married at speed and then have an inalienable right to be a citizen of the British Isles with all the benefits involved. All one needed was a compliant and not too expensive partner – the cost ranged from £250 to £1,000. It was only afterwards that the police could check up and then, of course, it was usually too late. Another officer had told PC Baines that there were some thousand cases country-wide due for investigation. The police could only look into twenty to thirty a year. There were far more important calls on their time.

So PC Baines was not feeling particularly friendly as he rang the bell of Number 11. Also, he had had a bad argument with his wife that morning about the amount of sweets their small son ate. Like Ivanka before him, he did not notice that the front door was freshly painted. He saw only that the stonework of the house was in a deplorable state.

It was Helen who opened the door, out of breath as usual from running downstairs from the attic room.

PC Baines explained that he had come to see Mikhail and Ivanka, who had given the police station this address as a married woman. His fresh young face looked stern under its helmet. He would see Mikhail first, if Helen would kindly inform him.

'Oh yes, of course . . .' The Irishman was asleep in his room as usual. Ivanka . . . well, Ivanka would be at Luli's where she had spent every night since the wedding. What to do? Mikhail would know. Helen showed the policeman into the saloon and asked him to wait.

Mikhail was sitting at the table in their room and if he was in despair because yet another batch of poems had been returned that morning with only a printed rejection slip pinned to them, he did not show it.

'Mikhail, Mikhail, there's a policeman downstairs. He wants to see you – *and* Ivanka. She ought to be here, Mikhail.'

Mikhail did not like Ivanka either, but he said immediately: 'We hev to telephone she.'

'But the 'phone's in the saloon, Mikhail. I can't take him anywhere else.'

Mikhail thought for a moment. Then he said: 'Mek it wit Cerrolin, swithearrt. I shut it doorr to seloon.' He smiled. This reminded him of a Feydeau farce, he said. He liked it.

Helen thought that he would like it less when he saw the plump and stony face of PC Baines.

He followed her downstairs and greeted the policeman warmly, enfolding his limp hand in his own strong grasp, flashing him a radiant smile. Then he exchanged an exaggeratedly meaningful look with Helen before he closed the door of the saloon behind them both.

Helen shut the front door as quietly as she could and did the same with the gate. Then she ran along the pavement to Number 9 next door.

As usual, Caroline was delighted to see her, as if all the boredom of ordinary life could be shelved for the moment.

'Come in, Helen. Like a coffee?'

'Got to make a 'phone call, Caroline. Can I use yours?'

'Of course.' And because Caroline was longing to find out why Helen couldn't use the telephone next door and also why she looked so flustered, she suggested: 'Why don't you use the one in the kitchen?'

Jack and Bill were seated at the table there, drinking coffee, eating Bourbon biscuits and talking to Caroline's mother, who kept a fixed social smile on her face.

'This is what I'd do, dear: send them all back. I'd pay for their tickets. After all, it'd be an investment. That would only be fair, dear, even though you and I know it's not a fair world. Enough's enough, dear. They've had their chance. It

144

hasn't worked. And look what they've done to the crime rate here, dear. Just look at it . . .'

'Is that you, Ivanka? . . . Oh, I'm *so* glad you're in . . . What! You haven't got up yet? . . . Now listen, you've got to come straight round to Stefan's house now. There's a policeman there. You're supposed to be living there, Ivanka . . . Yes, that's a good idea . . . Bring a whole lot . . . But come quick . . . He's talking to Mikhail now but he's going to want to see you *and* Kevin pretty soon . . . Yes, *very* soon, Ivanka . . . No, that doesn't matter. . . *He's* not going to notice if you're not properly made-up. . . Just please come quickly . . .'

Next door in the saloon, Mikhail and the policeman were sitting on wooden chairs one each side of the fireplace scattered with wood ash. Mikhail had already offered the policeman coffee, tea and plum brandy. All had been refused.

Now Mikhail suggested even more persuasively, eyes gleaming with passion, white teeth flashing, that PC Baines might be tempted by some excellent black olives from Italy (but bought from the local Cypriot delicatessen). And he had some sheep's-milk cheese too. Was very very tasty. Should he make a small hors d'oeuvre?

'I won't have anything, thank you.'

'Is surre?'

'Quite sure.'

PC Baines had a list of questions written in his notebook which he removed from his top pocket and settled on his plump thighs.

When he had first arrived in England, Mikhail had been seen by the Home Office. It had taken many hours for one of its representatives, and another from the security service, to interview him before they had deemed him a deserving case for sanctuary. Until he applied for naturalisation, for which he would be eligible after five years, permission to stay would be renewed every six to twelve months and his passport would continue to bear the description 'stateless'. At that point, Special Branch would start taking an interest in him again. Until then he was a case for the local police station, to be seen every three or four months, depending on pressure of work.

'Your English seems to be coming along quite satisfactorily . . . Are you still attending language school?'

'Oh yes, ich Turrsday ivenink . . . End I hev it frriend . . . You see it she. . . She helpink me. . . She givink me lessons . . .'

'Oh yes?' PC Baines made a note in his book: a confirmation of an idea which had occurred to him when he had met Helen earlier.

'Can you supply me with the name of your language school, and also the individual in charge?'

'Indivit . . . ?

'The name of the language school.' PC Baines could check the rest for himself. All he wanted to verify was if the establishment was a reputable one; and he would also find out if any of Mikhail's less trustworthy compatriots – those known to have connections with the embassy in London – were involved with it.

He tucked the card Mikhail gave him into the notebook.

'Do you associate much with members of your own community – other exiles?' The point of this question was to try and ascertain how well Mikhail was integrating.

'Uh?'

Outside the house, Helen was pacing agitatedly up and down the pavement, waiting to smuggle Ivanka in as soon as she arrived. Caroline had followed her, fat baby straddling one hip.

'Promise you'll tell me what it's all about when it's over, Helen. Gosh, there's always something going on in that house, isn't there? Never a dull moment. With us it's only a leaking loo and heaven *knows* when they'll get around to

146

fixing it . . . *Wish* you'd tell me why that perfectly frightful girl's suddenly got to come round here . . . I've never *seen* such a tart.'

'Oh – thank goodness!' Far down the street Helen could see a figure topped by a gleaming floss of blonde hair and weighed down on one side by a large suitcase edging slowly along the pavement. Ivanka put the suitcase down, and could be seen looking around her helplessly as if waiting for a strong chivalrous man suddenly to materialise. There was no one. Ivanka picked up the case again and, severely hampered by her tight skirt and high heels, resumed her slow passage up Shipka Avenue. As she came closer, they could see that her mouth, hastily smeared with shocking pink lipstick, was alternately pouting and snarling. Whatever she was muttering to herself, it was not polite.

How did Mikhail spend his spare time? PC Baines wanted to know. After all, there must be a lot of it. Being paid by the State, Mikhail wasn't supposed to have a job. A little later on, PC Baines would try to find out if he was moonlighting.

'Oh, I em worrkink!' said Mikhail in surprise.

'Is that so?'

'All the time I mek it worrk. Frrom yearrly in morrnink I don't stop it worrk.' Mikhail added proudly: 'I don't hev it no prroplem worrkink . . .'

Now they heard a scuffling sound in the hall outside, the clip of high heels against its tessellated floor, a noise as if a heavy object were being dragged up the stairs.

Ivanka wrinkled her nose in disgust as they pushed open the door of the Irishman's bedroom. Yes, he was here all right: a fat mound under the pile of dirty sheets and blankets. There were empty bottles rolled all over the floor and the smell of the alcohol was a relief compared with the other odours.

After much negotiation, the Irishman had received £750

from Luli (whose generous Arab lover had also paid extra for the cost of a special marriage licence) and a sizeable portion of it had already been spent on drink though, as yet, Stefan had received none of his long overdue back payments of rent.

'Tis rrevoltink pick! . . . Wek up!' and Ivanka pushed at the Irishman's large round back with a spiky scarlet nail.

'Have you ever *seen* such an absolute dump?' asked Caroline unnecessarily. The baby in her arms was pulling at her dark curls and she buried her nose in the warm folded flesh of his short neck as people in earlier times used to sniff at pomanders.

Ivanka had opened her suitcase and was pulling out garments. There were satin French knickers in all colours; wisps of matching brassieres; transparent nightdresses heavy with lace and ribbons. With revulsion plainly registered on her face – which, like Luli's, looked much younger without its coating of rouge and foundation – Ivanka swept a bunch of dirty socks and underpants off the only chair in the room and replaced it with a neat pile of her own underclothes. Then she took dresses on hangers out of the case and draped them from a hook fixed to the inside of the door. She had known she should bring a suitcase of clothes – Luli, experienced in these matters, had warned her.

Then she shut the case and shoved it under the Irishman's bed, wincing as, on its passage, it encountered unmentionable objects all tangled up with great woolly balls of dust and hair.

She pushed at him again.

'Kevin! Kevin!'

'We'd better go,' said Helen. 'Well, *you'd* better, Caroline. I'll come with you.'

As they trod softly down the uncarpeted stairs, Caroline noted the imposing proportions of the stairwell, identical to her own under peeling wallpaper and chipped paint; the splendid carved oak bannisters which, in her house, had been stripped and varnished.

148

'Where's the case?' she whispered and, in explanation, tilted an imaginary bottle to her lips.

'Still asleep.'

'Gosh, Helen, this house! Now I want you to swear that as soon as that policeman's gone you're going to come and tell me all about it. I want to know every detail. I simply don't believe the drama of your life!'

Closeted in the saloon, Mikhail and the policeman again heard soft footsteps outside the door and then a strange gurgling coo which sounded exactly like – but, of course, could not possibly be – a baby. If the conversation they were involved in had been less serious, then PC Baines might have remarked on it. But it had no bearing on his presence here and, besides, he wanted to get on with the interview.

'So you haven't been approached by anyone from the embassy?'

'No . . .' If the policeman had been older, less impatient, had perhaps suffered more, then Mikhail might have confided some of his fears. But they were only fears and there was nothing which could be proved. So there seemed little point in telling this scrubbed-looking cross young man about the feelings he had of being watched, followed, kept tabs on.

'In cases like this,' PC Baines was saying, a little pompously, 'it's usually necessary to prove persecution.' He gave Mikhail a stern look. 'The majority of persons like yourself are opportunists.'

Mikhail nodded, not knowing what the word meant, his whole face alive, registering the policeman's every reaction.

'It won't be necessary for *you* to do that.' PC Baines did not explain why because he did not know: being very junior, he had not been given the full low-down on Mikhail's case. 'Have you received any threats?'

'Trrets?' repeated Mikhail, looking as solemn and bored as the policeman.

'Has any person approached you and threatened your life?'

149

'Oh – no. Not perrson what I see it.' For this was true.

And so, without picking up the thread of a hint, PC Baines passed smoothly on to the next matter, which was warning Mikhail that his rent and living expenses would not be paid for ever. The time would come quite soon when he must find himself a job. Had he any idea, PC Baines asked, what sort of job that might be? If not, then perhaps Mikhail ought to start thinking about the matter. What were his special talents? he asked. Was he, for example, any good at carpentry?

Upstairs, Ivanka was still trying to awaken the Irishman.

'Get up, Kevin! You bin ped lotta money. What you doink lyink heerre like lezzy pick? Is disgustink. You arre filty. What I doink wit you?'

'Oh shut up, woman!' muttered the Irishman, stirring at last. He rolled over and sat up in his dirty vest. One hand rasped at the stubble on his face, then scratched his woolly head. He belched.

'End tis is my wonderrful husband!' said Ivanka. 'The men what I wetted forr all of my life! Look at tis wonderrful time what he givink me! Is beautiful rroom! So grrecious! End he is so culturred, so stylish, so smarrt!'

'Oh shut up!' Then the Irishman said to Helen who had put her head around the door: 'Not you, darling. Will you get this terrible woman out of here now?'

'Kevin, you must get up – quick. There's a policeman downstairs. He's come to check that your marriage to Ivanka is valid. He's almost finished with Mikhail. I said I'd fetch you both. Please hurry. And you'd better shave . . .'

When, five minutes later, PC Baines was introduced to the newly married couple in the saloon, he thought to himself with a pang of envy he did not acknowledge that they both looked as if they had only just got out of bed (which was

150

indeed true): she only half made-up, he with pieces of bloody cottonwool adhering to his chin.

He unsmilingly accepted the Irishman's assurance that 'We're very much in love, officer – it was a lightning romance. I knew as soon as I clapped eyes on the girl that she was the one for me.' And when he soon afterwards inspected the room in which they said they lived, he noted irrefutable evidence of Ivanka's presence. They were an odd couple. Their way of life was certainly insalubrious. But he had seen far worse.

On his return to the police station three blocks away, PC Baines reported that the marriage of Ivanka Kinchev and Kevin O'Malley appeared to be genuine, and that Mikhail Tironov was settling down satisfactorily with no problems.

Chapter Nineteen

On the morning of the party to celebrate Ivanka's marriage, Dimiter received a letter from his homeland.

The moment that he saw the coarse floppy white envelope with familiar orange and brown stamps, sloping loopy script flowing across its whole face, he thought with strange happiness mixed with grief that it must be a last letter from his mother, found after her death, perhaps, and posted by a well-wisher: a message from beyond the grave. For, what with all the opening and reading and re-sealing, letters from that country sometimes took several weeks to reach their destination.

But when he looked more closely, he saw that it was not his mother's writing. This similar script belonged to his aunt Anka who had broken the terrible news to him less than three weeks ago, and here was her name and address written carefully on the back of the envelope.

Dimiter braced himself. She would be writing to tell him of his mother's last days and hours on this earth. That would be typical of his practical and emotional aunt Anka – and he wanted to know, truly he did.

What he was quite unprepared for was the photographs.

Three large black and white photographs, matt in texture, were tucked into a rough flimsy sheet of off-white paper scored with faint blue squares. More like lavatory paper than writing paper, his mother had always written her letters on it too. The photographs had been taken at his mother's funeral. Dimiter shut his eyes – screwed them up tightly as if he never wanted to open them again – and then, with a blank expression perfected in the country of his birth, where people learnt to hide their true feelings, he examined them.

The first picture showed his mother in close-up: lying on a bier of flowers and leaves, her eyes closed, her expression resigned. She might have been asleep – corpses were buried so quickly in that country. Within two days of a death, the funeral would be arranged: and so it was quite acceptable to have open coffins, as was the tradition. As she lay there, half-hidden in the mass of flowers and leaves, a hand – Anka's? – stole out from the top left-hand corner of the photograph to touch her cheek.

The second picture showed Dimiter's two uncles lowering the bier to the ground, surrounded by more familiar faces. Snow fell, the white flakes caught for ever in space by the camera. It might have been a scene from another much earlier era. The women wore black shawls wrapped around their heads and shoulders, the men soft black homburgs. They all looked at the camera with an expression which could not have been fear but which looked so like it; and in each one of those faces of his mother's brothers and sisters and cousins Dimiter saw fragments of hers.

The last photograph showed a tall priest in a long black robe, a round black flat-topped hat, a scarf of gold brocade: blessing the body before it was lowered into the grave and covered with earth, some thrown by the mourners who traditionally scattered three handfuls each. There were the same observers, standing back a little now, gazes bent on the form on the bier; and, again, some glanced at the camera with that expression so close to fear but mingled with another which seemed to demand: 'Why aren't you here with us? What stopped you from coming?'

Dimiter pushed the photographs into a drawer. Then, like a person who must eat a piece of chocolate straight after taking bitter medicine, he went to his mantelpiece where other pictures of his mother had been arranged on every space of it since her death.

There were photographs taken before he had been born:

the girl his mother had once been smiling shyly at cameras probably held first by her parents and then by his father.

She directed a sweet earnest gaze at him from between long thick plaits as a schoolgirl; she flirted with the cameraman in a sprigged dress, her hair cut short and curled; and, later on in time, here was he himself held tenderly and proudly in her arms as a baby. Here were both of his parents, a little stiff and solemn in their touching youth; and here was his mother as he knew her best, dignified in black.

She grew old in the course of that procession along the mantelpiece. Had that schoolgirl, that pretty teenager, that young mother any premonition at all that in the distant future the one she loved best, he who came from her own body, would be prevented even from paying his last respects to her by a system she had never properly understood?

Dimiter brushed away tears with the back of his hand. It hadn't worked. He wouldn't remember her like this. For the rest of his life, he knew that his dominating memory would be of the eternally resigned face half-sunk in flowers and leaves and the fearful accusing expressions of the mourners. Always.

But Dimiter said nothing at all of this to anybody in Number 11 Shipka Avenue. They did not, after all, even know that his mother had died.

He was always quiet. He had been even more so over the past three weeks. Now nobody remarked on the fact that in all the buzz of preparations surrounding the party he moved about like a ghost, only deriving comfort from the elaborate creation of the sheep's-milk cheese pastries which were his speciality.

Besides, he was not the only one with problems.

'But what am I to do?' Stefan was asking Mikhail as he seasoned the same bean soup he had made the first time Helen came to this house. His dark hair looked oddly oily tonight, though he had washed it in honour of the party. This was because he had used conditioner instead of shampoo: a frequent mistake of his.

'I have asked him ten times to pay me. He just laughs.' He sucked noisily on a spoon with which he had dipped out a little of the soup to taste. 'Oh, this was no good, this idea. He is not a decent person. He is a psychopath, a vulture, a moral cripple. He will ruin me . . .'

To Helen he explained: 'Tis chip stuff drrinkink it all my cesh. What I em doink wit tis peasant?' And he continued seasoning his soup, adding a little grating of this and a tiny pinch of that, making it as perfect as possible so as to be fit to serve at the party to celebrate the marriage of his Irish lodger to Ivanka.

'Well, at least he might bring a bottle or two this time,' said Helen, who was preoccupied with other matters.

And Mikhail, similarly abstracted, said: 'Well he can always go and live at Luli's with his wife. That would teach them both.'

'Only me!' called Caroline Johnston, wandering in through the front door which had been left on the latch. 'Hello Michael, Helen . . . Oh *doesn't* it all look simply scrumptious! What's this? Aubergine? Super! – but I'm going to pong of garlic for days! Stephen won't want to come near me. I'll sue you for breaking up my marriage, Michael!'

'Stivven is comink, Cerrolin?' asked Mikhail.

'Well – no, Michael. He's terribly sorry but he can't. I think something's going on at the office. Of course he never tells me a thing. I'm only the wife. Honestly!'

Then keeping at a good distance in the tiny kitchen from Stefan whom, like Dimiter, she had not addressed, she asked: 'Where's the bride?'

'On her way,' answered Helen.

'Tis is forrmelity,' said Stefan. 'You know it tis, Cerrolin. Ivanka don't stay merrried wit tis chip stuff forr lonk.' He threw in a couple of his favourite expressions from his native country while scattering a handful of chopped parsley into his soup. Ivanka had a hedgehog in her knickers *and* she knew where the lobsters hibernated.

155

'I see,' said Caroline, trying to memorise what he had said to tell Stephen later – or perhaps not.

'He sayink Ivanka lookink forr welty hosbend nomberr two,' Mikhail explained, ignoring the meaning of the first expression. Ivanka was an ambitious girl. Then: 'Wherre yourr motterr is, Cerrolin?'

'Oh, babysitting.'

'You hev to brrink it she.'

'And have fun? I mean, I adore my mother but no thanks.'

'Your motterr livink wit you?' asked Dimiter. These were the first words he had uttered today.

'Yes. For my sins!'

'You arre locky.' But he said it so gently, so quietly, that there was no way in which it could be interpreted as a reprimand.

'Hello hello hello!' – and here was Christo, forehead gleaming with perspiration even on a cold evening such as this, untwining a long cashmere scarf from his neck, slinging his heavy Harris tweed overcoat over the newel post in the hall. 'My goodness, the weather is becoming sharp. It is really inclement, is it not?'

What a curious person he was, Helen thought as they all went into the saloon where there was more room. He was the only one she knew hardly at all: perhaps because he came to Number 11 Shipka Avenue infrequently but more probably because, in emulation of what he perceived of the English, he hid his real self under layers of polite small talk.

'He comes in and out of here every so often,' she thought, 'usually managing to upset someone or other in the process.' It occurred to her that perhaps this was his way of distancing himself from the other exiles.

'Here's a small contribution.' Christo took four bottles of red wine from a carrier bag. In this respect, thought Helen, he was not at all like the English, who did not rank meanness as one of the worst faults.

The Irishman appeared from his room upstairs. He hadn't brought a bottle. He hadn't even shaved.

'Congratulations!' said Caroline effusively, still having not really taken in the true nature of this marriage.

'Thank you! And here she is – my gorgeous bride!' For, in a rush of scented air, Ivanka and Luli came into the saloon.

'What a portrait of taste and style!' said the Irishman, sounding sincere.

The hair of both women – the one jet black, the other white blonde – stood out from their heads in backcombed masses of waves and curls. Luli wore lilac, Ivanka white as befitted a bride, purple eyeshadow to match Luli on her slightly hooded lids. On their feet they both displayed tiny high-heeled gold sandals.

'Tenk you, darrlink,' said Luli warmly, but her sister smiled wearily like a beautiful courtesan bored with too many compliments, then frowned and batted away Stefan who was attempting to kiss the plump flesh exposed by her low neckline.

He called this portion of a woman's anatomy 'the delta of the Danube', he explained to Caroline who hurriedly turned away.

'Are you well?' Christo asked Luli in their own language.

'What is well?' she replied with a gay laugh. She kissed each person in the room, even including Caroline, and handed over more drink, her own record-player, and a sheaf of records. 'Is anyone else coming?'

She exclaimed with delight when Stefan told her that two more of their countrymen in exile, who lived on the other side of London and did not drive, would be sharing a minicab to 11 Shipka Avenue. Stefan had also invited a schoolmate of Luli's who had married a minor English politician and might therefore be able to help Mikhail in the way of contacts. But Stefan did not tell Luli this – as he had not told Mikhail – because when he mentioned Mikhail would be present, the woman had immediately remembered a prior engagement.

Nor did he say that he had also invited three English girls he had encountered on the street yesterday. He did not really expect them to turn up, but one never knew.

He had not invited Hetty Clarke, but was delighted when she came, ostensibly delivering Neighbourhood Watch newsletters.

'Na you mekkink special newspepperrs concerrnink tis frree landrry? Is rrilly toughtful, Hetty.' He took the pile from her, dumped it behind the front door, and handed her a brimming glass of red wine.

It was all just as you would expect, thought Hetty, whose antennae seldom let her down when a party was in the offing. Julio Iglesias on the record-player, far too much noise and far too many people in this uncomfortable room whatshis-name called the saloon, the women ludicrously over-dressed and over-made-up, with the exception of Helen of course. Helen obviously held the same views on dressing as she herself did: people (meaning men) must take you as you were, which also meant you could eat what you wanted without feeling pressurised to stay slim.

Stefan pinched Hetty's ample bottom through her towel-ling trousers.

She gave him a glare, which he interpreted as an interested smile. 'Save me!' she murmured to Caroline Johnston who had moved towards her like a person marooned on a life raft heading for land.

'Told you!' hissed Caroline through bared teeth, like a ventriloquist.

Hetty, who often put garlic into her salads, noticed that Stefan smelt unpleasantly strongly of it. His lips were taking kissing directions towards her, he told her. He was getting much ocular pleasure from looking at her.

'Who is that?' she asked, to distract him.

Stefan explained it was Ivanka. He didn't tell her that the party was to celebrate Ivanka's wedding because he assumed she knew.

'And she's just come out?' said Hetty. 'Everyone else has been here for years, right? I'd like to talk to her.'

Hetty's house further down Shipka Avenue was comfort-able and modern: a base where she liked to entertain her mostly female friends with good food and wine that was not always plonk. Hetty lived well on alimony from her ex-husband (so much so that there was no need to contemplate remarriage); but she was a Marxist and had been so ever since beginning, but never completing, a sociology course two years ago as a mature student. In Hetty's opinion, the West could learn a lot from the East – to take only one example, look at the crèches which the State provided for working women there. Hetty often said the present system in Britain was rotten to the core and Mrs Thatcher a Fascist dictator. Like many of her friends, she had helped campaign for the Labour Party prior to the last general election though, regretfully, more and more people in Shipka Avenue these days displayed blue posters in their living-room windows.

Hetty felt she knew a great deal about the country the strange collection of people in this room had originally come from. Perhaps even more than they did. Only the other day, in the one decent Socialist newspaper which remained, there had been an article on it. Fresh winds of liberation prevailed there now, it had said. The young people listened to Western jazz in smart cafés sporting trendy clothes created by home-grown designers.

Not that Ivanka fitted that description. Ivanka looked as though she had been sartorially inspired by one of the cheaper American soaps, thought Hetty, curling her lip, as Stefan led her to Ivanka's side, followed by Caroline.

Luli, holding Ivanka's hand and patting it, did not appear to remember she had met Hetty before. But she cast her ravishing smile absentmindedly at Caroline. As for Ivanka, she turned down the corners of her pink pouting mouth appalled by Hetty's lack of style: mystified, as always, by Caroline.

'Next wik Luli tekkink me to furr sel.'

Yes, Luli told them, she wanted to buy her Ivanka something really special – with the help of a kind friend who had already assisted her greatly with a certain matter. Ivanka's silver fox was okay, she said, but she and Ivanka wanted to have a look at blue mink. It would be a wonderful contrast with Ivanka's beautiful hair, would it not? They were planning to spend a whole day trying on furs.

For a moment, Hetty (who espoused the cause of animal welfare) was unable to speak. Then she asked Ivanka earnestly: 'How do you find it here?'

'Heerre? Is rrevoltink. I not onderrstend how tis peasant be livink in tis way.'

'No. I meant how do you like being in England? Quite a change, I should think.'

Ivanka agreed. The fashions were much better, she said; as were the shops of course. Knightsbridge was beautiful; so was Oxford Street and Regent Street.

'I know it's quite easy to emigrate these days,' Hetty pursued doggedly. 'No problems with visas. I expect you got yours as soon as you applied for it, didn't you?'

'Why you want knowink tis tinks?' demanded Luli suddenly, looking as sullen as Ivanka but also fearful. 'Who you arre? Who tellink you to mek tese questions?' Then she caught Stefan by the sleeve, speaking in English to him in her agitation. 'Who tis perrson, Stefan? I see herr beforre. Why you hevvink herr in yourr home?'

'Look I only . . .' Hetty began. But Stefan interrupted, gabbling something at Luli which calmed her down. Her flat broad face became successively quizzical, surprised, amused. By the time the two unfamiliar exiles arrived – late because minicab drivers often took longer routes with foreign customers – she was heaving with suppressed mirth.

They were called Lubomir and Maria – she tall and gaunt, he so fat that his orange shirt decorated with crazy palm trees and rampaging camels gaped around the buttons over his hairy chest and diaphragm. He was a man of property, having amassed three houses in an unfashionable part of North London, which he let. She did translations for a firm which exported computers to Eastern Europe.

Maria was sure she could help Mikhail. She knew many eminent figures in the literary world, she told him. Perhaps

160

he would like to come over to her place one evening on his own and they could draw up a list of those it would be best to approach? A quiet meal, informal, though she had to admit she knew how to cook.

'That would be pleasant,' said Mikhail politely. He found it painful to look into Maria's mournful black eyes set far back in bluish hollows. That reminded him, he said, it was time for them to eat. If she would excuse him, he would fetch the food.

Always aware of Mikhail, Helen followed immediately to the kitchen. 'What was she saying, Mikhail? Stefan says she can help you.'

'I tink she tinkink how I cen help it she,' said Mikhail. 'But I em wise crrocodile. I em rrealisink it tis.' He put his arms around Helen and nuzzled her neck. Why didn't they vanish from this place? he suggested; he only wanted to be with her, his sweetheart, he said.

It would be so easy to believe him, Helen thought sadly, running the tips of her fingers over the thick soft hair which grew at the back of his head. She started to say they could do no such thing, if only because Caroline needed looking after, when Caroline herself appeared in the doorway.

'Hetty's gone!' she said in a tone which sounded suspiciously triumphant.

'Beforre tis mill?' exclaimed Mikhail, astonished.

'It was something Stefan said to her. She told me she'd never been so insulted in her life,' Caroline went on, enjoying herself. 'She said she'd better things to do with her evening and anyway Stefan was a randy little groper. He's just asked me what it means. What *could* I say? He'll probably ask you too, Helen.'

'Oh no! You're not going as well are you, Caroline?'

'Just try and chuck me out!' Then Caroline asked: 'Are *all* your parties like this?' thinking at the same time '*Why* did I believe there was something mysterious and exciting about this house and these people? I won't stay long.'

And Helen replied with her smile which managed to be

161

both radiant and apologetic: 'All of them!' – having no idea that this party was to be quite different and also the last for a long time. In fact, to the end of her days, Hetty Clarke would regret walking out early in a huff.

CHAPTER TWENTY

When Caroline's mother pushed open the door of Number 11 a little later on, it was partly to tell Caroline that James had woken up coughing but she had given him syrup and Caroline was not to worry: mostly because she wanted to view the set-up for herself.

Mikhail was coming out of the kitchen with a plate piled high with more bread and welcomed her warmly.

'Tis is rrill pleasurre. The kids is okay?'

'Oh yes, the children are quite all right. Stephen's back . . . No, he won't be coming, er. He's brought home a *quantity* of work and anyway . . . Well, just for a minute then . . . To say hello to everyone . . .'

Entering the saloon – so like the back half of the drawing-room of Number 9 in shape and period but so utterly different in decor and content – Caroline's mother saw her daughter's cross surprised face; three women who looked no better than they should be with their dyed hair and over-made-up faces, two of them extraordinarily unsuitably dressed for a simple supper party in what was frankly little more than a slum; various men one knew were foreigners – something about the hair and the shoes. There was also that shy girl who had made such a mistake in coming to live here, though she had to admit that the boyfriend who had just let her in had a lot of charm in an unusual sort of way.

Before she knew where she was, a plate piled high with brightly coloured oily smelly food was pushed into her hand. Someone offered her a chair by the fire. Another person provided her with wine.

'Mummy!'

'It's all right, Caro. Stephen's back. Well, what could I do, darling? . . . I only came to tell you – he insisted . . .' But Caroline went on looking annoyed even after her mother had explained all about James's cough.

'Do you know,' she told Mikhail, who had drawn up a chair by her side, 'Caro used to suffer from the most dreadful coughs and colds when she was little. I remember once . . .' As she told the familiar tale to Mikhail, who looked so interested and amused, it came out better than she ever remembered.

Sitting on the divan with vast plates of food balanced on their laps, Stefan and Lubomir were swapping stories about encounters with Englishwomen. They were the best in the world, said Stefan, only they didn't know what to do with themselves and, of course, their men were no good to them at all. It was one of his favourite topics. But Lubomir disagreed. They had no passion. None. They were like English yoghurt, he said, looking over his stomach at what remained on his plate.

Luli sat in a tight circle with her sister, her new brother-in-law, and Christo and Dimiter.

'You can't imagine how happy I am now,' she told the exiles in her low husky voice. She removed a thread of spiced spinach from between her front teeth with a long pearlised pink nail. 'Excuse me . . . I still can't believe I have my baby with me for ever. We have such fun together, Vanya and I. I am like a young girl again. We went dancing last night. Tomorrow we're going to the happy hour at the Hilton. I told my boss today "If I fall asleep at the desk, it's my little sister you should be ticking off." Oh, I am so happy, dear Mitko and Christo! Happy for the first time in years and years . . .'

'Gabble, gabble, gabble,' said the Irishman automatically, and Ivanka threw him another look of contempt.

'You know,' Luli went on, laughing, 'Vanya made us try on wigs the other day in Selfridges. Could you see me as a

164

redhead? Oh, I was sensational, wasn't I, sweetie? A knock-out. This is what will keep me young, you know ...' And Luli caressed the gleaming blonde head of her sister, who instantly took a small mirror out of her handbag and checked her coiffure was not out of order. 'I think of her in that place,' said Luli intensely, tears in her eyes, 'and I thank God she is no longer there. I think of them, those poor people ... I think of their sufferings and each night I go down on my knees and thank God for our good fortune.'

There was no response from either Christo or Dimiter.

Then Christo said with the painful little smile on his face which was habitual when he was about to make a crack at someone else's expense: 'Who cooked these *banitza*?' He pointed at one of Dimiter's pastries on his plate.

'You know who made them,' said Luli. 'Our Mitko always makes these delicious things' and, as she had caressed Ivanka a moment ago, she squeezed Dimiter's knee.

'They're too salty,' said Christo. 'Much much too salty. You don't know how to make these things. I've told you over and over again that you have to mix the sheep's-milk cheese with cream cheese. This is the correct way of making *banitza*.'

'Don't tell me how to do this,' said Dimiter, immediately looking far more upset than he should have done – and, as he spoke, he cut into a slab of lamb on his plate with one of the good sharp knives Mikhail had bought from the local supermarket.

'You make me laugh,' said Christo contemptuously, and he settled more comfortably on his elegantly clad knees one of the big plates with which Mikhail had also equipped the house. 'You say you want to open a restaurant. This is your dream, isn't it? The thing you see yourself doing in years to come? Not working as a little odd-job man but running a restaurant which everyone would come to?' Christo put on a fluting voice. ' "Oh this is so delicious, this new place," they would say to each other. "There's this little place just around the corner that's opened and they serve these pastries which are so salty that you need several glasses of wine to wash them down. But it's all free so it's okay!"

'Well, this is pathetic, you know? I tell you what you'll be doing in five years' time, Dimiter – just what you are now. You'll be living in this same house. You'll be scratching a living mending this and that and this is all. You'll live and die in Stefan's house.'

'Oh shut up!' said Dimiter loudly. Over on the other side of the room, Mikhail looked up suddenly, his grey eyes wide and fearful, and Caroline asked Helen: 'What *are* they going on about now?'

'Oh go fuck your mother and send a carbon copy to God!' replied Christo casually and automatically. In his old country, swearing was a much more inventive and poetic business. He was not to know that this familiar oath was just about the most unfortunate he could possibly have directed at Dimiter.

Out flashed Dimiter's knife. One moment it lay slack in his hand near a heap of lamb and aubergine, the next out it darted, burying itself in Christo's blue and white striped shirt, its precise location marked by its orange plastic handle, like a coloured pin on a police map. It seemed as if the knife acting on its own had accumulated all the energy needed for that terrible thrust. There sat Dimiter in his chair, silent and appalled, staring at the bright orange handle sticking out from the blue and white shirt which first became shadowed around the handle's base, then deep purple and finally bright fountaining scarlet. As a qualified doctor, Dimiter understood too well the damage that had been done.

Only Mikhail took in immediately what had happened. He leapt up, snatched a mass of paper napkins from the trestle table, drew the knife out infinitely gently while murmuring a litany of soothing noises to Christo, then pressed the napkins to the wound.

'Call an ambulance,' he shouted to Stefan over his shoulder and the music which still tinkled on: a thousand Capri violins, shockingly inappropriate. 'Now!'

'But why?' whimpered Christo, staring in disbelief at the

166

blood trickling over his fingers where he had touched his chest. 'Why me, Mitko? Why me? Why don't you stick a knife into Stefan, who's stolen all your girlfriends one by one? Oh yes, you knew this – you must have known it. But why me, Mitko? Why hurt me?' Christo's voice sank to a whisper. 'What have I done to you, Mitko? What have I ever done? This was only a joke, you know. Just a little tease in good fun. I don't understand, Mitko . . . I don't understand . . .'

Over by the fire, Caroline's mother sat like a statue, her fork piled with delicious morsels stuck in space, halfway to her mouth. Now one could see the strong family likeness between mother and daughter – who had precisely the same look of polite horror on her face.

Stefan snatched up the telephone and, with trembling fingers, dialled 999.

'Help!' he said and, as he spoke, he sobbed like Christo. 'A men hev bin stebbed! Plizz send it embulence na! – strreta-way!' and somehow or other he managed to give the correct address.

Luli was crying too as she cradled Christo in her arms. He lay on the floor, his face as white as the napkins had been before they turned sodden scarlet. Luli's glass beads bumped against his nose.

'It's okay, my Christo. It doesn't hurt so much, does it? No! You be a brave boy like I know you are. Soon an ambulance will come to take you to hospital where they'll make it all better. Don't you worry, my pumpkin, don't you worry . . . Your Luli's here to look after you and keep you safe till they come . . .'

It was Helen who comforted Dimiter. But she did it with actions and not words because she did not know what to say to him, the one she had believed the gentlest of them all. What could you say to someone who had committed such a violent and terrible act? She came and knelt before him, clasped his cold hands in hers and looked into his blank eyes with her own shocked ones.

167

'Tea!' said Caroline's mother suddenly and loudly from her seat by the fire. 'That's what we all need – a cup of strong hot tea with plenty of sugar in it. I know where the kitchen is. Now you come with me, Caro, and give me a hand' – and she heaved herself to her feet, not looking at all vague or even arthritic. Mikhail had treated her with great and unaccustomed respect – and perhaps because of this, she suddenly appeared able to command it. For Caroline followed her obediently, just like the child her mother was always telling her she had once been.

Lubomir and Maria were putting pillows collected from Stefan's bedroom under Christo's head. 'Gently, you donkey!' Maria said sharply as they covered his body with an old brown army blanket laced with moth-holes; and Lubomir grumbled to the prone still figure: 'Women! Even at a time like this they find something to fight about!'

Suddenly Ivanka let out a wail of terror and clutched at Luli's arm, as if what had happened had turned her back into a child too. She and Luli clung together, blue-black hair nudging stiffly against glistening white blonde, mascara staining powdery cheeks shadowed with rouge.

Only the Irishman behaved as if nothing had happened, continuing to work his way through his plate and take large gulps from his glass, which he had refilled twice with red wine since the accident. Maybe he too was in shock and this was his own particular way of reacting to it.

They heard the sirens approaching from a long way off. The noise came nearer and nearer, turned into the street, and was abruptly silenced like a musical toy confiscated by an infuriated parent.

Then came the sound of the sagging gate being dragged across the path, steps – a lot of them – and a hammering on the front door.

Helen opened it to six policemen in uniform.

'A man's been stabbed – is that right?' one asked, as if he disliked her.

'Yes, but we asked for an ambulance.' Behind them, she

could see the lamps on at least three police cars flashing their blue beams over the street: on and off, on and off, as if a child were playing with a light switch.

They pushed past her.

'Is an ambulance coming?' she asked, and another replied 'Yes it's coming' as he followed his colleagues into the saloon.

Now another siren – solitary, thinner, an echo of the others – could be heard. As Helen stood watching by the open front door, an ambulance drew up on the opposite side of the street where there was room to park, the police cars having taken up all the space outside Number 11.

Half a dozen neighbours from the other houses had gathered there. Hetty Clarke was among them, still clutching her sheaf of Neighbourhood Watch newsletters which she had retrieved from behind Number 11's front door before leaving so abruptly.

'But I was there!' she kept repeating. 'I was there!'

She had already begun work on her anecdote, testing out the rough draft on the three households where she dropped newsletters later. The rich brew of outrageous male chauvinist piggery, right-wing views and blinkered materialism, flavoured with racism (her own), had gone down pretty well: everyone was interested in what went on in that crumbling house, Hetty had discovered. Hetty always painted herself the timid bystander in such sagas – 'You won't believe what he said to me . . . so I just sat there like a little mouse' and so on and so forth. But now her concoction seemed a pale gruel. For a crime had been committed in that sordid place and she of all people had missed out on it, and only just. Shifting impatiently from one foot to the other, she watched as two men got out of the ambulance, opened the doors at its back and slid through them a stretcher stacked with neatly folded blankets.

It was the warm scarlet colour of those blankets which prompted another neighbour – a young lawyer from Number 14 – to cross the road and approach Helen.

'Can you tell us what's going on?'

169

'Someone's hurt.'

'But the police cars—'

'He was stabbed.'

She watched shock strike him dumb, but only momentarily. He rejoined the others and, like a man spreading a contagious disease, passed a dose of shock to each of them in turn. Hetty spoke at length and they murmured among themselves, cast scared looks at Number 11, its front door wide open to the night, and noted that it had no carpet in the hall or up the stairs. For everyone except Hetty, it was the first glimpse they had ever had of its interior.

In the saloon, the ambulancemen tucked Christo neatly into their stretcher after first checking his pulse and taking his blood pressure. Their soothing competence contrasted with the edgy aggression of the six policemen who had surrounded Dimiter like a flock of crows. He was not unconscious like Christo, but seemed just as incapable of speech. He did not appear to absorb the questions fired at him. He was traumatised by his own action, and very soon they gave up. They would take him with them to the police station, after asking for his passport.

It was Mikhail who went to fetch it, and so it was he who saw the parade of photographs of Dimiter's mother, passing through life. Mikhail opened the door of a shallow built-in cupboard and half a dozen double rolls of soft lavatory paper burst out. There were tins of ham and ratatouille stacked on another shelf; dried sausages dangling from a hook. Mikhail replaced the lavatory paper. He knew Dimiter's history and understood the neuroses of those who had served time in the harsh prisons of his native land.

The passport was pushed into the drawer of a table along with assorted coins, Dimiter's national insurance card, and three photographs taken at a funeral. Mikhail looked from the face on the bier to the faces on the mantelpiece. It would have been impossible for an observer to read his expression: to decide whether pity or anger was there, or both. Then he picked up the passport and went downstairs.

170

They were going with Dimiter, he told Helen. There was some explaining to do to the police. He needed her to translate for him.

'Okay,' she agreed wearily.

The ambulancemen left first. Christo's face, poking out of a scarlet shroud, was now a ghastly greenish grey. It frightened the neighbours opposite, though Hetty – constantly reminding them of her inside knowledge – said he was quite pale naturally. It was a pity, remarked someone, that the local hospital had recently closed down. It was a good half-hour's journey to the nearest casualty department, agreed another; and they all had an absorbing discussion on the shortcomings of the National Health Service whilst keeping a watchful eye on developments at Number 11.

The tea Caroline's mother had made for the exiles, who did not drink it, was appreciated by the policemen. They took short statements all round and asked everyone present to come down to the station the following day to give longer ones. They had difficulty in understanding Stefan, who was still weeping sporadically.

To the neighbours, it was like a live whodunnit. They had seen the victim, clearly (to everyone except Hetty) on his way out of this world. In a minute that horde of policemen would bring out the murderer but, without conferring, each one of them was quite certain who it would be. It could only be the sullen dark one who was always drunk – *and* lecherous too, they understood from Hetty – and had disturbed the peace of the street night after night and let down its rising status with his appallingly dilapidated house. They stared at the open door of Number 11, its empty hall lit by a swinging unshaded electric lightbulb, hardly daring to blink in case they missed something.

It came as a real shock when Dimiter emerged, entirely surrounded by tall policemen like a tiny statesman particularly vulnerable to assassination. This was the man who had unblocked one of their kitchen sinks only last week; constructed those strong cupboards in another's daughter's bedroom – and yes, they had to admit he did do a good job. It

171

couldn't be him: the one they contacted each time something needed fixing in their houses. They had never properly talked to him beyond requesting his presence and paying for it – and they had to admit he was a lot cheaper than most. Hetty said he had always been weird and you had to watch out for those quiet ones. But to have had a murderer in their houses without knowing it!

He was hustled into the first car. Mikhail and Helen were allowed to travel in the third. The neighbours watched the glossy black cars draw away, lights still flashing, and deplored the need, at this hour, to switch on the sirens again. They saw a short, voluptuous, middle-aged woman in a tight lilac dress with strikingly black hair cascading over her shoulders emerge into the hall of Number 11 and glance across at them. She recognised Hetty and immediately slapped one palm on to the inside of her elbow so that her plump white forearm and tightly clenched fist shot up in a reflex action. To Luli's mind, it was too much of a coincidence that the police had turned up uninvited, when they had only asked for an ambulance, so soon after Hetty's questioning of Ivanka about how she had arrived in Britain. Police were the same the world over, thought Luli – who would have snorted with derision at the image presented to the children at the local church school of the friendly neighbourhood bobby. True, that bunch had seemed only to be interested in Dimiter, but still . . . As for the collection of vultures standing with Hetty . . .

'Charming!' said Hetty, as the door slammed shut, and the others murmured 'Well!' and 'Yes!'

Then they all went back to their own warm houses with a fresh appreciation of their comfort and elegance, but also a profound sense of unease.

In the saloon, the remaining exiles were obviously settling in for a long night. They weren't speaking English at all now. They talked rapidly, excitedly: as if, in the hours of that night still left, they would never have enough time to say all they wished to say. They no longer appeared so distraught.

172

The Irishman was deeply asleep. His woolly head lay on the trestle table next to an empty plate. Occasionally he farted gently.

'Time to go,' said Caroline's mother.

She and her daughter tried to say goodbye: to edge into the conversation – more like a competition – in which Ivanka, cuddled and patted by Luli, was currently the star performer. Then they gave up the attempt and crept quietly out.

'Oh Mummy,' said Caroline as they walked along the pavement to the house next door; and she linked her arm through her mother's, something she had not done for many years. 'It was—' She searched through her vocabulary for a word which would accurately describe the shock and horror of what they had witnessed and could only come up with 'unreal', even though the experience had been more real to her than anything in her life so far except perhaps the births of her children.

'It was unreal,' she repeated, fitting her key into the lock of her own neat front door.

CHAPTER TWENTY-ONE

When Helen and Mikhail returned to Number 11 Shipka Avenue at last, it was four o'clock in the morning and all was dark and silent.

'Where are they?' asked Helen, tucking the change from the minicab fare into her purse. 'I was sure they'd still be here.'

Mikhail did not answer.

'They can't be asleep,' she said as they glanced into the empty saloon which was in utter disarray. Smeared plates were piled crookedly on to every surface. Clearly a second meal had been eaten, for no food remained. It was unpleasant to see the tomato and lipstick which stained the white paper napkins scrunched up and flung everywhere. But the blood which had spilt on to the wooden floor had been wiped up, though not thoroughly; and the blood-soaked blanket which had wrapped Christo had been removed. No alcohol remained: not in the bottom of a single one of the glasses scattered about.

'Oh, they must have run out of drink. They've probably gone to Luli's – all of them, even Kevin.'

Still Mikhail said nothing, but Helen went on talking.

'We'd better go to bed, hadn't we? You must be so tired, Mikhail. I know I am. Shall I get us a hot drink? Would that be a good idea?'

At last Mikhail spoke and she dared to look at him. He needed a brandy, he said. All his vitality and cheerfulness seemed to have leaked away. He looked as Dimiter had done

174

when they finally left him: pale and blank as if nothing had ever made him either happy or sad.

'That's just about the last thing we'd ever be able to find in this house,' Helen tried to joke.

'I see it brrendy in rroom of Dimiter.' Mikhail had spotted it in the cupboard when he fetched the passport. He was sure, he said, that Dimiter wouldn't mind.

'Of course not,' said Helen soothingly. She longed to take Mikhail in her arms, but did not recognise this cold white stranger. So, hiding her terror, she behaved formally and also as if nothing had happened. 'Shall I get it?'

'I get it.' He started slowly up the uncarpeted stairs, the sound of his shoes on the hard wood over-loud in the house which was quite empty except for them.

'Well, I'll come up too.'

She checked that the front door was closed. She could not lock it because the others were out but, for some reason, greatly wanted to. She switched off all the lights and then followed him.

Mikhail was sitting on their bed. In his loosely clasped hands he held what Helen at first thought was a toy.

It must have been a present from Dimiter's mother, along with the jars of jams and pickles he saved for special occasions. It was a little wooden man. His torso was a polished cone, his feet tiny planks slotted on to pegs for legs, and a carved nose sprang from his egg-shaped head. He wore a hat of brown synthetic fur and more of the same was glued around his cone-shaped body to resemble the edges of a long coat. On his back was fixed a miniature plaited raffia basket for carrying firewood, and tucked into this was a small bottle of plum brandy.

No, said Mikhail, it wasn't correct for him to drink it. He should put it back.

'I'm sure Dimiter wouldn't mind.' Helen shuddered. 'It's so cold. After all,' she went on, 'we can fill up the bottle tomorrow with more brandy. We can get it from Luli. We don't even have to tell him.'

'Okay,' said Mikhail, and in his dead and empty voice she thought she could detect a faint note of gratitude.

He offered it to her first.

'Well, a little.' She tipped the narrow mouthpiece to her lips and felt the peppery brandy numb her mouth and throat, leaving behind a warm pervasive taste more almond than plum.

Mikhail took a long draught himself. Then he put the bottle on the table beside the bed and slumped, staring at the floor.

'Bed?' suggested Helen brightly.

She longed to discuss the happenings of the night: Mikhail's discovery of Dimiter's tragedy, and the effect his own statement to the police might have. Surely now that they knew the circumstances of the attack they would be lenient? But she seemed quite unable to begin without a cue from Mikhail. It had been easy to be happy and confident and good when treated with an abundance of optimism and energy and, above all, kindness. But now those supports had been abruptly removed, Helen was lost in a sea of self-doubt, beginning to wonder what sort of a relationship it had ever been. Her voice sounded different, even to her.

Feeling strangely modest, she undressed with her back to Mikhail, pulling a nightdress over her head. Then she got into the bed and tried not to look at him with eyes which, she knew, revealed far too much.

He rose with an effort and removed a dark jacket Christo had given him, ran his hands through his black hair, looked briefly into the mirror above the mantelpiece. He sighed deeply and she realised she had never heard him do that before. Then he unbuttoned his checked woollen shirt (one of her many presents to him) and folded it before laying it on the old armchair where he always put his clothes at night. Next came the cotton T-shirt he wore underneath for extra warmth, his belt, his smart grey trousers, the only pair which were not jeans and had been donned in honour of the party.

He made a sudden horrified exclamation in his own

language and caught up the shirt he had folded so neatly, threw it down on the floor. There were spots of dried blood there as well as on the trousers. Not much of it, but spatters everywhere.

'What, Mikhail?'

'Nottink.' Everything could wait until tomorrow.

He stood in woollen vest and Y-fronts, then moved towards the curtains.

'Let's leave them open,' suggested Helen, grateful for something to say. 'It's almost morning.'

'Okay.' He sounded as if it didn't matter to him at all.

He climbed into bed, reached for the bottle of brandy once more, switched off the light and lay flat on his back while she shut her eyes tightly as if by so doing she could blank out everything that was happening. She knew she would not be able to sleep at all, but thought with resignation that she would have to pretend to be asleep until it was time to get up.

It never occurred to Helen that Mikhail would want to make love that night and she was quite unprepared for it. One moment he lay at her side not touching her, seeming hardly to breathe, an abstracted stranger. The next, he had turned suddenly towards her and was kissing her, breathing the scent of almonds into her mouth, desperately seeking her body with his own cold one through layers of obstructive wool.

'Oh Mikhail, I love you!' she said, quite unable to stop herself.

But he didn't hear, or perhaps he pretended not to. Already confidence was returning and she thought: 'What does it matter? What does anything matter but here and now?'

Before, Mikhail had been a dream lover. He had come into her life just as she had given up all hope of that kind of happiness and been everything she had never known in a man before. This wasn't the same Mikhail, and neither was he making love to the girl he always called his sweetheart. She knew she, Helen, was incidental. She didn't even feel like a person. She had the strange sensation that Mikhail was making love to his past and, in the dawning light which seeped into their attic room, she saw in his staring eyes so close to hers no recognition at all. He looked beyond her to a time before he had known her. There was no tenderness, though more passion than there had ever been between them. And when it was over, she didn't feel used or abused or any of those things another girl might have felt with another man in similar circumstances. All she thought as she lay bruised and pleasured against Mikhail's body, now damp with sweat, his heart pounding, was 'Now it will be all right.'

He had spoken only once during that wild and violent embrace, and she just made out the words half-sobbed, half-muttered against her ear: 'I buyed it the knife.'

CHAPTER TWENTY-TWO

'Oh!' exclaimed Caroline. 'How are you? Everything all right?'

She behaved as if Helen was the last person she had expected to encounter on a quick sortie to the pakky delly, which was what she and Stephen called the twenty-four-hour supermarket.

'Well – just about.'

'That girl looks perfectly ghastly,' thought Caroline. It struck her that Helen looked as if she was afraid someone might beat her: just like a labrador the Johnstons had once got from the dogs' home and later had to return because of its anti-social habits. But she asked casually: 'Sure?' It wasn't as if one didn't have one's own problems.

'Well—' Then Helen said: 'Haven't seen you for a long time, Caroline.'

'Ages,' agreed Caroline. Not since the night of the stabbing which was more than four weeks ago now.

'Well, it's all been—'

'Don't I know!'

They stood in the street outside the two houses, Caroline frowning and kicking with one neat foot the shopping basket on wheels her mother had given her for Christmas, Helen trying to smile but only succeeding in looking more pathetic, in Caroline's eyes.

'How's— is he better?' Caroline asked finally. She still had not registered Christo's name, but she had heard via a neighbour across the street, who had read it in the local newspaper, that Christo's wound had not been fatal.

'Oh yes. Thank goodness. The knife missed his heart by about half an inch. I went to see him yesterday, as a matter of fact. He's quite cheerful. They say he can come out of hospital soon.'

'Well, that's super – absolutely super. And—?'

'They haven't decided exactly what to do about Dimiter yet. At the worst, he'll be charged with attempted murder. It might not come to that. At the moment, he's just waiting – and of course he doesn't like being kept in a cell.'

'So – it's all turned out all right. Sort of . . .' Caroline laughed nervously.

'I suppose so.' Then Helen said in a rush: 'Have you got time for a coffee, Caroline?'

'Awfully sorry. Got to rush. Let's meet soon – very soon. But must dash now. See you' – and Caroline was off down the street before Helen could say anything further, her grey pleated skirt swinging frantically under her navy jacket.

Helen turned sadly and went back into Number 11.

She had been watching for Caroline, waiting to seize the moment when she would emerge from her house: not knowing that Caroline had believed the coast to be clear and had been avoiding Helen ever since the stabbing. Helen could not know the reason was as much to do with what had happened the day afterwards.

The following evening, Stephen had broken the news that he would shortly be made redundant. The office was cutting down, he had suspected it for some time. He had not told Caroline before, he had said, because he hadn't known how to and, though he did not add this, because traditionally one didn't make a fuss about such things. In their set, one made light of them in inverse proportion to the way one made heavy weather of trivial matters. It was how things were.

Helen shut the front door of Number 11 behind her and kicked away the thick heap of circulars with one foot. The house had the same still, useless air about it she had sensed that first morning when she came for coffee with Mikhail. She had the strange feeling that nothing had changed since then and the events of the intervening months were no more than a dream.

She decided to make tea for everyone. It was appropriate to start the day and at past noon everyone else was still in bed at Number 11.

She was filling the kettle when the telephone began to ring. It rang constantly these days: dozens and dozens of wrong numbers. Why else should callers hang up immediately when she or anyone else who happened to be around answered? Mikhail did not like to answer the telephone nowadays. He never did any more.

'Hello . . . hello . . . hello . . .' Click. Buzz. It was hard not to agree with Stefan that the British telephone system was the most inefficient in the world.

Stefan received his tea first because his bedroom was nearest the kitchen, on the ground floor.

As usual, it was a sobering experience to enter his crowded stuffy bedroom though he himself was still quite drunk from the night before.

'What is?' he shouted, starting out of bed with a wild look in his red-veined eyes. This was invariably his immediate reaction on being woken. Then, when he understood it was only Helen, he lay back on his grubby pillows gasping with relief. What had happened to him in his past, she wondered, that he behaved like this? Perhaps she should leave him to wake up in his own time? But, on the other hand, he was always pleased to see her.

'How you arre, darrlink?'

'Oh – okay, Stefan.'

'Tis is tea what you arre mekkink?' He took the cup and saucer and it rattled in his hand.

'Yes. Like always.'

'Oh.' As usual, he put it on the table beside his bed where it would grow cold and scummy and never be drunk.

'How are you feeling?'

'Oh! I em yill! Rrilly I em yill.' Then, as always when one of the exiles felt even slightly off colour, suspicion struck. He was thinking there was something strange with this illness, he told Helen intensely. He had never ever felt like this before, he said – even though he often felt ill in the mornings, almost always because he had drunk too much the night before.

'Do you think it's a touch of the 'flu perhaps?'

'Tis was trregical tink what heppen,' said Stefan. *This* was what was making him ill maybe, he went on. Yes, maybe. This awful thing which had happened between Christo and Dimiter. It was worse, much worse, than if an Englishman had stabbed Christo. It had been awful for his nerves – awful. Did Helen know he had not slept one blink for thirty-six hours now? 'I em lyink heerre tinkink of tis trregical tinks. Poorr Mitko. Poorr poorr Mitko . . .'

'And poor Christo too!'

'Yes. I em sayink it tis . . .'

Stefan stared gloomily at the window of his room. Helen had drawn back the ancient heavy brown brocade curtains made by the previous owner of the house. The room smelt of stale cigarette smoke and gin, as if the window had never been opened; whereas the wardrobe looked as if it had never been shut, with its swinging doors bearing down on the hard high bed. There were ashtrays crammed with cigarette ends on the bedside table, cardboard boxes packed with dusty programmes from the Royal Opera House on the floor, clothes flung everywhere. The only patch of order was Stefan's shoe rack, where dozens of highly polished shoes were arranged in lines according to colour: cream, beige and light brown on the top shelves; burgundy, dark brown, navy blue and deep shiny ebony on the bottom.

This conversation had become a ritual. In the morning – or rather, early afternoon – Stefan was always deeply gloomy about what Dimiter had done to Christo and how they had both suffered, particularly Dimiter. His own health had suffered too, he claimed. But by about six o'clock he was sufficiently cheered to have a drink; and the rest of the evening passed in a haze of alcohol and conversation (almost always about the stabbing), usually round at Luli's these days.

Mostly, Helen merely listened. But this morning she decided to depart from the ritual.

'Stefan, I'm worried about Mikhail . . .'

'Uh?'

'He's – not himself, Stefan . . .'

'Uh?'

'Would you like coffee rather than tea, Stefan?' Plainly he was in no mood yet for any sort of real discussion.

'Oh! – would be merrvellous, Helen.'

When she returned with the coffee, Stefan already looked more sprightly. He had lit a cigarette. Yes, he said as if their conversation had never been interrupted, he could certainly get a good price for this house. Actually, it was unbearable, the cold. Maybe he would move before next winter came along or maybe he would import his own central heating, he said with a sly wink. Mikhail was a lucky man to have a woman who was comfy as well as cultured.

'Stefan, I have to talk to you about Mikhail. There isn't anyone else who would understand.' As she had known it would, this made Stefan concentrate all his attention on what she was saying.

'He's – given up, Stefan. Look at him – he sleeps all day. He's not working. He's not interested any more. He won't talk to me about it. He's become like—' But she stopped because she had been about to say 'the rest of you here.'

'Tis tink what heppen,' said Stefan, 'was offul forr Mikhail also.'

'But it was more than a month ago now, Stefan! Christo's recovering. They'll be lenient with Dimiter, I'm sure they will . . .'

Stefan took a long noisy drink from his cup, wiped his mouth with the sleeve of his red and white striped pyjamas, lit another cigarette from the first.

Mikhail hadn't been in this country for so long, he said.

'What? I don't understand you.'

It was only eight months since he had arrived, he said. He explained that everyone coming from East to West experienced a huge culture shock. It was the biggest problem – this psychological one – of going into exile. Some people never came through it. Look at himself! Maybe he had never recovered from the shock. He thought so sometimes. But actually he was not cheap stuff. No! He might be a drunk, but he knew what was truth, what was beauty. Did Helen know, he said, gesturing at the old programmes on the floor, that he used to be a leading opera critic? In his previous life, that was. Did she know that? No! He wasn't going to these things any more – what was the point? – but he was an expert, an authority.

'But Mikhail! Talk to me about Mikhail, Stefan!'

Usually, said Stefan, this reaction – the sort of reaction Mikhail was having now – occurred earlier. Perhaps within the first three months. But Mikhail had had Helen helping him with his work, caring for him, and so there had been a delay. What had happened between Christo and Dimiter, he told her, had given Mikhail a huge shock and so he was having the reaction now. It hadn't helped having no success with his poetry – and Stefan said he knew all about the dejection letters.

He went on: 'Oh, I em destrroyet also. I em yill because of tis offul tink . . .'

'But Mikhail was always so positive!' Helen protested. 'So ambitious. Oh, I know there've been disappointments. But he'll make it. I know he'll make it! After all, it's Mikhail who made me see that anything's possible if you want it badly enough. He can't give up now!'

'Oh Helen,' said Stefan sadly, 'you arre child.' Like Mikhail, he pointed out.

She knew nothing of this cruel world, he said. But then, he too had been a child when he first came to the West. He had thought he could be best. He had believed he could do anything. Now, he said with a little smile, he was a lost cause – and he was not alone. Dimiter was truly a lost cause now, poor Dimiter, God help him; and there was poor Christo who had tried so hard to be an Englishman with no chance ever of succeeding. As for Luli and Ivanka – well, they were happy now they were together, shopping and flirting, but Luli could only stand it here if she could continue going back and forth. He wouldn't go into the reasons why she could do that – it was a shady business – but it wouldn't be so easy for Ivanka. Wait and see how *she* was in three months' time! Oh, he didn't regret leaving his country – no, he would never say that, never! And this was the most free country in the world, as he well knew. But his native country was in his blood – how could he forget it? That country had made him what he was. And the worst thing of all, he said, was that people here knew nothing about his native country, nothing at all: nor of the cruel system which had forced him to leave. They didn't care – didn't want to be told. The worst thing was that they weren't even interested – even they talked awful rubbish about Socialist paradises. Like Hetty, he said, that night when poor Dimiter had stabbed poor Christo. She had a good heart, but he had gone crazy listening to her. Actually, he had told her to fuck off, the hen – and this was why she had left in an awful temper. He had finished by telling her that the proof of her freedom was that she could talk such rubbish with impunity.

Then he sank back on to his pillows with a groan. 'Oh, I em yill, Helen. Rrilly I em yill . . .'

There was nothing more to be gained from Stefan. Helen left him lying in his bed staring blackly round his room and chain-smoking. She poured three more cups of tea in the kitchen and then carried them upstairs on a tray.

One was for the Irishman, still deeply asleep. She drew his curtains, shook his shoulder, left the tea beside his bed. The other two were for herself and Mikhail.

Mikhail was awake. He lay staring at the sloping ceiling with his slanting grey eyes. The room looked strangely bare.

The timetable had gone, as had the pieces of paper with English words, growing daily more complicated, which had previously been pinned on the walls. Mikhail had removed them all.

'Here, Mikhail.'

'Oh swithearrt.' But there was no feeling in the endearment, as in time past. He said it automatically, the way he took the cup of tea from her hand.

'How are you feeling?'

'Okay.' But he looked a different person — the more so because yesterday he had cut his beautiful black hair to a stubble with a pair of nail scissors. All his radiance and warmth had disappeared as if they had never been. There was no trace of the enthusiasm that had once danced in those grey eyes, the optimism and gaiety which had rendered his flashing white smile an utterly irresistible weapon. This Mikhail, slow and dull, seemed hardly to be alive. And that night of passion after the accident might not have occurred at all. There had been no repetition of it. Mikhail and Helen had slept together since the way brother and sister are supposed to do.

'What would you like to work on today?'

'Always you say it tis.' He stretched his lips, bared his teeth a little, but it was not a smile.

'I've done my column for the week. I'm here to help you, Mikhail. We can work on something new. What do you think?'

'Oh Helen . . .' He touched her hand with his lips and she felt the bristles on cheeks that had not been shaved for a week. 'Always I rrememberr it everrtink what you done forr me. Neverr I forrget it tis.'

'Why do you say that?' she asked, terrified but managing to sound almost normal.

He went on kissing her hands, scratching them with his beard.

'Why do you say that, Mikhail? Why?'

He was going back, he said; and at last he looked into her eyes. He didn't know how to tell her this, but he had made up his mind. He was going back to his native country. He had no choice, he said, none at all.

CHAPTER TWENTY-THREE

'We have to talk,' said Caroline Johnston to her husband, unaware that next door, at almost that moment, Helen was saying just these words to Mikhail.

Talk, serious talk, was strictly limited in Number 9 Shipka Avenue and if, as so often happened, one was too tired to cash in on the ration – well, that was it and one didn't talk. But tonight, with the children in bed and Caroline's mother having at last retired to her room, they had to talk. Even so, Caroline busied herself at the same time with making a batch of cakes promised for the church fête tomorrow.

'One can't simply go on pretending nothing's happened, you know. We have to make plans, decide what we're going to do . . .'

Outside in the blackness, wind raced around the house in a frenzy, creaking the timbers and rattling the hundred-year-old slates on the roof. In a cold fury, it shook the wooden fences in the garden and the trellis atop them woven with the dusty brown bones of the vine next door. Come the spring in a couple of months green fronds would shoot up and out in all directions and try to snake into all the other gardens.

'I mean, what's going to happen about the mortgage? And the boys' education? Mummy's got a bit of money but not enough for all that. Not nearly enough. Oh *bloody* hell!' Caroline had just realised while dribbling very liquid cake mixture into pleated greaseproof paper cups that, having made double the amount specified in the recipe, she had forgotten proportionately to increase the flour. 'Oh well,' she said, shooting the cakes into the oven after only a moment's hesitation, 'they'll just jolly well have to lump it. I can always pretend James made them.'

'I'll get some sort of golden handshake,' said Stephen. 'Not that much though – haven't been with the firm long enough. Knew I shouldn't have moved from the old one. Should have listened to my instinct.'

'But it was such an opportunity. Compared with the rest of our friends, you were earning peanuts. No, you had to move, Stephen. Oh I don't *believe* this!' For, at that crucial moment, there came the tenth telephone call of the evening.

Long before Stephen heard about his redundancy, Caroline had planned a special event for the following weekend: a breast-feeding gathering on the common. True, the weather was not good; but, in Caroline's eyes, that would further make the point that breast-feeding was something women ought to feel happy and confident about doing anywhere, at any time. A picnic was planned. Caroline was co-ordinating the affair and so more local women than ever had been telephoning their house.

'Hello . . . Yup . . . Oh, super! . . . So you'll make some carrot cake, will you? . . . No, Miranda's already making tofuburgers . . . Well, we haven't actually thought about what we're going to do with the littlies yet – the big littlies, that is . . . Yup, I've made photostat copies of a leaflet I've put together – facts and figures about why we should all breast-feed – in case people want to know what's going on . . . No, don't give it a *thought*. No, not doing a thing . . . Don't be silly, that's what I'm *here* for . . .'

'What I em doink heerre?' asked Mikhail. He went on: 'I don't hev it no choosink' and, in spite of all her distress, Helen automatically corrected him.

'Any alternative, Mikhail. "I don't have any alternative." But why don't you have any alternative? Why?'

Like the Johnstons next door, they had waited until there was privacy and quiet in which to talk. They sat upstairs in

189

their room: Helen on the bed, Mikhail in the chair at the rickety table where they had so often worked, while the rest of the house lay dark and empty beneath them.

What was he doing here? Mikhail repeated. All the time he worked, he said, but no one wanted to know nothing about this work. It was as if he was writing in space and writing was the most important thing in this life for him, he told Helen: for him, it was important like breathing. He sighed deeply, covered his face with his hands. He couldn't be a writer in England. He knew this now. But why couldn't he? he asked reasonably as if he really did not understand. After all, she earned a good living writing about cookery, but she couldn't cook. Why couldn't he be a poet? But it was not possible – he knew this now – and soon he would be forty years old. He thought of this all the time. How much time did he have? Was only a short time. He knew this, he said. You didn't go on having talent for ever. And now he thought he must spend this short time that was left writing in a language and a world which he knew.

'But you *can't* go back, Mikhail! I can't believe you're thinking of it seriously! You've got a sentence on your head. You'd be imprisoned immediately or worse, Mikhail, much much worse.'

She stared at him, her eyes full of fear and passion but her voice steadfastly calm. 'You wouldn't be able to write then, Mikhail. And do you think anything you ever wrote again would be published there? I saw that newspaper Luli brought back. I've heard them all talk about it.'

There was a long long silence.

Then he said: 'I don't be belonkink wit tis worrld, Helen.'

'How can we talk about it?' asked Stephen. 'There's always something else going on, Caro. If it's not the children, it's your mother. Or those appalling characters next door. Or this breast-feeding counselling lark. I really think those women you've never met mean more to you than I do. Oh

190

yes, I do. And I can't talk to you about my real feelings, Caro. In answer to your question: I can't.'

'Well, what are they?' asked Caroline. 'Come on Stephen – I'm listening. I really am listening now.'

'I don't know,' said Stephen after a long pause. 'That's part of the problem. I don't know . . .'

Yes, Mikhail agreed, this thing that had happened with Dimiter and Christo had made up his mind. It had been so awful. So tragical for one of them to attack his own kind. This thing had told him everything that was wrong with this country.

'What Mikhail? Tell me' and a quite separate part of Helen marvelled at this ability to talk about something which mattered so much as if it had nothing to do with her whatsoever.

'Poorr poorr Mitko,' said Mikhail. Why hadn't he told them what had happened with his poor mother? Why didn't he talk about it to them, his friends? Mikhail said he thought it was because Dimiter had been living here for so long: he thought he had to behave like everyone else in this country.

'What do you mean?'

'What it is, tis pless?' Mikhail demanded and, as he launched into the longest speech she had ever heard him make in English, she perceived a different character altogether from the one she knew beginning to emerge: bitter and resentful, as if the carefully constructed layers of his new personality were all at once starting to crack and crumble off like the paint on the outside of the house.

He did not understand this place, this country, he said. He did not understand it at all. He knew what colour underpants his neighbours wore, he said, because he saw them dressing each morning in their bedrooms which had no net curtains. He knew how they spent their evenings, too, because before they drew the real curtains he could see them in their saloons watching television, night after night. He could probably

191

guess to the last penny how much money they had because of the cars they owned, the furniture he could see through the windows. But he knew nothing – nothing at all – about them *inside*. Everyone lived in boxes in this country, he said: each cut off from his neighbour, alone. No one – not one – understood what was real friendship. Also, he said, people saved everything up here. They saved their feelings, their thoughts, and always – of course – their money. For what? he asked. For who? For when? What were they called – those cotton blankets that were used to wrap the dead? Ah yes. Thank you, Helen. Shrouds had no pockets. And he was not spending the rest of his life in this cold atmosphere.

'But Stefan? The others?' And, again, the observant analytical side of her applauded the vocabulary he had amassed, his idiosyncratic mastery of her language.

Stefan was a disaster, pronounced Mikhail. Like his house. A sick person. If he thought he might end like Stefan he would kill himself. But even so, underneath all the rubbish, Stefan understood what life was for. Even Stefan. He couldn't stand Stefan for much of the time, he said, he drove him crazy; but he loved him with all his heart. Stefan was more of a person than anyone English he had ever met.

'We are not talking about ourselves,' Helen told herself resolutely at this point. 'This conversation is about something entirely separate from what was between us.' She did not allow what Mikhail had just said to hurt her. She managed to say gently: 'You haven't given yourself enough time, Mikhail. It's too soon to decide what you really feel.'

'End,' Mikhail went on as if she had not spoken, 'tey arre Philistines.' He went on to point out that, in this country, people could read whatever they liked, see whatever they wanted in the way of plays and films – unless it was exceptionally pornographic, and he meant exceptionally. What did they do with this precious freedom? They chose to fill their brains with rubbish. He told Helen that in his country people would queue for a whole day for the chance of seeing or reading something good and real. But in this

192

country, he said, people seemed afraid of the good and real, like they were afraid of talking to each other from the heart. He compared them with dead people. All they cared about was having a good pension and looking okay in the eyes of their neighbours. The only deep feelings they had, he said bitterly, was for their cats and dogs. He had seen a woman in the butcher's the other day buying best fillet of beef for her cat. She told everyone in the shop and no one thought it was tragical. And Mikhail went on to say he'd tell Helen another thing: people helped each other in his old country. They might hate each other – often did – but they helped each other. This pitiful Neighbourhood Watch business would be unheard of there. In his old country, people didn't have to be told to wear badges on their houses to remind them of the existence of their neighbours. And another thing: no one there treated old people the way they were treated here. That grandmother from next door, for example: she had to talk to herself because no one else would. Once he'd seen her in the baker's trying to talk to the woman behind the counter – only a little conversation about the sort of bread her daughter had liked as a child – but no one, not one person, would listen to her.

'We don't have to have this sort of life,' said Caroline slowly. 'Well, we don't have to Stephen, do we?'

The thought was so novel, so disturbing, that she rose from her chair abruptly and put the kettle on. They had already had two cups of tea each, just as Helen and Mikhail next door had already drunk a quarter of a bottle of whisky. They had consumed half a tin of wholemeal biscuits too, because it was comforting to eat when one talked as one had never talked before.

'Listen to that!' She peered through the garden door into the roaring dark and dimly saw her shrubs bending back and forth as if exercising. Somewhere in the neighbourhood a burglar alarm began shrilling, tripped off by the wind. 'Do you think the fence is going to hold?' For the common fence Jack and Bill had eventually mended, three months after they had promised to, could be heard cracking as it swayed, even through a layer of glass.

'I suppose,' said Stephen, his total lack of interest a sign of just how worried he was about other matters.

'I've always wanted to live in the country,' said Caroline suddenly. 'Well it's in you, you know, if you were brought up there yourself. And it would be super for the children to keep proper animals. Maybe even a pony. *Think* how James would love it!'

'Steady on, Caro. Don't count your—'

'*And* chickens!' agreed Caroline excitedly. 'Oh yes, Stephen! We could do everything ourselves then it wouldn't be expensive at all. Couldn't we think about it? If we sold this house ... The Robbins got £115,000 for Number 22 and that was at least three months ago.'

'And the boys' education?' asked Stephen with a bitter little smile. 'I don't know where you're thinking of moving to, Caro, but that *is* one of our main priorities – remember?'

'But if you haven't got a job,' Caroline pointed out, 'then we're not going to be able to afford it anyway. Oh, you might get another and we could hang around living off whatever money you get while we're waiting. But it's jolly difficult to get a job these days – the sort of job you had before, I mean – one knows that. *Or* we could use the money *and* what we'd get for this house – and remember it's in perfect condition, Stephen, perfect – to set up on our own. We could grow everything too. Oh do think about it, darling. I know it sounds funny but it would be super to think of somewhere as home – real home – at last. And if there isn't going to be the money to pay for the sort of education we wanted for the boys – well, they're going to have to make the best of what there is. I mean, other people manage somehow – don't they?'

'Hold on, Caro!' Stephen stared in astonishment at his wife. This extraordinary vivacity suited her. 'Hold *on*! You're

194

bananas! You know that? And I thought you loved it here –
near all your friends.'

'I don't think,' said Caroline slowly, 'that I could bear to
feel I didn't belong. I mean, half the fun was we were all in
the same boat. I couldn't *take* being pitied, Stephen. I don't
think I could take that at all . . .'

They sat in their attic room, feet from each other, while the
old house shifted and sighed around them.

Helen looked at Mikhail's pale angry face and thought
that she had never really known him. Precisely because they
did not share the same language, she had fancied that they
enjoyed some mysterious kind of communication: that, even
though many mundane matters could not be understood, the
most important ones were. What a fool she was. Why had he
stayed with her even for a day? Mikhail had not shown her
his real self because he had believed that – starting all over
again in a new environment – he could be whatever he
wanted, not what he was. But she had been just as dishonest
herself. All she had been to Mikhail was a tool to help him
realise his ambitions, and she had fallen happily into the role.
Not once had she expressed any wishes or hopes for herself.
And now it was almost over.

'When will you go?' she asked in a quiet dreary voice, as if
the question had nothing to do with her at all.

'Soon.'

'How?'

He would go to the embassy, said Mikhail. His embassy in
Queen's Gate. He tipped the bottle of whisky, drank deeply
and went on talking as if he were alone. If only, he mused,
we could know at the time what was the best moment in all
our life – could recognise it when it happened and be sure we
could hope for no greater. If only. He sighed. Probably Helen
hadn't had that best time yet so probably she didn't know
what he was talking about, he said gently and, feeling his
interest light on her briefly, Helen almost wept because she

thought he had quite forgotten her, and understood her so little.

It wasn't possible to escape from himself, Mikhail went on. He had thought it was possible – and he smiled at his naïveté. But now, he said, he realised that wherever he went, he would take himself too. Even if he found a new planet, it would be the same.

'But you don't have to go there – not *there*!'

'I onderrstend it terre. I em no useful heerre. I can't mek it nottink heerre.'

Only one matter remained for discussion. But Helen had already decided she would not discuss it, even though merely thinking about it filled her with panic. How could she talk about it to Mikhail, who never looked at her or touched her and acted as if the two of them together had never existed? She tried to put it aside: in fact, compared with Mikhail's imminent departure, it seemed almost minor.

Then he changed it all: shook the picture she had formed of him and them into little pieces as if it had been part of a kaleidoscope. 'Always I love it you, swithearrt,' he said.

'But I thought—'

What had she thought? This had nothing to do with his decision to return.

'I thought you loved your wife,' she said, dragging the words out, forcing them to be said. For this, of course, was partly the reason he had decided to go back, though he had not said so. She had always known it.

'You tink I love it my wife?' He sounded astounded and a small smile actually flickered over his pale, set face.

'Ivanka told me—'

'Ivanka! What she tellink it you tis chip bitch?'

'She said she was beautiful, your wife. Ivanka couldn't understand why you were with me.' As she spoke, Helen gave a deprecating smile, for she had never been able to understand why either.

'Listen,' said Mikhail with passion, 'I *hetted* it my wife!' Really, he assured her. She was awful. Vain like Ivanka.

Always thinking of how people were seeing her. Only caring about clothes, make-up, hair . . . Didn't care nothing about him. Only liked the wealthy life he could give her. Besides, it was already finished when he left. *And* he was pretty sure she was having a lover . . . If his English had been up to it, he would have told Helen that it was her own diffidence and lack of vanity, such a sweet contrast to his wife's spoilt narcissism, which had attracted him in the first place.

'Oh Mikhail!'

'Do I say I don't love it you?'

'You didn't ever say you did.'

Mikhail looked horrified. 'You tink I lettink you mek it everrtink what you done forr me witout I love it you? Oh, swithearrt! What you tink I em!'

Helen brushed away a tear. What Mikhail had just said turned her in that moment from someone who waited dully for whatever blows fate might dish out into another who would fight for what she wanted.

'Mikhail, there's something you should know . . .'

'Uh?'

She took a deep breath. 'I'm afraid I might be pregnant.' Not 'I might be' but 'I'm afraid I might be' because she could not entirely cast off her old apologetic self.

'Uhh!'

She didn't dare look at him or even try to interpret his reaction, but already she knew she had made a mistake in telling him.

'That night when Dimiter got stabbed, Mikhail,' she went on almost inaudibly. 'It must have happened then because I'm always so careful. I'm two weeks late, Mikhail. It's never happened to me before – I'm always so regular. I feel pregnant though I don't know what it feels like. I wasn't going to tell you but . . .' She trailed off miserably, looking down at her bare feet.

'Why you don't tell it me tis?'

'I couldn't' – still not daring to meet his eyes – 'I feel such a fool. I never thought—'

But this was big stuff, Mikhail said. Important. He grasped her shoulders and tried to force her to look at him, but she drooped her head. Did she mean to say that he and she were having a child and she had known it for two weeks and hadn't told him?

'You don't mind?'

Mind? Mind! Didn't she realise, he said, gabbling with excitement, that this was the best news he had ever had in his whole life? And, at last confronting him, she saw his face transformed by joy, the white bitter one banished as if it had never been. Always he had wanted a child, he told her. Always. But his wife hadn't wanted it because of spoiling the figure. And now he had one! Their child. Special child. Child of love. Oh, they had to make a big party to celebrate this! It was the best thing that had ever happened for him!

'But Mikhail!' exclaimed Helen, uncertain whether to laugh or cry. 'You've spent the whole evening explaining to me why you've decided you're not going to stay here with me. You've said you're going back to your country!'

'I? I go beck? I liv it you when you hevvink it ourr child!' She had to be mad, a sick person, he said, to be saying this. Why did she say it? It was very upsetting for him that she should accuse him of such things, he told her with tears of pain in his grey eyes.

'You're the crazy one, Mikhail,' said Helen, and she stroked his stubbly head where it lay in her lap, his ear to her belly as if even now he hoped to detect signs of the life that was there. 'No, we're both crazy.' And, sitting with her future there, in that tiny attic room, she began to dream of how it would all be.

CHAPTER TWENTY-FOUR

Just after one o'clock the next morning, the chimney stack shared by Numbers 9 and 11 Shipka Avenue toppled and fell. Jack had repeatedly assured the Johnstons that it was quite safe for the time being: at least until he had finished his current job of replumbing a bathroom in Norwood, by which time Stefan might have got around to studying his estimate. But the force of the wind that night was too much for the old stack, the mortar of which had long since crumbled away. It was just a leaning pile of bricks and at three minutes past one it rumbled into the two gardens in an avalanche of stone and dust.

Every one of the inhabitants of the two houses was jerked out of sleep as if by a giant shake to the shoulder. They heard the crash in their dreams. (In Caroline's mother's, it fitted neatly into a saga involving saving the children, trapped in a runaway car.) They awoke the moment it was over; and they thought, all of them, 'Was it a bomb?' and then 'Did I imagine it?'

Mikhail and Helen, curled naked in each other's arms, started up and, for a moment, Helen saw a look of utter terror on his face: the sort of expression, magnified many times, which Stefan had in the mornings when she woke him. She knew all about Mikhail's horrors now. The old Mikhail – the person he had decided to be – would not have admitted fear. Like pessimism and self-doubt, defeat and despair, he had not allowed it to exist for him. But the new Mikhail, the real one, told her about the sense of being watched and followed; the numerous calls, before he stopped answering the telephone, from the anonymous stranger who threatened him in his own language. Helen understood now why he had hung the blanket over the French windows in the saloon: in case his persecutors managed to squeeze and scramble their way into the overgrown garden, there to crouch in the dark and witness the nightly play. It was why he had been so watchful, too, of what he ate and drank: particularly when Luli was around. They specialised in building up an atmosphere of mistrust, he told Helen. In the end, you had no idea who were your real friends and that was exactly what they wanted.

He might always be at risk, he said – for, after all, other less well-known exiles were known to be harassed too. But when Helen asked him to promise to talk to the police, he agreed. He would do it tomorrow and, if she came with him, would insist on seeing a senior officer who would take these things seriously.

Stephen Johnston was the only one who realised immediately what had happened. He had not been deeply asleep because, since falling under the threat of redundancy, he had lost the habit of it. He opened his eyes wide like a doll just picked up from a horizontal position and said: 'Oh bloody hell! Bloody bloody hell! That's the last straw – the last bloody straw! I'll kill that little wanker next door . . .'

'What?' exclaimed Caroline, clutching the baby who, as so often before, had spent the night in their bed, nuzzled to her breast whenever he whimpered.

'I'll kill him! I'll teach him to ignore my letters! I'll take him to court for this! Could have killed someone!'

The bolts on the two back doors were shot back within seconds of each other and separate bands of sleep-smeared figures in a strange assortment of nightwear stumbled out into the cold gardens.

What they saw stopped speech, but only temporarily. The stack had crashed on to the common dividing fence and flattened it, so that the two gardens were now effectively one. Bricks were scattered in orange jumbles over a wide area.

They lay dark and slimy among smashed lilies at the bottom of the Johnstons' miniature pond; all cracked and dirty in the golden sandpit; in suffocating heaps on beds of lovingly reared flowers; and one had landed neatly on the baby's plastic truck, chipping the seat.

The mess was all the more shocking in the garden of Number 9, usually so orderly. In Number 11's, it seemed fitting somehow. In the weeks since the stabbing, Mikhail had not touched the garden and, relieved, it had begun to return to its former wild state. There were bricks everywhere too, but they belonged among the weeds and dandelions. In a short time, they would look as if they had always been there.

'Oh!' said Helen softly, clutching Mikhail's arm.

'I have *never* in my entire life seen such an appalling mess,' said Caroline.

And Stephen demanded: 'Where is he? Where's your friend? He's got a lot to answer for, I can tell you!'

'Wherre Stefan?' Mikhail asked Helen. 'No heerre. I tink is wit Luli.'

'Yes, must be.' That was where he had gone with the Irishman the evening before, leaving them alone to talk. That evening belonged to different people – she could not relate to it. 'I'll 'phone him shall I, Mikhail?'

'Yes' – but as she started towards the house, he clutched at her arm and peered upwards, carefully checking that no more bricks could come suddenly tumbling down before he let her go.

'I'll kill Jack too,' said Stephen. 'Him and his "Not a chance of it coming down, dear"! I'll finish him! I'll sue him as well! I'll put him out of business!'

'So typical,' remarked Caroline's mother in soothing tones; but whether it was Jack's or Stefan's behaviour which was typical, she did not say. She might even have been referring to Stephen, who had a short fuse as she often pointed out. 'It's chilly out here, isn't it? Caro, you're not nearly warmly wrapped up enough, darling. Now wouldn't it be a good idea to make some tea? I'm sure we could all do with a cup.'

'Mummy!'

So Caroline's mother retreated to the kitchen of Number 9 to fill the kettle but leave the gas unlit, count up the clean mugs in one of the pine cupboards, touch the tin where the tea bags were kept, but otherwise do nothing.

'He's coming,' said Helen, returning to Mikhail who put his arm around her. 'Right away. He sounded a bit—'

'Drunk,' supplied Stephen bitterly. 'Yes, I'm sure. So what else is new? Well, he's got a lot of explaining to do. Now – I've kept dated copies of every note I put through his letterbox asking him if we could jointly agree on paying for the stack to be mended. I've proof. Our house isn't just somewhere to live for us, you know. It's our main asset. Our only real asset. Isn't it, Caro?'

'Mmm,' agreed Caroline abstractedly. She was wondering why Helen and Mikhail looked quite so unconcerned and happy. They leant against each other in the devastated gardens exchanging secret smiles and every so often whispering in each others' ears. A blanket was draped over their shoulders and they had quite obviously been naked before they had pulled on the most minimal of day garments: a long T-shirt for Helen, a pair of old jeans for Mikhail. They looked – complete.

Stefan kept to his word and turned up within five minutes.

Luli and Ivanka had also come to inspect the damage, picking their way through the rubble in absurdly high heels, murmuring in a deliciously shocked way to each other; and, through the French windows, a light sprang on in the saloon and the Irishman could be seen launching himself heavily on to the divan bed.

'Oh,' said Stefan, as if commenting on something quite unimportant. He tottered slightly in his old mackintosh and peaked tweed cap. His eyes were half-closed and Stephen could smell the alcohol from yards away.

'Is that all you can say? Look! Just look what you've done to my house and garden through your criminal neglect!'

'What it tis crinimal neclect?' asked Stefan pleasantly, slurring the words. 'Is bick mess heerre. Why we don't go in seloon wherre is morre comfy? I tink I em hevvink it a little Scotch.'

'This is your house too!' shouted Stephen. 'Use your eyes, man! – Look at it! Well, you're going to regret this. I'll see you do. I'll teach you to think you can live on an island and ignore all the rest of us. You're here now, you know. You've got to fit in with *us*. Not the other way round. You and your singing and your mess. I've had it, I tell you. I've had it right up to here!'

'Stephen!' said Caroline, for he was getting dangerously cross. She turned to Helen: 'Can't you get Michael to talk to him? I don't think he's taken in a word Stephen's said.'

Helen murmured to Mikhail and then they all watched as he spoke rapidly to Stefan – Stephen with an 'I told you so' expression on his face, waiting grimly to see the effect when Mikhail informed Stefan that he, Stephen, was going to sue him for every penny he hadn't got.

To his amazement, he saw an incredulous light spark in Stefan's bloodshot eyes which, in a moment, spread over that sullen visage folded in on itself and transformed it into a portrait of radiant sentimental happiness. Stefan took Helen in his arms and kissed her once, twice, thrice – and would have gone on indefinitely if Helen had not pulled back, smiling. And then! – well, he could hardly believe this – Stefan put his hands on Mikhail's shoulders and actually kissed him on the lips. Now Stefan babbled away at the two over-dressed and over-made-up women hovering in the background and they too darted forward with exclamations of pleasure and tenderly kissed first Helen and then Mikhail. The one with the bus-conductress black hair (as he and Caroline always described it to each other) stroked Helen's stomach with a white hand tipped with scarlet; and the other one with hair like yellow candyfloss patted Mikhail on the shoulder as if to say 'Well done!'

It was Helen who explained.

'I'm sorry,' she said to Caroline with just a trace of her old diffidence. 'I'm pregnant. Well, it hasn't been confirmed yet and I'm only about a month gone. But, well, we're very pleased.'

'Helen!'

To Stephen's amazement, he saw his own wife kiss Helen and then, a little shyly and self-consciously, Mikhail.

'Are your boobs sore?' she demanded in front of everyone. 'Have you gone off coffee? Do you feel sort of bloated? Well you *are*, Helen, you *are*! Oh, this is simply wonderful! Heavenly news. *Oh*, you are *lucky*!'

'I tink we hev to celebrrate it tis,' said Mikhail. 'Na, I hev it rrill good salami in frridge. Is excellent.' There were also some cold roast peppers and, naturally, black olives. Should he make a small hors d'oeuvre for everyone?

'End I fetch it tis liquid frrom Scotland,' added Stefan. 'Why we don't go in seloon?' Still beaming all over his face, he began to lead the way out of the ruined gardens.

'Have you all gone completely mad?' demanded Stephen. But no one took any notice.

'The girl's not even married,' he went on to himself. 'But *he* is. What sort of life's it going to have anyway? *If* it's there at all, poor little bugger, which I doubt. And *that's* more important than *this*? I give up. Really, I give up.' But all the same, he followed the others into the saloon of Number 11, the first time he had ever been into that house.

'Tommy's is best,' he heard his wife say. '*And* it's local. Now I want you to promise me something, Helen. There's this perfectly frightful new lobby which is trying to make us all go back to having epidurals and being drugged up to the eyeballs – just when we'd changed all that. Now you're not to listen to a word they say. Childbirth is *the* most wonderful experience there is and it's *not* painful. Well, it is sort of but it's not really, if you see what I mean. It's more like hard

204

work. You have to work like *stink*. But look what you get – look at James and William. Oh you *are* lucky! Oh I *do* envy you!'

Unobtrusively, Caroline's mother had joined them, having removed the rollers from her hair and powdered her nose. 'I think it's all right. Just for a moment. The children are sound asleep again, bless them . . .'

'I tink will be dotterr,' Mikhail told her as he pressed delicacies on her and. watched her glass sternly. He had a strong feeling it would be a girl. He knew what kind of child he wanted, he said: not smart, you know, knowing everything – but soft, sweet, innocent, like Helen. And he would be very strict, he went on, love gleaming in his eyes – he wouldn't make a mistake spoiling this kid.

Luli – loving, giving Luli, who had informed on Mikhail's movements ever since he came to England and would continue to do so because she, of all the exiles, admitted her homesickness and could not bear to say goodbye to her native land – promised to knit the baby a shawl. And her sister Ivanka, who had been granted an exit visa from her country on condition she tried to persuade Mikhail to go back to it, said she would make a dress and embroider it. And Mikhail, who suspected all this but also understood and forgave it, kissed them both and called them his friends.

He was lucky, he told Helen, sheltering in his arms, and Stefan, beaming at his side, to have such friends – and he included the Johnstons, who had avoided any real contact with his lover until she was no longer their lodger, and the Irishman, snoring on the divan bed, who was allowed to behave like no other lodger. Tomorrow, said Mikhail, he would get messages to Christo, in hospital, and Dimiter, in police custody. He knew they would be delighted too.

'I'll never understand them,' said Stephen as he warily accepted a cube of sheep's-milk cheese dusted with paprika from Stefan. 'Never . . .'

But when Caroline said 'Don't you remember how absolutely thrilled we were when we heard we were expecting James?', he agreed 'Well, yes, maybe. But still . . .'

Outside in the gardens the bricks lay undisturbed, pressing into the soft earth. Tomorrow was another day.

Only then was it discovered that, in its massive rush from roof to ground, the chimney stack had completely severed the main stem of the vine – killed the *Polygonum baldschuanicum* which had dominated the garden of Number 11 for so long and threatened all the neighbouring ones. Its branches became dry and brittle, the tiny buds rippling them withered and died.

It was the second good thing to come out of all this mess, remarked Caroline's mother to no one in particular.

CHAPTER TWENTY-FIVE

'Is gorrgeous,' pronounced Stefan. 'Is goink to be grret beauty. Tis kid will be brrekkink it all hearrts.'

'Oh Stefan!' Helen laughed. She looked at her daughter curled up like a little mouse in the cot beside her hospital bed, wanting to believe him but at the same time thinking herself ridiculous.

'She don't look like Mikhail,' said Ivanka, making something suspicious out of it as she ate another of the strawberries she and Luli had brought.

'She doesn't look like me either,' said Helen with another laugh. She added, looking radiant: 'Thank goodness!'

'Tis little rrebbit lookit like herrself,' said Mikhail. For the hundredth time he bent over his black-haired blue-eyed daughter and gazed at her with awe. Then he stroked her satiny cheek and looked suddenly fearful. 'Is okay, switheartt? She don't be movink forr lonk time.'

'She's asleep, Mikhail! She sleeps a lot.'

'I check.' He put his ear to his sleeping daughter's mouth and felt her slight warm breath, noted that her little chest rose and fell, and relaxed.

'But she is engel!' exclaimed Luli, a picture in pink – a startling contrast to Ivanka, who wore orange. 'She is best bebby whateverr I see, Helen.'

'She's wonderful,' agreed Helen with gratitude. During her pregnancy she had often feared for the contentment of a baby conceived during a night of such passionate misery. Then, following that train of thought, she said: 'How about Dimiter!'

This was not believable, Luli affirmed. Ah fate! It was a strange strange business, this fate! If there hadn't been this awful business with poor Christo, poor Dimiter wouldn't have gone to prison! If he hadn't gone to prison, he wouldn't be so happy now!

'She is not yonk,' said Stefan who, at this time of day – afternoon visiting hours – appeared deeply gloomy except when he looked at the baby.

'So what?' said Helen. 'He's happy. And I don't think he likes them young anyway – unlike you, Stefan!'

Dimiter's sad story had been picked up by the national press. Moved by it, a middle-aged widow had written to him in prison. Dimiter had replied, conscious of his poor spelling and grammar, and a friendship had begun which quickly became a romance, first on paper and then in reality. Two weeks ago, after serving a much reduced sentence, Dimiter had married the widow and set off for a new life in Bournemouth where she owned a small tea-shop near the sea-front. In years to come, her customers would become fond of Dimiter's sheep's-milk cheese pastries which would always, from now on, contain cream cheese.

'I tink I hev it to get merrried,' said Stefan, thinking of Dimiter and his new wife and looking at Helen and Mikhail who, though unmarried, were closer to each other than any married couple he knew.

'But then you couldn't move to a bachelor flat, Stefan,' pointed out Helen who, enveloped in happiness, had lost nearly all her old diffidence. 'Have you thought of that?'

'Tis is true,' he agreed sadly, staring down at the mirrored surface of his shoes. As a matter of fact, Stefan was not a bachelor. Years ago, out of affection, he had married Luli so that she could stay in Britain – just as, for a substantial financial consideration, the Irishman later married Ivanka. Stefan was in a position to give Luli nationality: the only one of the exiles to have decided to renounce completely the land where he had been born. The marriage was a secret. It explained his special hold over Luli and when, later, Mikhail and Helen asked him to become godfather to their baby, he shared this honour, privately, with his wife.

'More champagne,' said Mikhail, who had brought a bottle to the hospital on every visit since his baby had been born.

'Ah chempagne!' Luli stared down at her golden fizzing glass. 'My Vanya is crre-etted forr drrinkink chempagne!' And she looked at Ivanka, sitting next to her, with very much the same expression as Mikhail bestowed on his baby.

'Christo's coming tomorrow,' said Helen.

'Ah Christo!' And Luli exclaimed again with a certain awe: 'Ah fet! Is strrenge strrenge business!'

The stabbing would recur again and again in the exiles' conversation, but never when Christo was there – and this was often, as he had clung closer to them since. When his old father was allowed out on a visit in six months' time in one of those arbitrary decisions the authorities in his native land sometimes made (perhaps influenced by the fact that if Christo's father stayed in the West they would no longer be obliged to pay him a small pension), his fellow exiles were the first to hear the good tidings.

'So much news,' said Helen. She and Mikhail no longer lived at Number 11 Shipka Avenue. Two months before the baby was due, they had moved to a small rented flat nearby in spite of Stefan's protests. 'Why you do it tis? You don't like it heerre? Why you west it yourr cesh? I em worrrit forr you. How you live?'

But they had wanted to be on their own and, besides, money was no great problem. Mikhail had discovered a talent for carpentry, just as that young policeman had seemed to predict, and Helen had negotiated for a full-time job with her magazine. She would become fashion editor: there was a vacancy to be filled.

'You wrritink ebout feshion!' exclaimed Ivanka now, in disbelief. 'Firrst you wrritink ebout cookink, Helen, end you don't cook. End na you wrritink ebout feshion . . .' She did not finish the sentence, looking at Helen, as always, with a sort of puzzled contempt. But now it was mixed with reluctant affection.

'Tis is lend of opporrtunity,' said Mikhail. There was no bitterness in his tone. It was a joke.

'And how about *your* new job, Ivanka?' asked Helen quickly. Luli's rich Arab friend Hassan had paid for Ivanka to take a course to become a beautician.

Luli answered for her sister, as usual. Her Vanya was a natural for this work. She was so quick, so talented. Last night she had made Luli a special make-up for going on the town. 'You see me, Helen, end you don't be rrecognisink me – I em so fency!' And Ivanka smiled faintly, accustomed to the praise.

'And Kevin?' asked Helen. 'Do you see much of him?' She was tired. Her swollen breasts ached and she shifted her position over the rubber ring she sat on. She longed to be alone with Mikhail and the baby. But they were so kind, all these visitors, so generous. They had come – as they always went anywhere – loaded with gifts of every sort: for her as well as for the baby. She loved them – all of them. Yes she did. But now she was tired.

Luli's face became flat and heavy. Always he was asking for money, she said. Really this whole business had been big mistake. But what could they do? It had been the only solution. Really, she conceded, they had to be grateful he didn't want to live with them. Then her black eyes sparkled and narrowed and her smile – like a tender snarl – transformed her full square face, making it almost triangular. 'But tis is not imporrtent. *Tis* is what metterr – tis swit little beauty!' She beamed down at the tiny face in the cot. 'Ah, my pumpkin! Yourr enty Luli mekkink you sometink rrilly special wit herr knittink niddles.' She asked Helen anxiously: 'You like yellow, Helen? Is good colourr forr bebby, no?'

'But tis chip stuff still livink wit *me*,' said Stefan dourly, not distracted. 'Tis Irrish peasant neverr payink it me tis cesh what he owink me. Na is yuge debt – yuge!' On top of this now enormous debt consisting of back rent, he went on, this peasant was eating his food, drinking his drink – and he was

210

cunning like a fox. Had he told Helen this pig had run up an awful bill on his telephone? He thought he had to buy a big lock for this thing. He was driving him mad, he said. Really this peasant was driving him mad – and the new lodger wasn't much better. He was a real cheap production. These young people from his old country were a big disappointment these days. And his house was a disaster, a disaster. Did Helen know the gas board had come and sealed off the gas pipe with a plug because some idiot who came to read the meter said it was dangerous? He had straight away pulled the plug out and was using the stove like normal. Of course nothing had happened. Idiot!

He paused, out of breath, then winced as another baby in the ward let out wail after wail like a pair of squeaky bellows.

'See it what excellent child *I* em hevvink,' said Mikhail proudly. Then, in their own language, to the visitors: 'Helen is exhausted. She had a bad time, this girl, you know. I don't want to be rude but I think it's time to go. She needs to keep her strength for feeding this little rabbit of ours.' He appealed to them with his melting eyes and flashing smile. 'You're not offended? It's all new, this business. She's not used to it yet.'

'Of course,' said Stefan. 'In fact my nerves can't take this awful noise for much longer.'

'This is understood,' said Luli, and she rose immediately with Ivanka.

'Oh,' said Helen wearily, 'do you have to go?'

'We hev, my darrlink.' Luli bent to kiss her, brushing her unmade-up cheeks with her stiff hair, leaving a scent of musk which would cling to Helen's white nightdress for hours.

She watched them leave: Stefan wrapped in his dirty raincoat, peaked cap perched on his head, stumbling along in shiny black shoes; the two women tottering on their high heels, violent patches of colour in that predominantly white and grey hospital ward. She saw the other girls in the other beds – talking to their visitors – stare curiously and knew they were thinking 'Oh, foreign. That explains it.'

211

Stefan gave a last thumbs-up sign, his fingers deep blue from Luli's hair dye. Then they were gone.

'I should?' asked Mikhail, hovering over his baby, longing to hold her close to him once more.

'Of course, darling. It's probably time for her to be fed.'

He unwrapped the baby tenderly from its blankets, lifted it, and heard a soft mew that was certainly not a complaint.

'She *is* hungry,' said Helen with satisfaction, opening the front of her nightdress. She took the baby from Mikhail and put it to her breast. Such a natural feeling to put flesh to flesh.

Alone with her new family, she already felt calmer. She smiled at Mikhail and he beamed back. No need for words.

She looked like a proper mother now, Mikhail thought with love. Not a girl any more. He noted the mouth still a little swollen from her labour (which had been long and painful), the tender calm expression in her eyes as she gazed down at the snuffling gulping baby. 'A man is not a man until he has fought in a war,' Stefan was fond of saying, 'a woman is not a woman until she has given birth.'

'Oh!' Helen exclaimed softly, not to disturb the baby. She put out a hand to touch yellow roses which had been arranged in a vase together with the red carnations Dimiter and his new wife had sent. 'These are from the Johnstons. And Caroline sent a letter with their card. Want to see?'

'Okay,' said Mikhail, knowing he wouldn't be able to comprehend it all. But some of the old pride remained. Understanding this, Helen watched as he pored over the letter, taking his time, smiling at her and the baby every so often.

'Oh Helen!' Caroline had written, '*I am so thrilled*' (underlined three times) 'for you both! I simply can't wait to see her and will try to get up to London just as soon as I possibly can. Couldn't get much out of Michael on the 'phone, he was *so* excited – *sweet*! How did it all go? *Wonderful*, isn't it? And those breathing exercises really work, don't they? Did you manage to stop them from giving you drugs? *Ghastly*, aren't they, the way they try and inflict them on us? And did you use a birthing chair? *Think* they've got them at Tommy's. How's your milk? Now don't panic if it doesn't come, Helen' (at this point, Mikhail looked at his baby drawing contentedly at Helen's breast). '*Everyone* has problems at the beginning. The thing is to simply *persevere*. And don't listen to them in the hospital if they tell you to keep to a four-hour schedule. Just give her the breast *whenever* she wants it. *Listen* to me going on! But I do know about this, Helen.'

'So much ink,' thought Mikhail as he went on to the next bit.

'Well, it's been *quite* a change for us. It's absolutely a new life. *So* exciting. It's the tiniest house you ever saw in your whole life – only three bedrooms so Mummy has to double up with William. We're still working like *stink* to get it straight. But the boys adore it and Fred's in his element – lots of lovely rabbits to chase. I've discovered this simply marvellous invention called coconut matting – *just* as good as carpet. Can't *think* why no one's told me about it before. Imagine, Helen, we've got *a dozen chickens*! Did have two dozen, but Stephen didn't fix the run quite right and a badger got in last month – *what* a bore. He's up to his eyes planning what we're going to plant in our tiny patch. He'll probably decide on cabbages, so *be prepared* when I come up to London (don't know *when* that will be) cos I seem to remember Michael makes something perfectly heavenly with cabbages.'

Now the baby was nuzzling Helen's shoulder and she was stroking its miniature rounded back as she had been taught by the nurses, supporting its wobbling head with the palm of her other hand. Mikhail watched entranced as the baby burped, and then admiringly as Helen put it to her other breast. He would have liked to go on watching for ever but went back to the letter.

'I don't miss the Avenue at all, Helen, and Stephen seems to like it here too but you know what an old worryguts he is. Everything seems so sort of simple to me now tho he says if we don't make a go of this we'll end up on the S.S. *No* joke! But there's a simply marvellous village school here – *so* handy when the boys get to school age and it'll be nice to have them around. Actually James has started going to a sort of nursery someone runs in her drawing-room. *She's* the wife of our postman, but *sweet*. It's super having more time to myself because James is a tiny bit wild these days. William is divine as always and I'm still feeding him myself tho Stephen keeps telling me I shouldn't. And talking of that, Helen, you've made me feel jolly broody! I'm working on Stephen (!!!) because I really feel we can afford another now. Sounds *bananas*, doesn't it?!

'I miss my job, Helen. But I've had a brainwave to earn some pennies. Can you believe it – *no one* teaches breathing exercises round here! So I'm going to start classes myself. Not an *enormous* reaction from people I've talked to so far but I'm working on it. And Mummy's making trillions of cushions because of course I'll be teaching in the drawing-room and the coconut matting is a tiny bit scratchy . . .'

'I tink is enoff,' said Mikhail at this point, and Helen smiled because she too had found it hard to read beyond the fourth densely scrawled and underlined page.

'So many changes,' she said sleepily.

Mikhail agreed absentmindedly that it was a big change for the Johnstons, all his thoughts on his baby. He still could not believe she was here. He would never believe it, he thought. He was sure that each time he looked at her, for the rest of his life, he would experience this sense of awe and gratitude. She was the best poem he had ever produced, he had told Stefan.

'It's funny, darling,' said Helen, passing the baby into his waiting arms. 'You came here because you wanted to change your life. But you changed everyone else's. Some strange things happened. It didn't seem like they were for the good at the time; but out of them came wonderful things, not least – oh darling, we're going to *have* to decide on a name for the rabbit soon.' Her eyes were closing. 'Everything changed after you,' she murmured. 'Everything.' And she slept.

EPILOGUE

This was the house where their mother and he had met, Mikhail would tell his three children each time they visited Number 11 Shipka Avenue. It became a landmark in their lives: a crumbling palace full of shocking surprises where they were wonderfully spoilt by their Uncle Stefan (of whom they had long since ceased to be afraid).

It was one of the places their father often took them – like Speakers' Corner at Hyde Park. 'Tis is prroof you arre in frree countrry,' he would inform them sternly, whilst they stared at the orators in uncomprehending boredom. 'Heerre you may say anytink beforre all pipple – anytink! Even you tink Prrime Ministerr deserrvink to be trrottled.' He took them to the pond on the common, too, to marvel at the fishermen who eternally hoped to catch fish where none had ever been sighted. Mikhail was reminded of himself when he had first arrived in England.

That time of illusions was gone. If he wrote poetry now, which was seldom, he showed it to no one but Helen. It was better this way. Better, too, for her to try to ignore the bitter black moods when he would ask of no one in particular why, when for the first time in his life he could write without restriction, none cared to listen. But to Helen's growing embarrassment he had always to explain himself to strangers. Once, he would tell them, every glittering reward had been his. They better believe it. Oh yes! What car had they? He had had Mercedes. Unheard of! And Helen would blush painfully at the all too frequent response: 'So you're a carpenter now.'

But in a private and most unexceptional way, Mikhail was happier than he would have believed possible living where he was, doing what he did. He was an ordinary man these days: sometimes short-tempered and gloomy – himself. But he loved his common-law wife and, as for his children, they were his real hopes for the future now.

He was afraid, he told Helen when she was heavily pregnant with their second child, a boy, and just for a moment there came into her blue eyes – so calm and confident now – the same lost unsure look of her youth.

'Afraid, Mikhail?'

Yes. He loved his first child so greatly that he couldn't believe he could love another so much.

With Helen's career going so well, it was he who took care of the children. It made sense since he was earning so much less than her. He could fit his carpentry into the noise and clutter they had brought in their wake. Sometimes, though, in the midst of coaxing them with spoonfuls of spicy food then getting them ready to go to the one o'clock club on the common where mothers took other children, he would think 'Now they'll be serving lunch in the Writers' Club.' Images would come to him as if he were watching a film about someone else – his old well-dressed self making a spectacular entrance, dropping a casual but precious word at this and that table as he made his leisurely way to his own, where he and a few favourites would be fawned over by his waiter. Mikhail's face would darken and he would wrestle with the knotted laces on a tiny shoe as if he wanted to rip them apart. But then a child would cry or call his name (so strange to be called 'Daddy'), and as he went to attend to it he would breathe deeply, remind himself: 'This is my real life – all this.'

It was amazing how people talked to him now. It was as if these little children clinging around his neck and to his knees represented a badge of membership. They were boring in the extreme, the conversations he had, sitting in the sun on the common, about feeding and smacking and potty-training (once, even, breast-feeding) – but it was a sweet boredom because it arose out of his children.

Often, Mikhail would tell his British children of the grandparents they had never met. For them, this old couple who spoke an entirely foreign language came to symbolise the good forces in countless stories. Baba made a magic tisane out of herbs and flowers, Mikhail told his little son who suffered from severe sore throats; and, as for the roses grown in that faraway garden, you could almost smell their over-poweringly sweet scent from here!

One day very soon, Mikhail's English friends assured him, he could take his children to his old country on a visit. 'Really!' It was as if they knew the situation far better than he. 'It's all changing now' – and they used the word '*glasnost*' easily and with confidence.

Mikhail did not believe it was changing, although he too thought 'One day I will go back' – just as he still secretly felt 'One day I shall be recognised here as a poet' – because he could not bear to think otherwise. He agreed with the rest of the exiles that not until the whole system crumbled to give way to another would it really be different – and, mindful of this, he went on avoiding dark and lonely streets and treated new arrivals from his old country with considerably more caution than did Stefan.

As for Stefan, he went on living in Number 11 Shipka Avenue, which returned to what it had been before Mikhail came. New lodgers moved in, some of them exiles, all of them cheap stuff, and he would tell them gloomily over delicious bean soup in the saloon that his house was a disaster. He bought a deep wide second-hand armchair to hide the new ravages of the dry rot. Weeds sprang up in the garden and honeysuckle on the run from an obsessive pruner next door made coiling overtures in imitation of the vine. Another of the gutters collapsed, crashing on to the bricks still scattered in the garden, and the black paint with which Mikhail had coated the front door became pitted and scratched around the keyhole where Stefan and the Irishman mis-aimed their keys after drunken nights at Luli's. The hedge met across the gate again and it became difficult to open the front door because of the heaps of circulars: more and more these days from estate agents, who longed to be able to advertise the house as 'nds. tot. ren. but gt. poss. and in v. des. loc.', and from property developers posing as estate agents.

Shipka Avenue really was fashionable now. No longer on the move, it had got where it had been heading. Nannies moved in with the new families and it became impossible to park because so many households ran two cars. The older inhabitants said they deplored the changes in the street but they liked the new value of their houses which, sooner or later, they would cash in on.

Number 11 was still spoken of as 'an eyesore' and 'a disgrace' and its owner certainly had some unsociable habits. But a sort of tolerance operated these days. In the neighbours' eyes it had acquired an odd distinction. They did not know it was a place where dreams had glistened and faded. To them it was 'the house of the stabbing': a sight to be pointed out in not so hushed tones to visitors to the street. But quite soon the story of what really happened that night became so embroidered with re-telling as to be almost unrecognisable. There had been a woman involved of course! According to the most popular version, there had been an attempted rape. Why else should one of the foreigners have gone for another, his friend, with a flick-knife? Although a few of the neighbours (like the previous owners of Number 9) were no strangers to misfortune, they could not understand – or would not. Besides, that nice chap who used to live at Number 11 and was so touchingly fond of his children said he never regretted leaving his country – never. That's what he always insisted.

Perhaps the abyss which separated their two worlds was too great.